The Girl Behind The Curtain

Also by Stella Knightley

The Girl Behind The Mask
The Girl Behind The Fan

About the author

Stella Knightley is the author of twenty-six novels published under other names. *The Girl Behind The Curtain* is the third and final book in the *Hidden Women* series, which blends the daring stories of historical women of note with an erotically-charged contemporary love affair which will delight the fans of *Fifty Shades*. Stella grew up in the west of England and now lives in London.

STELLA KNIGHTLEY

The Girl Behind
The Curtain

HODDER

First published in Great Britain in 2013 by Hodder & Stoughton
An Hachette UK company

First published in paperback in 2013

1

A CIP catalogue record for this title is available from the British Library

Paperback ISBN 978 1 444 77709 3
Ebook ISBN 978 1 444 77708 6

Printed and bound by Clays Ltd, St Ives plc

Hodder & Stoughton policy is to use papers that are natural, renewable and
recyclable products and made from wood grown in sustainable forests. The
logging and manufacturing processes are expected to conform to the
environmental regulations of the country of origin.

Hodder & Stoughton Ltd
338 Euston Road
London NW1 3BH

www.hodder.co.uk

To Marguerite Finnigan

Prologue

It was Friday night at the Boom Boom Club. It had been a good evening. The amateur cabaret extravaganzas always brought in a crowd. Sometimes, the club's regular performers wondered whether the audience didn't actually prefer to watch amateurs making fools of themselves to the professionals who had honed their craft over years. That night had been especially great entertainment. The elderly twin brothers dressed as sisters, who sang the old weepies before ending their set with a frighteningly high-kicking can-can routine, had put in a special appearance. The crowd bayed for an encore. The sister-brothers obliged three times.

Jerry Schluter, the club's owner, watched from the wings with Kitty Katkin, his biggest star, as Marlene the cross-dressing mistress/master of ceremonies introduced another familiar figure: a young man dressed as Jean Harlow, who was convinced he should be in Hollywood even though he couldn't hold a note. Marlene egged him on. The crowd were going wild, knowing that he would be simply terrible. They howled with laughter even as he took centre stage. Several were weeping with hilarity by the time he reached his second wavering verse.

Herr Schluter watched proceedings with a sad smile on his face. He shook his head. 'It never fails to surprise me that this is what the people want,' he said. 'Delusion and humiliation. Just another freak show.'

Kitty nodded. Like her boss, she found the proceedings on amateur nights rather poignant at times but she knew that they kept the club going. And the club provided her livelihood. And it was where she'd found true love.

The young man dressed as Jean Harlow was persuaded to indulge in such an awful encore that a corpulent man on one of the tables in the front row laughed himself into a coughing fit.

'You'd better get on there and calm them all down,' Schluter told Kitty.

Kitty tipped her silver hat at him and indicated to Marlene, who was consoling the amateur crooner, that she was ready to take the stage.

'Ladies and gentlemen.' Marlene began her introduction. 'That last act was a difficult one to follow, but here at the Boom Boom Club, we are always striving to go one better than before. And I think you will all have to agree that it doesn't get much more magnificent than our next star, our very own English songbird, the beautiful, the mellifluous, the incomparable . . . Kitty Katkin!'

Marlene started the welcoming applause. The audience whooped and cheered. Backstage, Kitty gave a little shimmy of excitement, as she always did when she was about to perform. Her perfect red bobbed wig settled back into place and she stepped out. Right leg first.

Just that.

The crowd went crazy as Kitty's long white leg appeared

through the gap in the curtains. Her calf and thigh were suggestively bare. Her elegant high-arched foot was encased in a dancing shoe covered in shimmering rhinestones. Next out snaked an arm, festooned with glittering bracelets to match the shoe. Leg and arm moved up and down in unison, as though hoist by the same invisible puppet string. Kitty had the crowd enchanted with only two limbs. Then out popped her head.

'Kitty! Kitty!' the fat man in the front row called. 'Marry me, Kitty. I love you.'

Kitty tweaked the corners of her glossy red mouth into a living-doll smile.

There were plenty of men in the audience who would have loved to spend an evening looking into the naughty eyes beneath that straight red fringe, but Kitty Katkin's heart belonged to one man only. Kitty met his gaze right now. Her darling Otto was in his usual place at the piano in the orchestra pit, leading the band through the intro to her opening song. Every high-sung word of love or longing that came from Kitty's mouth that night would be directed straight at him. When his blue eyes met her own, her smile was suddenly very real.

Kitty launched into her first song, which was 'Burlington Bertie' with much ruder lyrics and a very lewd dance.

'I'm Burlington Bertie, the boys say I'm dirty . . .'

The crowd may have been delighted by the pratfalls of the cabaret wannabes but they could tell that Kitty was a cut above. They clapped along. They whooped whenever she flicked out a long leg. They hollered when she threw in a handstand that revealed the Union Flag sewn onto her knickers. Kitty's act was part ballet, part opera, part clown. The audience laughed and swooned and shouted for more. She had them in the palm of her hand.

All the time she was thinking of Otto, performing for Otto and imagining what they would do together when they were alone.

Kitty had three numbers to sing that evening. Her glittering silver costume was carefully constructed and held together only by poppers so that her long slit skirt disappeared with the flick of a wrist. By turning her hat round, she went from city gent to cowboy. Beneath her neat little waistcoat was a daring, skintight basque.

It wasn't quite a striptease but it was enough to send every man in the room – at least every man who wasn't interested in other men – home with the idea that he had been royally and rudely entertained. During her last song, Kitty would always turn her back on the audience and unclip her basque so that they could kid themselves she had been topless in front of them, though in fact they hadn't seen a thing. No one got to see Kitty's body except Otto. It was always and only for him.

Kitty brought the house down with her comedy galloping as she sang along to 'The Last Round-Up', a cowboy ballad she'd pinched from the Ziegfeld Follies and given her own special twist with a filthy new libretto. It was all building up to a wonderful finale, but that Friday night, Kitty would not be ending her act with 'Goodnight Sweetheart', the song with which she always closed the show. As Kitty was finding her mark on the centre of the stage and thanking her fellow performers and the audience for their support, Otto began to play a different tune. It was Irving Berlin's 'The Song is Ended'. It was *their* song.

For a moment Kitty was confused. She looked at Otto enquiringly. He looked back at her and gave the slightest nod, a nod so small and so subtle that only she could see it. Kitty briefly checked out the rest of the band. They had taken the change of music in their stride and were following Otto as a good orchestra always follows a great conductor. He had their absolute trust.

Kitty glanced to the side of the stage. Marlene and Schluter looked back at her. Marlene's eyes were steely. Her jaw was set. Schluter looked weary and resigned. He nodded just as Otto had done, then he disappeared into the darkness. Behind the scenes, Kitty knew, the entire backstage crew would be swinging into action.

Taking a deep breath, Kitty centred herself. 'Goodnight Sweetheart' was the song she had planned to sing, indeed, *wanted* to sing but 'The Song is Ended' was always going to be the real finale. She felt the backs of her eyes start to sting and tried to fight the tears with a smile. No one must notice that anything was different, even though Otto had always reassured her that if she *did* cry the crowd would just assume it was part of the act. 'The Song is Ended' was one of those tunes that got you right in the heart. It was so full of love and longing.

Kitty began to sing.

Oh so many moments of bliss, she thought as she wobbled through the first line. Must it really all come to an end? Right now? Like this? She wasn't ready for it. Otto had been telling her for weeks that she must always be ready because the moment *would* come and it would not wait for anyone to say their last goodbyes.

'I never want to say a last goodbye to you,' Kitty had told him. She'd pummelled him with her fists whenever he suggested it. But now it was happening. Though the lights made the audience indistinct to her, Kitty thought she could see dark shapes moving at the very back of the room, drawing closer, paying no respect to the fact that the show wasn't finished yet. Not quite. She sang on.

Kitty's heart was breaking. Every word was important to her now. Every single note must reach Otto's ears and caress him as though those notes were kisses. She was so glad they'd been so happy before the show. They'd made love in her little room on the top floor of the Hotel Frankfort. When she pushed a stray strand of hair away from her face, Kitty could still smell the scent of Otto's sweet skin on her hand.

Now Otto threw in an instrumental passage, as he had always warned her he might when they discussed how this moment could be. He was buying time for the people behind the curtains. For Marlene and Schluter and Isadora and Old Hans. Kitty wished he could play for ever. She watched Otto's hands moving over the keyboard and heard in every note he played a love song just for her.

And then suddenly it was the last verse. Kitty's voice cracked as she sang the song's final line. But she couldn't let it end on such a sad note. She wouldn't. She added a flourish. A final line of her own, over the top of Otto's fading chords. 'But I'll be coming back for you, dear.' She looked right at him and blew him a kiss.

Then the crowd began to applaud and there wasn't a second to lose. Kitty bowed quickly, curtly, and exited stage left at a run. The crowd continued to clap. They wanted her back. Another bow. Another encore.

'More more more!' they yelled.

But there would be no encore. Not tonight. Maybe not ever. Kitty was already on her way down to the basement.

Upstairs in the theatre, a gunshot rang out.

I

Berlin, last September

Another month, another country. If it's September, it must be Berlin, I said to myself, mocking the touring rock stars who claim they only know which town they're in by consulting the day on the calendar. I was beginning to feel a little bit like that. I had started the year in London, then moved to spend two months in Venice. I'd followed that with two months in Paris, then back to London again and now Berlin.

The plan was that I was going to be in Berlin for the long term. I was in Germany to teach English to support myself as I began a new project, studying the experiences of British expats in the capital between the two world wars. It was a project I was looking forward to undertaking, but I couldn't help but feel a little nervous as the plane touched down. Another country, another adventure? Or another dose of heartache?

Thanks to my friend Clare, who had been living in Berlin since we finished our undergraduate degrees in London almost a decade earlier, I would at least be arriving in the city with some idea of what to do and where to go. Clare had already helped me to find a flat to rent. She'd actually offered to have me stay at her place for as long as I needed, but I'd done enough couchsurfing in London over the spring and summer and I didn't feel like imposing. I wanted a place of my own. Somewhere I could stay for as long as I wanted. A home.

Clare couldn't meet me at the airport that first day because she had to work, but she had sent very detailed instructions on how to get to my new place. She'd been kind enough to spend some time there too, checking it would have everything I needed and filling the kitchen cupboards with essentials. She had also made an inspection of the landlord. The elderly man, who was called Herr Schmidt, lived on the ground floor of the building. That kind of arrangement – a live-in landlord – could be difficult, but Clare didn't think he would be too much trouble.

'And if he is,' she said, 'you'll easily outrun him. He must be ninety-five if he's a day.'

I was grateful that she'd checked out the flat *and* the landlord. It made me feel just a little less lonely when I arrived on the Hufelandstrasse in the Prenzlauer Berg and pressed the doorbell. My first impression was certainly good; the outside of the tall white building was very clean and tidy and the neighbourhood seemed quiet and safe. Clare had explained to me that the area was the Berlin equivalent of London's 'Nappy Valley' between Clapham and Wandsworth Commons – lots of young families chose to live there. It might not be the hippest part of town, but it was very nice.

It was a short while before Herr Schmidt answered the door. He was exactly as Clare had described him. Easily in his nineties. He walked with a cane but he was by no means a helpless old man. He was beautifully dressed in smartly pressed clothes. He was still tall and only slightly stooped with age. He looked well-fed and, indeed, I could smell something delicious wafting into the hall from his kitchen on the ground floor.

'Fräulein Thomson,' he greeted me. 'I am very glad to meet you. Welcome to Berlin.'

He gave me a small nod. He had such bearing that I found I wanted to curtsey in response, but I made do with a nod of my own. Bizarrely, I found I was slightly lost for words. Herr Schmidt had the most startling blue eyes, almost aquamarine.

'Do you have much luggage?' he asked, breaking the spell.

'Oh no,' I said. 'This is it.'

'I'll take it for you.'

There was no way I was going to let him try to drag my heavy case up the stairs. 'I can manage,' I insisted.

Still, we did an awkward little dance in the doorway as he tried to take my bag off me. Eventually, I let him wheel it into the hallway. I sensed it was important to him to feel that he was treating me as an esteemed guest rather than a lodger.

'Your rooms are upstairs,' he explained to me. 'But first perhaps you would like to share some coffee and cake.'

I certainly wasn't going to say no. I was hungry. I hadn't eaten the plastic-covered roll that passed for breakfast on the plane from Heathrow. Plus, I wanted to get to know my new landlord. I was relieved that I immediately felt comfortable in his company. It's funny how we make such judgements, isn't it? We can look at someone's face for just a second and know at once we'll get along. That's how I felt about Herr Schmidt; there was kindness in his incredible blue eyes. I was also intrigued. He spoke good English – there had to be a story there. It was lucky too, since my German still left quite a bit to be desired. My first month in the city would be full of one-to-one German lessons to bring me up to speed. I was sure I would learn as much from my English-language students as they would learn from me.

'So you are going to be working at the university?' he asked me.

'Yes.' I explained the nature of my project.

Herr Schmidt nodded. 'Well, you will find plenty to

interest you here. The 1930s were a fascinating time to be living in this city.'

'So I've heard. I'm very keen to explore the juxtaposition of the decadence of the legendary nightlife and the political change,' I said, hoping I didn't sound too pretentious.

Herr Schmidt smiled distantly. 'There was certainly plenty of change,' he said.

And then he changed the subject by offering me another slice of cake.

The cake was delicious. I didn't need to be encouraged to have more than one piece. After that, Herr Schmidt offered to show me my new apartment. Between us, we carried my suitcase up the narrow stairs. He opened the door to my flat and waved me inside. There was, as Clare had promised, everything a girl could need (including Nutella in the cupboard, as I would later discover). The four small rooms – bedroom, bathroom, kitchen and study – were light and immaculate. Though the furniture was a little old-fashioned, it was charmingly solid. I liked the idea that it might have been around during the period I was hoping to write about.

'How long have you lived in this house, Herr Schmidt?' I asked him when he had finished pointing out how everything worked.

'All my life,' he told me. 'I was born here.'

I decided not to ask exactly when that might have been.

'That's pretty rare these days,' I said. 'To be born at home and then live in the same house one's whole life.'

'I suppose it is.'

He seemed sad at the thought. Perhaps it was the memory of all the people who had lived in the house with him. As far as I could tell, I would be the only lodger. The only other person in the building, in fact. The rest of the place was empty. But once upon a time it must have teemed with people: his parents, his siblings, maybe even his own wife and children, though he hadn't mentioned them.

'I hope you'll be very happy here,' he said.

I assured him that I would.

And I did feel that I could be happy in Berlin. Since leaving Paris – upset by my final meeting with Marco Donato and angry that I'd only got my job researching Augustine du Vert because of him – I had been killing time in the UK. I was eager to make a start on a new life.

I was tired from a day spent travelling, but after Herr Schmidt left to go back downstairs I unpacked my case, knowing I was unlikely to feel much more energetic the next morning. I hung my clothes in the narrow wooden wardrobe that seemed to have been made to accommodate the belongings of someone with much smaller shoulders. I imagined the wardrobe's original owner, who must have been a good deal more fine-boned than me, hanging gossamer-light frocks cut on the bias where I now hung my jeans and a couple of black dresses. I placed my underwear in a drawer lined with floral paper that was faded and brittle with age. It might have been put there by Herr Schmidt's mother. I don't know why I assumed that the room's first occupant must have been a woman but there was definitely something feminine in the atmosphere.

I'd brought with me framed photographs of my sister and my parents. I set those on the dressing table, with its speckled old mirror. Herr Schmidt had put a small vase of flowers on the well-polished top. It was a kind touch. It made me like him even more. It also made me well up just a little, as for some reason it put me in mind of the flowers on Augustine du Vert's grave at Père Lachaise. I put my overly emotional reaction down to fatigue.

Later, I set up my laptop on the table in the little study I would doubtless come to know very well. There was wireless, thank goodness. I'd worried that someone of Herr Schmidt's age might not bother with the Internet, but he'd told me he'd had it installed at the behest of his great-nephew, who had assured him it was a non-negotiable requirement for any modern lodger. I had felt oddly comforted by the thought that Herr Schmidt had relatives somewhere. Until he mentioned the nephew, he had seemed worryingly self-contained.

I logged on and checked my emails. I sent Mum a message to let her know I was safely installed. I let my sister know the same. I attached a photograph, taken with my phone, of the little study and another of the kitchen, small and so neat – for now, anyway. I texted Clare to thank her for filling my fridge and cupboards with so many goodies. It was very kind of her. I was lucky to have such a good friend.

After that, with a cup of tea in hand, I looked out of my new bedroom window. It had a wide sill that was the perfect seat, made cosy by the velvet curtains.

I was in the former East Berlin and some of the architecture I'd seen on my way to the Hufelandstrasse did have a distinct touch of the Soviet to it. But there was a large park just down the road from the house – the Volkspark Friedrichshain – and there were tall trees on either side of the street. The September sun was still warm and welcoming and the pavement was busy with locals going about their business. As I looked out, a couple walked by with their children: two in the pram and an older sibling who was entertaining the babies with a song. The parents embraced. How happy they seemed. Ordinary people leading ordinary lives, bolstered by their ordinary love for one another. Extraordinarily ordinary love. Wasn't that what Marco had wished for me?

*   *   *

13

Oh Marco. I couldn't even *think* his name without sighing. What was he doing right then? Closing my eyes for a second, I could see him quite clearly as he had been at our last – our only – face-to-face meeting, when we sat opposite each other in his office. He had held my hands and looked into my face. It should have been the moment we confirmed our love for one another. Instead it was the moment he declared himself out of the game.

Was Berlin where I would find the love he thought I wanted? I felt as though, ever since I had broken up with Steven in London almost a year before, I had been on the run in one way or another. Literally, as I moved from country to country, and perhaps psychologically too, investing my heart in the impossible dream that was Mr Marco Donato. The love I longed for seemed to dangle in front of me, like the carrot on the stick that remains out of reach no matter how fast the donkey runs.

I still thought about Marco every single day. Now, of course, I knew what he looked like – I'd burst in on him in his secret lair and seen his partly burnt face and withered hand – and that had added all sorts of complications to my feelings. I had fallen in love with his mind and told myself that his exterior did not matter. Not to me. Not to us . . . In any case, once you know someone, you look beyond their face, don't you? You look directly into their eyes. The eyes don't change. It's why your best friends never seem to age, no matter how long you know them. When we met face to face for the first time, however, in the office hidden in the library walls, Marco had been altogether less optimistic. He had said some things that shocked me to the core. He'd accused me of wanting to 'rescue' him for all the wrong reasons. He said he thought I liked the idea of the attention being with him would bring. What better way to feel beautiful than to stand alongside someone so damaged?

Marco's words had seemed so cruel and so hurtful. But with the benefit of time and distance, I wasn't so sure he was wrong after all. I had gone over our conversation many times and had to admit there were elements of truth to his accusations. Was it possible that I had latched onto him in order to boost my own self-esteem?

I hoped that wasn't the case. Though I had to admit that when Marco was in hospital, all those years ago, long before I knew who he was and what role he would come to play in my life, I had felt proud of my efforts to keep him going through his recovery. It *had* made me feel good about myself to be looking after him. And when I got to Venice, having broken up with Steven, God knows I needed something to make me feel good about myself again. But that wasn't what had drawn me back to Marco in particular, was it? It couldn't have been. When Marco and I began to write to one another, I'd had no idea he was the same Italian man who had wound up in the hospital where I had worked during my school holidays. No idea at all. How could I?

No, I told myself for the hundredth time. I had not fallen for Marco Donato because he seemed like a lost soul or someone who needed rescuing and I thought it might make me feel better to be that rescuer. I had just fallen for his wit and his charm . . .

And for the face in the old photographs I found online, a small voice reminded me. The model-handsome face that no longer existed. Even alone in my room in Berlin, I blushed with shame as I remembered how excited I had been at the idea that someone as glamorous and good-looking as the man in those pictures might be interested in someone like me.

But what did that matter any more? After I insisted that he see me, Marco had sent me away in such a determined and final manner that I could do nothing other than believe he sincerely hoped he'd never see me again. I had heard nothing from him since. The crazy fantasies we had shared were fast fading even in my overactive imagination. It was time for me to move on.

2

The Adlon Hotel, Berlin
Monday 9th May 1932

Dear Mummy,

I am writing to you from Berlin! I'm sure Papa has
told you I'm to be cut off altogether after the incident
in Munich, but I know you won't take any notice of
him. I feel certain you will want to know how I am
getting on, so I'm writing to let you know that I am
getting along very well indeed.

Of course, Cord has been looking after me here in
the big city and I'm sure we will be engaged just as soon
as he has finished his training. I know that when Papa
finally meets Cord in person, he will understand
absolutely why I fell for the lovely man. He's not just tall
and handsome, he's clever and very polite. Papa will be
glad I didn't come back to do the season and end up
with some chinless wimp like Eleanor's husband. I know
she is my cousin and I should be more generous, but
really, Mummy, I'm sure you agree.

I must go now. Cord has promised to take me to a
cultural evening at the Opera and he's picking me up
in ten minutes. Please write soon and if you could

send a few quid at the same time, it would be gratefully received. Only on a temporary basis, of course. This hotel is expensive so Cord is going to arrange for me to stay with his relations until we can organise a wedding and get a place of our own. I am also looking for work as a bilingual secretary. I'm sure I'll have something within the week.

Give my love to the dogs and to Papa, even if he says he doesn't want it.

Your loving daughter,

Katherine

Katherine Hazleton, Kitty to her friends, sealed the envelope and took it to the post office, where she spent far more than she could afford on sending the letter back to England. She prayed that it would yield some kind of return. She was sure it would. Her mother had always been a soft touch compared to her papa. Kitty had no doubt whatsoever that Mrs Hazleton would defy her father's inevitable furious decree that Kitty should be cut off without a penny.

Her crime? Kitty had fallen in love. His name was Cord Von Cord. Kitty met him in Munich. Cord was visiting his aunt, who ran the boarding house where Kitty was staying while she attended finishing school. Cord was a medical student. He was tall and blond and very, very good-looking in that chiselled German way. Totally swoonsome, is how Kitty described him to her finishing-school roommate, Miranda. And he was scrupulously well-mannered too. At least, until after dark.

Kitty and Cord had been caught in her bedroom. Nothing had happened – not even, much to Kitty's disappointment, a proper tongue-filled kiss – but Cord's aunt simply would not believe it. A young lady alone in a bedroom with a man! Oh, the scandal! She sent Cord straight back to Berlin with a flea in his ear and telephoned Kitty's parents the very next morning. Rather than wait around for her father to pick her up and face the long journey home to Surrey, listening to a lecture all the way, Kitty did a bunk, using the last of her cash to catch a train to Berlin where she took a room at the Adlon (the only Berlin hotel Kitty had ever heard of) and waited for Cord to come and justify her impulsive move.

Well, Cord did come to the hotel and he did tell Kitty that he loved her. They went to bed properly this time and did everything Kitty could imagine and quite a few other things beside. Who knew such dreadful acts could be so pleasurable! But then Cord told her that while he loved her passionately, he rather wished she hadn't followed him to Berlin because, actually, he was already engaged to be married to someone else. He was sorry he'd neglected to mention it. His wedding would take place in two weeks.

How stupid Kitty felt then. She felt even more stupid two days later when her mother still hadn't written with money and what little cash she had was almost run through. Perhaps it had been a mistake to pretend that Cord was planning to marry her. Perhaps the truth would have elicited a quicker response. The Adlon was terribly expensive and the manager flatly refused to give her credit, no matter who her father was. After three nights, Kitty moved out of the hotel and went to look for cheaper lodgings. She had to look for a very long time; the best parts of Berlin were suddenly closed to her. In the end, after a horrible day, dragging her suitcase for what felt like fifty miles, she checked into an absolute fleapit at the wrong end of the Kurfürstendamm – the legendary Ku'damm spoken of by the finishing school's more experienced girls. It was awful. The only running water was coming down the *inside* of the walls. There was no fiancé, no bilingual office job and definitely no cultural evenings at the Opera. Kitty was all alone and absolutely skint.

But she still had her inner fire, is what she told herself as she gingerly lifted a grey blanket to check for bedbugs. Surviving in Berlin should be no problem at all. So what if she wasn't in the best part of town? She had her street smarts and her savvy and she had just enough German to get by.

And to get into trouble, as it happened.

When Kitty booked into the Hotel Frankfort in the late afternoon, she found the neighbourhood shabby but otherwise unremarkable. As soon as night fell, however, the street outside was transformed. During the day, the locals shuffled grey-faced about their errands. In the evenings, everybody perked up and the street was transformed into a market, though not a market selling anything that Kitty would have wanted to buy.

But she had to go out. She was hungry and even the food her horrid hotel offered at a discount for residents was way beyond her budget. She put on her boots – the green boots her mother had bought for her on their last trip to London – and strode out onto the street. It was important, she told herself, to convey an air of confidence. When you tried to make yourself inconspicuous, that was when you marked yourself out as a victim. If you walked tall and with a purpose, no one would bother you. That was the theory. Alas, Kitty's theory was wrong.

It started within a few feet of the hotel door. The catcalling and the whispers. One ruffian even went so far as to grab her arm and ask her, with incredible impudence, 'How much?'

'Unhand me,' she told him, speaking English loudly and slowly, in the way that had won and was losing an empire. She shook him off and continued on her way. He followed her halfway down the street, making terrible kissing noises as he stuck close like a dog at her heels.

At last Kitty spotted a respectable-looking restaurant and quickly slipped inside. But while she was reading the menu, an elderly man came and sat right opposite her and made no bones at all about his desires. He called her 'mistress'. She told him to leave her in peace. She wasn't interested in having any company that night.

Perhaps he didn't understand Kitty's accent. Far from leaving her alone, the old man reached for her hand and pleaded. She *must* let him sit with her. He had been waiting his whole life for someone so lovely. He would spend the rest of his days in her service if she'd only say 'yes' to him. When should he start?

'If you want to be of service to me,' she told him in her best schoolgirl German, 'you can tell that waiter to come over here and take my order. I've been waiting far too long.'

To Kitty's astonishment, the old man scuttled off and the waiter duly appeared, with the old man right behind him. Kitty gave her order and closed the menu with an irritated snap.

21

'I still don't want any company,' she told the old man, who was about to sit down opposite her again. She only wanted to fill in her diary. She had kept a daily diary since she was eleven years old and right then she had a lot to catch up with. 'Will you please leave me alone?' she asked. 'Go on. Shoo.' She waved him off.

With that, he fell to the floor at her feet and begged her not to send him away. He beseeched her. He would do whatever she required of him. She only had to say the word. All he asked was that she let him clean her boots with his tongue and after that he wanted nothing more than to lie prostrate upon the floor while she unleashed the contents of her bowels on to his head.

'What?'

Kitty stood up. The man was still clinging to her ankles.

'Unleash my what?'

Kitty's German vocabulary was fairly limited but she certainly knew '*Scheißen*'. The old man repeated his fondest wish and added actions to make his meaning even clearer.

Fearing that the old man was about to pull down his trousers in the middle of the dining room, Kitty flew into a panic. She swatted at him with her napkin. He seemed to think it was all part of the game. The more she whipped him about the head with the dirty white cloth, the harder he clung onto her. And then he started *licking* her boots. Actually trying to clean the leather with his tongue. It really was too much.

'Help!' Kitty screamed. 'Someone help me! Help! *Hilfe! Helft mir!*'

On the other side of the room, a young man, tall and

smartly dressed, decided it was time to come to Kitty's aid. He pulled the old man to his feet and, dusting him off quite gently, told him with a smile of wry amusement that he'd got the wrong girl.

'But she . . .' The old man gave Kitty's green leather boots one last longing glance.

'I know,' said the young man. 'But I don't think that's their meaning. She isn't from round here. You heard her accent. Let her get on with her dinner and look for your ideal mistress outside. This lady doesn't wish to be bothered.'

'She's asking for it, the way she's dressing . . .'

'How dare you!' said Kitty. 'Go away, you vile man.'

'You're a prick-tease, you are,' said Kitty's aged admirer.

The young man's face hardened. 'Come along, Grandpa.' He nodded towards the door and the old man slunk away. Kitty collapsed back down into her seat and fanned her pink cheeks with her hand.

'Thank you,' she said to the young man. 'I don't know what I would have done without you. That old chap was quite deranged,' she continued. 'Kept calling me "mistress". He wanted to lick my boots and have me . . .' Kitty pulled a face in place of the terrible word. 'You *know*. On *him*. Can you imagine?'

'I'd rather not. But it is what you were advertising,' said the young man after a pause. He pointed at her footwear. 'Green boots. Gold laces. Debasement and a bit of defecation.'

That was how Kitty came to be aware of the secret semaphore of footwear in Weimar Berlin.

'You should stay away from red boots too, if you're

23

going to frequent this establishment. Red or maroon means you're into flagellation.'

'Oh dear,' said Kitty. 'These are the only boots I've got.'

'In which case, best buy a longer skirt,' said Kitty's hero. 'Or dine somewhere else. All the old dominas hang out here when they're not busy.'

'Dominas? I don't think I understand you . . .'

'I have to go to work now,' he said. 'But it has been nice to talk to you, Miss . . .'

'Hazleton.' She held out her hand. 'Katherine Hazleton.'

'Otto Schmidt.'

With gentlemanly grace, the young man lifted her hand to his mouth and pretended to kiss it. 'Pleased to be of service.'

Kitty felt an unexpected tingle as for the first time she got a proper look at the young man's startlingly blue eyes. He smiled in a way that suggested mutual recognition. This was something more than two strangers making passing acquaintance. Kitty watched Otto Schmidt leave the restaurant and found herself wishing he might have stayed.

3

Venice, September last year

The Palazzo Donato was silent as ever. Outside, Venice carried on as it had always done, unchanged for centuries, entertaining all-comers from every country in the world. Late-summer tourists crowded the narrow streets and posed for photographs against the eternally romantic background of crumbling ochre buildings and sleek black gondolas in that perfect mellow light. The cafés of San Marco were doing a roaring trade. Meanwhile, liners as big as tower blocks docked at the Maritime Port and disgorged yet more visitors, keen to lay eyes on the most beautiful city on earth.

Unseen inside the courtyard garden of the Donato house, the roses were putting on one last show. The fountain was turned off; only the persistent drip that provided a shower for the dusty sparrows revealed that it still worked at all. The statues of Orpheus and Eurydice still reached for each other in vain. The gallery from where the palazzo's original owner, courtesan Ernesta, had once observed the comings and goings of her eminent guests, echoed only to the sound of Silvio the old retainer's footsteps as he went about his business like a monk.

Marco Donato had retreated to his life of seclusion again. There was one brief moment when it seemed as though Sarah the English girl's brave decision to burst into his hiding place and confront him might have worked. A couple of days after she left, Marco had spoken to his doctor about the possibility of surgery. Perhaps there was still something that could be done to wipe away the traces of the accident that had changed everything. The doctor confirmed that there had been advances. New techniques might bring a great deal of relief. But then the momentum died away. It had been much too long. That faint flicker of optimism was gone again and Marco turned his face to the wall, just as he had done for real in the private hospital all those years earlier. It was hopeless. The scars were far more than skin-deep.

Silvio knew better than to try to coax his master to talk about the situation. Though Marco had seen no one but Silvio and the doctor in years, Silvio would not dare to presume for himself the privileges of a friend. He just carried on as before. He rose at six to have his master's breakfast ready for seven. He made lunch at one and dinner at eight. He kept the house clean. He ran errands. He was Marco's connection with the outside world. But there was an interior world that he could never hope to penetrate.

While Silvio walked the corridors with his trusty wooden broom, Marco remained in his office. In the mornings, he dealt with his business interests. The Donato shipping line still reached every corner of the globe and there were many decisions to be made. Much responsibility. Marco hadn't lied to Sarah when he told her that he often spent what should have been his leisure time at work. When he did have free time, he read. For the most part he read history. The history of his own city, of Paris and of Germany. He used to draw but he hadn't picked up his sketchbook in months. Couldn't think of anything he wanted to look at for long enough to make a drawing of it. Not any more.

Marco stared at his last sketch of Sarah as though, if he

looked at it hard enough, it might just come to life. It was the picture he had drawn on the afternoon she had made herself vulnerable to him. He had drawn her sitting in the chair at the library desk. She had her legs open. Her long shirt dress was unbuttoned at the bodice. Her hands were hidden in the folds of her skirt. She was leaning back. Her head tipped. Hair streaming behind her. Her mouth was open. Her throat exposed.

As he looked at the drawing, a far clearer picture conjured itself in Marco's head. In his mind he could hear her as well as see her. He heard her breathing. He heard her whisper to herself as she read his instructions on the laptop screen. She had trusted him so much. But then he had trusted her too.

What would have happened if he'd dared to show himself to her that day, as she'd asked? Might they have made love for real? He thought about it often. He'd wanted her so much.

Each evening, after she left the library to go home, he would let himself into the library and take her place at the desk. He would read the pages she had been reading. He would brush them with his fingers, as though touching something she had touched so recently could somehow draw them closer.

Once, she left a glove behind. It had fallen unnoticed from the pocket of her coat as she dressed to go back to her apartment in the Dorsoduro and lay forgotten on the mat by the fire. As soon as he could, Marco went straight to retrieve it. He snatched it up and pressed it to his face as though it still contained Sarah's hand. There was a faint scent of perfume on the wool at the glove's wrist. Marco inhaled it. There was something familiar in its echo. He kept the glove, hoping that Sarah would think she had dropped it somewhere other than the palazzo. And when eventually he worked out that the perfume she wore was Iris Nobile by Acqua Di Parma, he had Silvio buy a bottle. It sat wrapped up in a desk drawer. A gift he never gave.

Marco still had the glove. It was in his bedroom, in the bedside cabinet. At one point, he had taken it out every night and held it for a moment before he went to sleep. Such a silly thing. The sort of thing a teenage girl would do, he berated himself, but it was the closest he had come to a woman's touch in so long. Until that night in February at the Martedì Grasso ball.

Sarah could have had no idea how hard it had been for him to make the decision to meet her at last. While Silvio oversaw arrangements for the party, Marco prepared a thousand opening lines. He was as frightened as any young boy planning to meet his first love. No; more frightened. He had so much to lose and so many reasons to expect that she would not want him. That's why he had chosen to throw the party. It was easy for him to entice her there and easy for him to disappear if it all went wrong. He'd sent the dress to mark her out – exactly as she had suspected – so that he would not have to risk wasting his confidence and energy on anyone but her. The possibility of rejection was so high. He'd felt sick with anxiety and yet he'd still decided that it was worth taking the risk. Sarah had enchanted him. Before he knew it, she would have finished her research and flown back to London. He wanted to give her a reason to stay. He had to make a move before she left.

If she had known how hard it was for him even to admit to himself that's what he desired, she would never have allowed what happened to happen.

Marco felt he had been waiting for hours when the girl in the dress arrived. Though she held a mask to her face, he knew at once that something was not right. The mask was not the one he had given her, for a start. And though she was the right height and the dress was the perfect fit, this girl did not move like Sarah. Sarah's way of moving was elegant but modest. This other girl – her friend Bea, as he would find out – sashayed into the room. She didn't so much walk as dance.

Marco had no time to evade her. He was too slow to move behind a bookcase and she spotted him as soon as she stepped into the room. She flirted with him. She was the kind of girl who would flirt with anyone, was Marco's guess. She dared him to take his mask off and when he refused, she made a grab for his hand.

Her face had said it all.

Marco had not looked in a mirror for a decade and that night was no exception. In order to reveal himself to Sarah, he had had to convince himself that it was not so bad. Bea's expression – her mouth open in shock when she saw his burnt hand – told him that he was kidding himself. His hand wasn't even the worst of it.

Once he had seen how Bea struggled to contain her reaction, there was no chance of him having the courage to meet Sarah that night. Bea was an intelligent woman. She didn't want to be seen to be horrified, but she was. She dropped his hand as though it was still burning. And then she was embarrassed, fleeing the scene like a child. Why should Sarah be any different? He no longer had the courage to find out.

How Marco had wished he could be whole again. Whole and perfect for Sarah. Then he would not have had to worry about rejection. He could have agreed to her early suggestions that they meet. They could have gone for a coffee, like two ordinary people. They would have had so much to talk about; they would have stayed together for the rest of the day. They would have walked back to her flat in the Dorsoduro and she would have invited him inside and offered him some wine.

After that, the actual seduction would have been a

formality. She would have glanced shyly downwards when he went to kiss her for the first time – women always did – but she would have acquiesced enthusiastically, giving in to the desire that had been building between them all day.

He would have followed her to the bedroom with the curious four-poster bed she had described to him in her emails. They would have undressed, marvelling at the perfection they found in one another. He would have kissed every inch of her body. He would have revelled in the beauty of her breasts. He had often imagined how soft they would be. They were so pale, untouched by the sun. The contrast of her rose-pink nipples was perfect.

By her side, he would have lain content for hours, just kissing her and tracing the outlines of her curves. To think of her touching him was almost too much. The thought of her hand around his penis made him catch his breath. The thought of her mouth seeking out his hardness made him close his eyes and let his own hand stray towards his crotch. To be inside her . . . He had no fonder wish.

From the moment Sarah walked into the courtyard garden of the Palazzo Donato, Marco had known he wanted to be with her. The gawky young girl who had haunted his bedside at the hospital had grown into a beautiful woman. She had such poise as she walked behind Silvio and when she looked up, as though she already knew of his hiding place, the sight of her heart-shaped face was like a punch to the solar plexus. From that moment, he was lost. A part of him he'd long forgotten began to come back to life.

In a funny way, to begin with it was uncomplicated. Flirting by email was so easy. It was the modern way. No one thought it odd any more if you didn't pick up the phone. But eventually, even text lovers have to meet face to face. He couldn't blame Sarah for wondering why he wouldn't come out from behind the safety of a screen. Of course, modest and shy as she was, she assumed it was because of some lack on her part.

How ridiculous. She was so perfect. He couldn't believe she'd ever thought she wasn't good enough for him. But she had compared herself to the stupid models in those decade-old photographs. If only he had been able to tell her what they were really like.

If only Sarah had known how much he wanted to be able to take her out and show her off and let her know how much he loved her from the pride he took from being beside her. He wanted to show her off to everyone and introduce her to old friends and family. But he couldn't imagine he would ever really be able to face the world again and, apart from Silvio, his friends and family had long since given up on him. He could not possibly have expected Sarah to join him in his isolation. She needed to be part of the real world. That is what Marco meant when he wished for Sarah an extraordinarily ordinary love.

But if she was willing to sacrifice the ordinary to be with him, then who was he to tell her not to? Perhaps it could work.

A small, rebellious part of Marco's brain kept trying to be heard above the rest. She had come back to him again and again. She had put her fears to one side and kept trying to break through. Who was he to tell her she was wrong? Perhaps she really did love him for his heart and his mind. Perhaps the way he looked really didn't matter to her. It wasn't impossible.

But then she did not know the whole truth, did she? She had not believed him when he told her his outer appearance was a manifestation of inner corruption and cowardice. If she knew the truth, she would finally see him differently and no

31

amount of kind-heartedness would be able to get past the way he looked then.

Marco silenced the optimistic voice again.

Alone in his secret office, he hid his favourite drawing of Sarah inside his own diary, alongside the real story. The ugly truth.

4

Berlin, September last year

I couldn't sleep on my first night in Germany. I got into bed, but the strange room and the unfamiliar sounds of the house settling down for the night meant I could only lie beneath the duvet with my eyes wide open, watching shadows pass across the ceiling, wondering if that noise I heard was a creaking pipe or footsteps on the stairs.

Eventually I gave in and got up. It was too late to watch television so I decided I would do some virtual housekeeping. My email in-box was full of messages I didn't need to keep. In the darkness of the night, with only the light of my screen to illuminate the room, I responded to all those emails I had been meaning to take care of for months. They weren't urgent, but they were still important. I made myself some camomile tea, then I set about bringing old friends and colleagues up to speed with what I was doing. I sent out belated birthday greetings – some so late it was easier to call them early for the following year – and gave my take on gossip doubtless long since gone cold. Apart from those who were closest to me, I had been neglecting my friendships over the past nine months. When Steven and I first broke up, I'd hidden myself away because I didn't want to have to explain what had happened. Then came my trip to Venice, then Paris, then a summer on the road. It was time to reconnect at last.

It was also time to do some weeding.

When I had finished dealing with the current emails, I turned my attention to those I had saved over the years. I had a file full of emails from Steven. Hundreds of them: from the effusive ten-page-long love poems we sent to each other at the very beginning of our relationship to the curt 'Please remember milk' notes that characterised the end. I didn't bother to open them but I decided against deleting them too. It no longer hurt me to see them and one day, I thought, I might like to reread some of the early ones.

But then I came to another file. It was titled 'Marco' and it contained everything we had ever written to each other that hadn't been committed to paper. It was home to all our emails and screen-grabs of our direct messages. Every digital missive we'd sent one another, from Marco's first response to my letter asking if I might visit the library, to my email telling him that I knew he was behind the 'out of the blue' job for the film company making Augustine du Vert's biopic. The only other things I had to remind me of our strange relationship were Marco's first and last handwritten letters: the first letter inviting me to the palazzo and the other asking me to give up on him and not come back again. They were tucked into my notebook, next to the rose I had stolen from his garden. The flower, which I had pressed between two pieces of paper, was now so dried out and delicate it was starting to crumble and I had read Marco's farewell letter so often that it too was in danger of falling apart, having been unfolded and folded so many times. I didn't need to open it again. I knew its sad paragraphs by heart.

I opened the computer file. The list of contents I found there was innocuous. Looking at it didn't hurt so much, but I knew that if I opened any one of them, I might feel differently.

February 1st, for example. Was that the day when we told each other how we lost our respective virginities? Was February 19th when I told him about the end of my relationship with Steven? I could no longer bear to look. Especially not at the direct messages we had sent each other that day in the library when Marco asked me to open the top left-hand drawer of the desk and I found a small black pebble-shaped vibrator waiting for my pleasure.

Thinking about that day made me close my eyes tightly to hold back the tears. I thought it had been the start of something. I had been so very wrong. After that day, everything seemed to fall apart.

I closed the Marco file. I hovered the cursor over it, ready to drag it into the trash can in the corner of the screen. It would have been so easy to leave it for another day but something in me wanted to make a definitive move right then. I dragged the file to the dustbin icon and quickly clicked on 'empty trash' so that there was no way I could go back and reinstate the files later. I felt a moment of heart-stopping horror as I heard the sound of scrunched-up paper that accompanied the virtual action. But then it was over. Marco was gone from my laptop.

After that, while I was still feeling brave, I took out the letters I'd read so many times and the pressed flower that had seemed such an important symbol of my feelings for the man in whose garden it had grown. I'd carried them from Venice to Paris and to London. Now I put them all into the bin in the kitchen, before I poured the fast-cooling remains of my camomile tea over the top of them, ruining them for ever. It was the only thing to do. The right thing.

It was about four o'clock in the morning by the time I went back to bed. By now, I was properly tired and it wasn't long before I fell asleep. In fact, I fell asleep in the middle of reading and would wake up with the imprint of my paperback pressed into my cheek. But until then, I slept deeply and dreamlessly. I was not bothered during the night by thoughts of Venice and my masked lover. No paramour came to call up to my window and entice me to join him in the shadowy felce of his sleek black gondola. No passionate stranger slid his hands all over my naked body as though he were playing a rare and delicate instrument. No man made music of my protestations, my acquiescence or my sighs of ecstasy and delight.

I slept. I woke up. In the morning the light through the thin curtains at my bedroom window was grey. I looked at my face in the mirror, creased and blurry with sleep. Time to face the day. The future.

5

The Hotel Frankfort, Berlin
Thursday 9th June 1932

Drat it. There's still nothing from Mother. I can't believe
my luck. Things have been very tight indeed, particularly
as I had to splash out on a pair of new boots to avoid
harassment every time I leave the hotel. Honestly, I
started to think that perhaps I should offer someone an
afternoon of enslavement and scatological entertainment just to be able to afford to move out of this fleapit
and into somewhere decent again. I am sure that nobody
looked at my boots in such a strange way when I was staying at the Hotel Adlon.

On Monday and Tuesday I went to all the secretarial
agencies I could find, but it turns out that my German is
nowhere near good enough to get me a position as a bilingual secretary. The woman I met at one place was quite
cruel about my lack of ability. She said that perhaps in
England people are happy to employ young women on
the basis of their looks alone, but in Germany a neat
appearance has to be backed up by solid administration
skills. In any case, the bitch continued, while my dress was
very fetching, it was far more suitable for a nightclub than

a respectable office. I suppose she had a point about that. I have been forced to wear some very strange combinations while I cannot afford to send my clothes to the cleaners. Oh Cord Von Cord! What you have reduced me to!

I can't believe Mummy hasn't sent a money order. She's usually such a softy. She can never resist a sob story, least of all from me – her only child! I can only think that perhaps she didn't get my last letter. Perhaps Papa intercepted the post and is trying to starve me into submission.

Well, more fool him, because I can hold out against his tyranny for far longer than he imagines. I am resourceful. I have proved that to myself in bucketloads this afternoon. I've only gone and got myself a job!

So perhaps it's not the kind of job my parents would have wished for me but I have no doubt that it will be interesting. I heard about it when I was trying to sneak past the hotel reception desk at lunchtime.

I owe nearly three weeks' rent and I just don't have it so I have been trying to avoid Enno, the hotel manager, as I go about my day. He has been very kind so far but I know he can't keep extending my credit for ever and the last thing I want is to find myself too much in his debt. He's completely cross-eyed and smells of sauerkraut. But today, he caught me. He saw me coming and hid behind the desk, knowing that if I didn't see him there, I might risk taking a look at the pigeonholes to see if I had any post. As I leaned over the desk to do exactly that, he grabbed me by the wrist, like the troll beneath the bridge grabbing the Billy Goats Gruff.

I screamed.

'Got you,' he said.

I screamed again. It was horrible. He scared me half to death. Still, he found me a chair and made me sit down on it. He waited until I had finished hyperventilating before he made his case.

'Fräulein Hazleton, you are a whole three weeks behind with your rent. The rules of this hotel are that bills are settled on a weekly basis. There are to be no exceptions.'

I nodded along to his speech.

'I cannot continue to extend you credit,' he said. 'My own job is now on the line.'

I burst into tears and cried very prettily but I knew I could test his patience no more.

'I'll move out this afternoon,' I said. 'I'm sure I will be perfectly fine under the railway arches.'

Poor Enno looked horrified. 'Hey hey!' he said. 'There's no need for that.'

He handed me his rather dirty handkerchief with which to dry my eyes.

'Look, a friend of mine is looking for waitresses in his bar,' Enno told me. 'I'm sure it is not the kind of work you're looking for, but it is better than nothing. It's a nice place. The staff are friendly. If you go over there this afternoon, I will wait until you have your first pay cheque before I ask you for money again.'

'Oh thank you, Enno.' It was such a kind offer, I had to say I'd take it up.

Enno's friend – a man named Jerry Schluter – owns a place called the Boom Boom Bar. I have passed it many times but never dared set foot inside. It doesn't look like the kind of place a girl should frequent on her own. But Enno assured me that no harm would come to me. The man who owns the Boom Boom and the guys and girls who work there are all good people, he said.

'They're just a little different, that's all.'

How different, I had no idea.

I arrived at the Boom Boom around three in the afternoon. The outside is very shabby. It also looked closed, but when I pressed my nose to the glass panel in the door, I saw there were people inside. I stepped into the lobby, with its worn-out carpet and velvet-flocked walls, and plastered on my most enthusiastic look. It was hard to hold that look for long. The floor was sticky and the air was redolent of spilled beer. I thought I might get drunk just from breathing.

A couple of people passed through the lobby without even looking at me, so I took my enthusiastic face off and coughed to get someone's attention.

'A-hem,' I said. 'A-hem!'

There was a woman on the counter. She had red hair piled high on her head in a number of tiny curls so that it looked like a dish of profiteroles (having lived off just one meal a day for the past week, I am starting to see food everywhere). When I asked her where I might find Herr Schluter, she answered me in an extraordinarily deep voice. And when she looked up, I saw she had five o'clock shadow. I couldn't hide my surprise.

'Yes, dear,' she said, in a bored sort of voice. 'I've got it all.' She grabbed at her crotch.

'Well, er, I'm . . . sorry,' I said. 'If I seemed at all rude. It's just that you remind me of my aunt.'

The redhead chuckled.

'She's got a dick as well, has she?'

'My father says he wouldn't be at all surprised,' I answered. The redhead grinned. I had the feeling I'd passed some kind of test.

'Who are you looking for, my darling?'

'I'm here to see Herr Schluter.'

'Down the corridor,' the redhead told me. 'Better make sure you knock.'

I hurried in the direction of Herr Schluter's office. I was already sure I didn't want any kind of job he could offer me but if I at least saw him, it might give me a little credit with Enno. Even a couple of days would be perfect. Mummy could write at any moment and then I wouldn't need to work at all . . . Still I knocked, as instructed.

I heard giggling in the room beyond. It was a little while before my call was answered by a scraggy-looking blonde, who waved me in and scuttled away.

Herr Schluter, a tiny man with a head as bald as an egg, was sitting with his feet on his desk. He looked me up and down. He pursed his lips. 'Enno told me you had tits,' was his idea of a greeting.

'Well!' I crossed my arms over my chest.

'Never mind,' said Herr Schluter. 'He was just trying to make sure I saw you. Tits are my thing, you see. But girls who look like boys appeal to plenty of people around here.'

'I didn't come here to be insulted,' I said.

'No,' said Herr Schluter. 'I understand you came here for a job. Have you worked as a waitress before?'

'Of course I haven't,' I said,

'There's no "of course" about it, as far as I'm concerned. You're living in the Hotel Frankfort and you haven't paid your bills in three weeks. You're in no position to play the society girl with me, Fräulein . . .'

'Hazleton.'

'Hazleton . . . So you've got no experience but I like your face. You seem quite plucky. If you want the job, you can start tonight.'

'What do I have to do?' I asked.

'Wait tables?' came the reply. 'Anything else you do in your own time and well off the premises. I don't want any trouble.'

'I'm sure I don't know what you're talking about.'

'You will,' he said. 'You will.'

After that, thank goodness, Herr Schluter got a little friendlier. He gave me a tour of the club. I could tell he was proud of the chipped gold tables and the tiny stage with its red velvet curtains. Then he showed me the kitchen. 'Where miracles happen,' he said. A chef with a filthy apron was peeling potatoes for the evening ahead. I was glad I'd never eaten there.

'Is this the new one?' the chef asked of me.

'I certainly hope so,' said Herr Schluter. 'English. A touch of class for the place, don't you think?'

'Heaven knows it needs it,' said the cook, who was called Hans. Old Hans, to be precise. It differentiated him from Young Hans, the stagehand who works the Boom Boom's curtains.

After he had finished the little tour, Herr Schluter told me to ask the man-woman on reception to find me a uniform. Since I was going to have to work with him/her, I thought I'd better ask his/her name.

'It's Marlene,' was the reply. 'Like Dietrich. And I am always referred to as "she".'

'Katherine Hazleton. Kitty,' I said, holding out my hand.

Marlene looked at my gloves, once white, now distinctly grey. There was a hole in the tip of one finger.

'Goodness me, you really do need this job,' she said.

Marlene took me down into the basement where the uniforms were kept. We passed a couple of dressing rooms. I couldn't resist peeking in. In one room, a young man about my age was coating his lashes with mascara. He was wearing a rather lovely silver dress. He caught me gawping and gave me a smile.

'That's Isadora. Like the dancer.'

'Hello, sweet thing,' Isadora called.

Isadora's friendly smile made me feel a little better. Likewise, Young Hans seemed rather nice. I began to feel as though my new job might not be so bad after all. Until Marlene handed me my uniform. The skirt barely covered my bottom.

'This isn't my size,' I told her.

Marlene assured me it was.

'But it shows my . . .'

'That's the idea, you silly sausage. All the better for earning those tips. You won't get by on your wages alone. You need to work the floor. You got any rollers? Your hair could do with being more . . .' Marlene mimed a bouffant.

I told her I didn't.

'Then come a bit early,' she said. 'And I'll fix you up.'

*   *   *

43

Now I'd better finish this diary entry and get myself to the Boom Boom so Marlene can indeed do my hair. I can hardly believe that tonight I start work as a waitress. A waitress in a transvestite club at that! Papa would be apoplectic. I think Mummy would be secretly impressed. All the same, I don't think I'll tell her when I write again tomorrow morning.

6

After the languid mystery of Venice and the haughty chic of Paris, Berlin felt much more like London and perhaps, if I cared to admit it, that's why it felt much more like it could be home.

My first few days there were blessed by brilliant late-summer sunshine. It was wonderfully warm: the sort of weather that makes you feel as though you're on holiday the moment you step out of the office.

I'd reported to my new boss and met my new colleagues but the university term had yet to begin. I had no students as yet, so, when I wasn't taking catch-up German lessons myself, I spent some time exploring the city. I'd visited before, on a school language-exchange trip and again to interview for the post I had just taken up, but I'd never done more than dash round the major monuments that were the top on any tourist's 'must do' list. I'd climbed to the top of the impressive glass dome of the Reichstag building and had my photograph taken by the Brandenburg Gate. I'd even posed with a fake soldier at Checkpoint Charlie. I hadn't been much more adventurous than that.

I was looking forward to getting to know Berlin a great deal better. It helped that I had some friends in the city already and they were eager to show me their favourite places.

There was Clare, of course, my friend since our undergraduate days. And then there was Harry. I met Harry when we worked together at Selfridges during one Christmas break. Extravagantly camp, he was a real Marmite person in that you either loved him or you hated him. Fortunately, I loved him from the moment we were set to work side by side, keeping control of the queue for Santa's grotto in Selfridges' toy department. He could always make me laugh.

Clare and Harry both loved the city and shared their enthusiasm at once. It certainly felt like a place with a great deal going for it. Compared to Paris, the population seemed much younger and less uptight. Compared to Venice, everyone seemed to have more energy and drive. The Venetians were content to rest on achievements past. I suppose it made sense that Berlin seemed to be looking more to the future, given what a complicated past Germany had.

The first weekend I was in town, I met Clare and Harry for a tour of the real Berlin. We met at the sombre and moving Berlin Wall monument on the Bernauer Strasse. I'd always thought of the Wall as just that: a wall. Seeing a preserved section of the wide strip of no-man's-land that had actually flanked the rather insignificant-looking Wall itself was surprising and chilling. There was a thick layer of sand, designed to make it impossible for an escapee to cross at speed or to do so without leaving a trace. There would have been dogs too and acres of barbed wire.

We walked from the Wall monument to the Mauerpark flea market, which was like a slightly more orderly version of Camden. There, Harry insisted on introducing me to the delights of various heavy German sausages. Suffice to say, we needed several beers to wash them down.

As we sat in a busy beer garden near the Kollwitzplatz, I

told Clare and Harry about my upcoming research project. They both felt sure they could help me find interesting subjects for interview. I told them about my travels too.

'You've been all over the place this year,' said Clare with a hint of wistful envy. 'What was Paris like? What was Venice like?'

I gave her the official line. They were both great cities and I'd had a great time. I'd got plenty of work done. She didn't need to know any more than that. I didn't mention Marco.

'Any man in your life?' Clare asked. 'I was surprised when you broke up with Steven. I always thought you guys were perfectly matched.'

'On the surface perhaps. You can never tell what's going on beneath.'

'A bit like Berlin,' said Harry. 'On the surface, everything's organised and orderly. Underneath, there's a raging heart. I tell you, Sarah. You are going to love being here. This city is totally crazy.'

At the end of the afternoon, we made plans to meet again later in the week, for a proper night out when Clare would take me to her favourite club. Harry made similar promises.

I went back to my new apartment alone. Passing Herr Schmidt's door, I heard the sound of a Chopin prelude drifting out to greet me. I'd seen the piano in Herr Schmidt's living room while we shared the cake but I'd had no idea he was such an accomplished player. The beautiful sound made my heart sting just a little. I hurried up the stairs before a wave of sadness could catch me.

I made myself a cup of tea and sat on the windowsill of my new bedroom, which had the best view of all the rooms I now lived in. I watched the wind in the tall trees of the Volkspark but my mind was elsewhere again.

What was Marco doing right now? Was life for him continuing as it had done for so long? A silent existence in a hidden room. Seeing only Silvio from day to day. Controlling his business interests from afar. Controlling himself, allowing no emotion to seep through and ruffle the calm of his orderly existence. Definitely no untidy love.

How had I fallen so deeply for someone I knew only at a distance? In real life, we had touched just once, when I reached out to take his hand as we sat in his study and he told me, at length and with more passion than I had imagined he had in his body, exactly why we could not and should not be together. Yet I felt as though we had been indulging in a wild, physical affair. When I thought about him, I could feel his hands all over me. I could almost smell him.

Alone in my room in Berlin, I fantasised about how it might have been, if Marco had not been so determined to hold me at arm's length.

From the brief episodes of cybersex we'd shared, I'd got the impression that he liked to be in command. He liked to tell me what to do. There was a huge part of me that responded to that commanding aspect of him. I wanted to hand over the control of my fulfilment to him. I found responding to his instructions so exciting.

'What are you wearing?' was how it began that day in the library. But as my thoughts drifted, I remembered the Dior dress that he had given me to wear to the Martedì Grasso ball. It was so tasteful and elegant. If I had ever imagined myself as a princess, it would have been in a dress like that, beautiful yet understated. He had chosen so well. Not only had he got my measurements right, he had tuned in to my most girlish fantasies when he picked out the dress of my dreams with its skirt like a waterfall of feathers. The dress now hung in Bea's wardrobe. She had offered to return it to me whenever I wanted but I was sure that I would never wear it if she did. Would it ever see the light of day – or evening – again?

As it was, I had worn the dress for just a few minutes. I'd put it on in my office at the university in Venice because Bea insisted that I should. When I looked at myself in the mirror that day, I did not know that Marco had been watching me for all those weeks. Did he imagine me as I saw myself then?

What if I had done everything differently? What if I had worn the dress as Marco planned and waited for him in the silent library, while the rest of his guests partied raucously in the courtyard? What might have happened?

He would have come to me. I was sure of that. I would have been wearing the *servetta muta*, the mask designed to keep its wearer quiet. He would have shown himself to me and the nature of my mask would have bought me time to take in his appearance without revealing my shock at the damaged living mask of frail flesh and paper-thin skin that was his face. Perhaps he would have taken my hand. The sound of his voice would have anchored me in the moment. It would not have taken long for me to see past the façade and greet him with the happiness I always felt at the thought of him and the written intimacy we had already shared.

He was ready for me that night. He must have been confident that against the romantic backdrop of the party, our first meeting would be a suitable beginning for a lifelong romance. Exactly how had he imagined it? Had he imagined me finally taking my mask away from my face and meeting him eye to eye? Stepping into his arms and breathing in the warm scent of expensive aftershave I now knew from the time I pressed his jacket to my face in his secret room? How would our first kiss have been?

And after we kissed? What then? Would he have locked the door to the library, so that we could make love on the desk at which I had spent so many hours?

I pictured him lifting me in his strong arms and carrying me there. I conjured a thought of him sitting me on the desktop and kissing me still as he unlaced the bodice of the perfect Dior gown. I imagined him loosening my breasts and caressing each of them in turn, burying his face in my cleavage, breathing me in.

Perhaps he wouldn't have stripped me naked that day. Instead, he might have pulled down the bodice to let my bosom free, then pushed up my skirt to reveal my soft white legs. I remembered how he'd once told me that to see a woman half-undressed could be just as erotic as seeing her entirely bared to the world.

I wanted to see him naked. I would have undone his trousers so that his penis sprang free, already hard for me and eager to be inside. I would have fallen to my knees in front of him and taken him into my mouth, delighting in the flavour of his strengthening flesh. I would have sucked him until he begged me to stop.

At last we would have lain down together on the rug by the fire, with the Dior dress beneath me to cushion me from the hard floor. On our glorious bed of silk, we would have joined our bodies together in the ultimate way. We would have locked eyes as he entered me, reminding ourselves that this was not just a physical act. It was not just our bodies we were joining.

As he slipped inside me, how complete I might have felt.

I would have wrapped my legs around him, holding him close to me. I would have grabbed his firm square buttocks and tried to speed up his thrusting, driving him deeper and deeper inside. I would have felt his orgasm building inside him. I would have heard the telltale change in his breathing and felt the urgency in his pace. At the same time, my own ecstasy would have been gathering in intensity. We would have come together, of course. Losing control like two swimmers caught up in a tremendous crashing wave, tumbling helplessly until we were swept back to shore, to find each other once again as we lay side by side in the shallows.

While I thought about all this – what might have been – my fingers strayed to the warm wet place between my legs. My heart rate quickened at the thought of Marco's hands on my body. My breath grew shallow and ragged. Ultimately, however, my orgasm arrived only in my imagination. In reality, it slipped away from me at the last moment. I could not let go of my sadness for long enough to come.

That first meeting in the library had not happened as it should have done because I didn't trust him. I didn't believe that Marco really wanted me. I thought he would be distracted by any girl in an amazing dress. So, rather than meet him myself, I sent Bea to test him and inadvertently I put him in a situation where he found himself humiliated. No wonder he had hardened his heart to me and decided not to make our love real.

The Hufelandstrasse grew dark as I sat on my windowsill. The house was silent. Outside, a car passed by and its halogen lights briefly illuminated my bedroom. The whole scene felt quite sad. That afternoon I had been full of optimism. Berlin offered a fresh start and new opportunities. But it's true what they say: you can't run away from the past. It just comes along in your suitcase. I may have been thousands of miles away from Venice but in my heart I was still very much there. It didn't matter that I had erased his emails and thrown away his letters. I still couldn't escape Marco Donato.

7

Berlin,
Saturday 18th June 1932

Dear Diary,

I have been at the Boom Boom Club for just over a week now and I think I am finally getting the hang of things. On my first night, I dropped seven plates between the kitchen and the tables. On my second night, I dropped six. Last night I didn't drop a single one. Thank heavens. Herr Schluter had given me a warning, saying I was costing him more than an evening's takings in crockery each night and much as he liked my accent, if the situation carried on, he would have to let me go.

Herr Schluter is very kind. He told me last night that I remind him of his niece in Vienna. That revelation was not, thank goodness, delivered as an excuse to sneak a hand onto my knee, as seems to happen whenever Daddy's friends get sentimental back in the gin-soaked salons of Surrey. No, Herr Schluter is a very upright man, which is odd when you consider his profession: running one of the most notorious cross-dressing clubs in Berlin. Marlene explained to me, however, that the underworld has its own codes of conduct and they are far more rigid than anything you might encounter in that which we call 'polite society'. For Herr Schluter to cross the line with me would be utterly beyond the pale. As inappropriate as it would have been were we both working in a tax office.

The scantily clad girl I saw leaving Schluter's office on the day I came for my interview was not, as I'd assumed, Schluter's much younger lover, but a hooker he has been helping to give up cocaine. Herr Schluter is like a father to many of the girls on the street. He is insistent that nobody at the Boom Boom takes drugs. Nobody even smokes. Far too dangerous in changing rooms full of papier mâché and feathers. Marlene assured me that I am utterly safe within the Boom Boom's velvet-flocked walls. Both physically and morally.

I think that Marlene is starting to like me since I gave her a lipstick. It's the one Mummy bought for me in London. It doesn't suit me in the least but on Marlene it looks rather wonderful. She in turn has promised to show me how to do my make-up. She said it is all very well my going for the natural look, but my eyes are magnificent and would look more amazing still with the application of proper eyeshadow and a set of those scratchy falsies that look like spider's legs. I can't wait to try them.

But the little kindnesses of Herr Schluter and Marlene aren't the only reasons I'm feeling happy about my job at the Boom Boom. On Fridays, the club hosts a talent evening when members of the audience are invited up onto the stage to do their party pieces. The club gets very busy. It seems that half of Berlin harbours a secret dream to sing. Anyway, on such nights Herr Schluter hires a special pianist. It's important to have someone who can play all the latest hits, since you never know what someone is going to ask for. The usual pianist is about a hundred years old and doesn't know anything written since the Great War and so he gets Friday evenings off.

So, the new pianist . . . As soon as he walked in I thought he looked familiar. It was only when he said to me, 'I see you've bought some new boots,' that I remembered exactly where we'd met before. It was Otto Schmidt, the handsome young man who saved me from that slavering beast in the café, that night when I did not know the first thing about how this city works and I went out inadvertently dressed like a 1920s domina.

I was slightly embarrassed to see him. I didn't suppose he would think I had gone up in the world from being mistaken for a prostitute to working in a transvestite bar, but, what the hell, he was going to be working alongside me! He must have been on his way to the Boom Boom when he left me that awful afternoon.

The ladies – by which I suppose I mean all the men who dress like ladies – all cooed when Otto Schmidt walked in.

'He's such a dreamboat,' sighed Marlene. 'If only he wasn't absolutely straight.'

'Heaven knows we've all tried to turn him,' said Isadora. 'He's got such big shoulders.'

'And a nice arse,' Marlene added.

I had to agree with them both, though of course I didn't say so out loud. Otto really is incredibly good-looking. His astonishingly blue eyes have everyone enchanted. Not only that, he is charming, well-mannered and incredibly intelligent. Turns out that he's not just a nightclub pianist. He's studying to be a lawyer. The job at the Boom Boom helps to pay for his education and to keep his widowed mother and little sister. I liked him when he rescued me and now I like him even more.

I think he likes me too. I caught him looking at me while Marlene was bantering with a contestant who had just sung '*Heute Nacht Oder Nie*' (which means, said Otto, 'Tell Me Tonight') without ever hitting upon the right note no matter how enthusiastically he warbled. Otto was very kind. I noticed that he changed key after the first verse in an attempt to flatter the singer, but the singer only changed his pitch so that he sounded as out of tune as before. It was a disaster. Marlene did a good job of pretending to be impressed though.

While the crowd was applauding and the next contestant took the stage, Otto played a little medley. He doesn't need music. He doesn't even need to look at his hands, so he looked straight at me instead. I blushed to my roots and nearly ruined my first breakage-free night by dropping a plate!

Marlene teased me backstage during her break.

'Perhaps you'll be the one who gets to find out what he's like after hours,' she said.

Otto's working again tomorrow. Herr Schluter says that the amateur talent nights are by far the best of the week as far as takings are concerned, so he's decided to have more of them. Tomorrow will be the Boom Boom's first 'Saturday of the Stars', with the stage open to anyone who thinks they can own it. I told him I thoroughly approve.

*   *   *

So that's all good. Still no news from Mother or Father, though. I will write Mummy another letter tomorrow. I will try to disguise my handwriting so that Papa doesn't guess it's from me right away and throw it in the dustbin without even opening, as I suspect he has been doing so far. That said, I'm not sure how I'm going to get away with the fact that the letter will have a German postmark. Never mind. I will write and write and write until Mummy writes back to me. In the meantime, I shall have to ask Herr Schluter for another small advance.

8

Berlin, last September

My second weekend in Berlin, I saw Clare and Harry again. Clare's birthday was coming up. Like me, she was turning thirty that year and she wanted to make a real event of it. Harry was full of plans.

'We'll have to go to the Boom Boom,' he said.

I was interested to know more.

'You'd love it,' he carried on. 'It's absolutely how you imagine the Berlin clubs of the early thirties. There was a club called the Boom Boom on the same spot back then.'

'But it was destroyed in the war?' I suggested.

'Oh no,' said Harry. 'It was destroyed long before then. Anyway, they've recreated it and every Friday night they have an amateur night. They did exactly the same thing in the original club apparently. Like a 1930s *X Factor*. Can you imagine?'

'*Berlin's Got Talent*,' Clare chipped in. 'There's nothing new in this world, as my grandmother used to say. Hey, Harry. That can be your birthday present to me. You can get up on stage at the Boom Boom and sing 'Happy Birthday' to me. In the style of Marilyn Monroe.'

Harry seemed to think it was a fantastic idea. He elaborated. 'The Boom Boom's speciality was transvestites. They were a huge draw in Weimar Berlin. There were thousands of clubs devoted to cross-dressers. It went the other way too. Perhaps Sarah could dress up as a man and sing something in the style of Frank Sinatra.'

'I can't sing,' I said quickly. 'Let alone in the style of Frank Sinatra.'

'Everyone can sing,' said Harry. 'That's the motto of the Boom Boom.'

'Wishful thinking,' said Clare. 'You've never heard anything quite so awful as the people who take the stage in that club. Susan Boyle spoiled it for everyone. Now every time someone a bit ugly or dowdy steps up from the crowd, you expect them to sing like an angel. Of course, they never do.'

'Well, in that case I'm definitely not singing,' I said.

Harry rolled his eyes.

'You're hardly Susan Boyle. In fact, I've been meaning to say, splitting up with Steven was really good for you. You've never looked so sexy.'

'Thank you,' I replied. 'It's a pity you're gay.'

'That makes my opinion much more valuable,' Harry insisted. 'At least you know I'm not telling you any old thing so you'll sleep with me. Perhaps it was Paris that did it. You've got that Euro-polish going on.'

'I think it was Venice, actually,' I said. I remembered my shopping trip with Bea and getting dressed up every day I went to the library just in case Marco deigned to drop in. 'Yes. Italy is definitely where it started.'

'Italian men are the most gorgeous on earth,' Harry declared. 'Even the dustbin men of Rome look like they've stepped out of an Armani ad. And as for the *carabinieri*. Those boots!' Harry laid his hand on his heart.

'Why are boots such a universal fetish?' Clare asked. 'Someone ought to do a paper on it.'

'I'm sure someone already has,' I said.

'Where do you stand on boots?' Harry asked me.

I laughed at his question, but for a brief moment, my thoughts went to my birthday in Paris and the shoes that Steven had bought me as a gift. They were boots, but not exactly the kind you'd wear to muck out a farmyard. And far from making me feel empowered, when I put them on I'd felt the very opposite of powerful. Unable to walk without tottering, I'd been anxious.

'I take the view that a girl should always wear shoes she can run in,' I said.

'So boring,' chimed Harry and Clare.

'Perhaps I am.'

We spent the rest of the evening making outrageous plans for Clare's birthday. Harry was in his element. He planned a performance that would bring the house down. Forget 'Happy Birthday'. He would sing 'Thank Heaven For Little Girls' and he would dress as one too, in a pink romper suit with a frilled white apron to match. Oh yes, he had the outfit already. He even had a curly blonde wig that he would wear beneath a frilled cap, along with his false eyelashes and glittering lipstick.

'I can't wait to see this,' I said.

'Don't think he won't do it,' Clare warned me. She pulled out her phone and brought up some photographs of Harry at his own birthday party. There he was dressed as Marilyn Monroe, in the iconic dress over the air-vent scene from *The Seven Year Itch*. He looked remarkably good in women's clothing. In fact, both Clare and I agreed, he looked far better than we would have done in the same get-up. It was the legs. He had much longer legs, with much more defined muscle tone than Clare and I could ever have achieved even with years in the gym. It was all down to that perfect balance of testosterone. Just as small boys always have the best eyelashes, the big boys get to have the best pins.

Harry preened as we looked at the evidence of his previous triumphs.

'In Berlin, I can be absolutely myself. This place. Individuality is in the air.'

I had to agree.

As we parted he said, 'Sleep tight, Ms White Bread.'

It was another warm night. Berlin really was experiencing an Indian summer. I went to bed with the windows closed but woke up again in the middle of the night, sweating and tangled in the bedclothes. I got out of bed with the intention of opening the window to let in some air. As I was struggling with the old casement, warped by the years, I saw a couple pause underneath the street-lamp across the road. She threw her arms round his neck. He kissed her passionately, bending her backwards as though in a dip at the end of an exotic tango. He held her in that position for quite some time as he explored her with his mouth.

They were clearly very hot for each other. She straightened up and continued to clutch at the fabric of his shirt as she kissed him with abandon. She devoured him and he couldn't seem to get enough of her. I felt a small stab of envy as I wondered if I would ever be kissed like that again.

Ms White Bread? I'd laughed at the time, but Harry's throw-away line had touched me in a far more personal way than he could have imagined.

I had been so confused about my desires since breaking up with Steven. I was conflicted, feeling both excited and ashamed by the way I'd responded to the whorish lingerie

Steven had me in for our trip to the swingers' club and the shoes he bought me to wear in Paris. Yet I had played with myself according to instructions on a laptop screen, for the pleasure of a man watching through a secret peephole. I must have known on some level that he would be watching. It was crazy to think otherwise. In fact, I had liked the idea that Marco had been watching me.

The drawings had given me quite a shock when I first discovered them. On the one hand, I might have felt violated. On the other hand, they were something quite different from photographs. A photograph required no effort. It required no real knowledge of the subject. A drawing required time. It required concentration. As I considered that, I had allowed my shock to fade so that instead I felt flattered by the thought that someone saw me as worthy of the effort the drawings took to produce. The thought of Marco's gaze was every bit as erotic to me as the thought of his actual touch.

I wondered what had happened to those pictures. Had Marco kept them or had he thrown them away as I had discarded his letters and the dried flower? I would probably never know. I liked to think that he had kept them and that he looked at them still. I hoped in some way they tormented him.

The following morning I had my first English-language student. Her name was Anna Fischer. When she arrived in my office, exactly on time, unlike any of the students I'd taken for tutorials in London or Venice, I was surprised to find that she looked familiar. It took a moment before I placed her as the girl I had seen being kissed beneath the lamp-post. She sat down somewhat heavily.

'Up all night,' she laughed.

I had the feeling I was going to like her.

9

Berlin,
Saturday 25th June 1932

Dear Diary,

Who would have thought I would be such a great hostess? It's only the end of my second week in the job and already customers are asking for me by name when they book their tables in the evening. They actually want to be in my section! It's quite flattering that they think I'm so good at my job, even if Marlene says what they are really hoping is that I will spill their drinks all over them so they can put in an extravagant claim to cover cleaning costs. I'm taking no notice of her. She can be the most terrible cow at times. But Isadora assures me that Marlene's caustic asides are actually a sign of great affection. She never bothers to tease people she doesn't like.

She has been teasing me about Otto endlessly. The usual pianist has been off sick, so Otto has been coming in every night of the week, not just when there's a talent show. And every time he walks into the club, Marlene whistles at him, then looks all innocent and pretends that the horrid whistle came from me. I don't think Otto believes her little ruse but it certainly makes me blush. It makes him blush as well. Marlene says that's a good sign. It means he likes me too.

'For goodness' sake,' she said when we were closing the club tonight. 'I wish you would both stop being so coy and get on with it.'

Otto is very shy, she's right. He is such a strange creature. On the one hand, he is rather straight. He is training to be a lawyer, after all, and his manners are absolutely impeccable. He is exactly the kind of young man my father would call 'solid'. He still lives at home with his widowed mother and two siblings. But he is working at the Boom Boom. That's a little odd, don't you think? I am sure he could have got himself a position at a more respectable establishment. He is easily as good as the pianist at the Adlon, so why did he not try to land a job somewhere like that?

I suppose I should just be glad that he didn't and that fate has decreed that we should wash up in the dodgy old Boom Boom together. A little flirtation certainly helps the evenings fly by. I live to see those heavenly blue eyes!

Berlin,
Friday 1st July 1932

Well, it happened at last! Tonight Otto offered to walk me home. Of course, I leapt at the chance to spend a little time on my own with him. When Marlene saw him helping me put on my coat, she gave me a very knowing look and stuck her tongue in the side of her cheek in a horrible lewd gesture. I shook my head at her, furious that she could try to spoil such a romantic moment with her crassness.

Otto, thankfully, didn't see her. He was too busy being a gentleman.

As we left the club together, he offered me his arm. I took it gratefully. My new shoes are still not terribly comfortable. And though Otto is very much taller than me, we soon fell into step. It was exciting to be so close to him. His arm felt firm and strong through his jacket. I leaned on him rather heavily as an excuse to snuggle up and get a sniff of him. He smells of soap and sandalwood.

It was a changeable sort of evening. It had been warm all day but now it threatened rain. I prayed it would hold off just for me. I wanted everything to be perfect. There have been nights this past week when the walk home from the club seemed very long indeed, but tonight it passed much too quickly. Perhaps it's because I was matching Otto's purposeful stride. Papa always used to complain I was a dawdler. Keeping up with Otto soon changed that. We got to the Hotel Frankfort in five minutes.

'This is where I live,' I said.

Otto frowned up at the crumbling façade, which threatens to drop a windowsill on the head of anyone who slams the door on their way out. 'But it's not a good place,' he said.

'Oh, it's not so bad,' I told him. 'Enno the manager looks after me. He's given me the best room in the house on the very lowest rate and he told me about the job at the Boom Boom.'

'Then I'm very grateful to him for that. But why are you here? How does an English girl like you, obviously from a good family, end up living in this part of Berlin? How could your family let you be here in this nasty hotel? How could they let you work in a nightclub?'

'They don't know,' I admitted. 'They don't know where I am at all! Well, they know I'm in Berlin because I've written to them at least twice a week since I got here, but last time I wrote I told my mother that I was about to move into an apartment with a nice girl called Hildebrand who found me a job as a bilingual secretary. I thought it might stop Mummy worrying. I thought the bit about the job might impress my father into sending me a little bonus.'

Otto laughed. 'Your German's not good enough to be a bilingual secretary,' he said, with typical Teutonic bluntness.

'Your English isn't so hot either,' I said.

'Well, in that case, perhaps we should both learn sign language so we can communicate properly.'

'Start with this,' I said, poking out my tongue.

'Why! You!' Otto pretended to make a grab for me. I darted out of the way. But not too far out of the way. I let him catch me. He did. For a moment we were pressed together and both breathing rather heavily but then he let me go again. I was very disappointed.

But we were still standing on the street and Otto seemed in no hurry to leave me. I toyed with the idea of inviting Otto in. Enno wouldn't care, I was sure. There were always twice as many people staying at the Frankfort as appeared on the official register. But I had the sudden thought that Otto would mind. He certainly wouldn't accept the invitation and, once I'd made it and he'd refused it, the evening would have come to an end. Worse still, he might think me too forward. Not the kind of girl who needed to be walked home again. So, instead, we stood on the pavement outside the hotel door, chatting about nothing in particular. Otto went into a long, rambling description of how he had come to learn his English. He asked how I had come to learn my German. I told him a bit about the finishing school in Munich. I'm afraid I might have given him the impression that my time at the finishing school finished properly. I certainly didn't mention that utter swine Cord Von Cord. I sensed that Otto would not approve of my ending up in Berlin because I'd followed a boy there. Especially not a boy who was engaged to someone else.

We stood on the pavement outside the hotel for the best part of an hour. In the end we had to make a decision because Otto spotted a policeman in the distance. Apparently there have been more policemen around lately and they are definitely a little stricter than they used to be. Of course, we weren't actually doing anything illegal, but neither of us wanted to have to explain ourselves if they assumed we were negotiating a price to spend the night together, rather than talking about the differences between German and English grammar.

'I think it's time for you to go inside,' said Otto.

I nodded my agreement. 'I think it is.'

'But first . . .'

He hesitated.

'What?' I asked.

'I have to do something.'

My eyes grew wide. Otto took me by the shoulders. I

assumed he was going to kiss me goodbye in the usual way: three kisses on the cheek. But instead he planted a smacker right on my mouth!

It was a good job he was holding me up because my knees buckled the moment his mouth touched mine.

It was a brief kiss – the policeman was getting closer – but oh such a wonderful one. He tasted of white wine and peppermint.

'Goodnight, sweet English rose,' he said as he let me go. He looked at me so intently. His eyes had gone a much darker blue. His gaze made my insides positively liquid.

And then the policeman was close enough that we could see he was reaching for his whistle.

'Go inside.' Otto gave me a little shove in the direction of the hotel door. 'I'll see you tomorrow.'

I cannot wait until tomorrow! What a magical night. What a fabulous kiss!

Forget Cord Von Cord. The beast. Now that I have kissed Otto, I can hardly believe that I was ever interested in such a pompous donkey. My knees never buckled when Cord kissed me goodnight. I never felt my heart beat so hard I thought it might burst out of my chest. Tonight's kiss was so different from any kiss I've had before. It's a sign that Otto and I are meant to be together. I'm sure of it. I can't wait to go in to work again!

IO

Berlin, last September

During my first term in Berlin, I would be taking eight
students for English lessons. They were mostly postgraduate
students, who were writing their theses in English with the
hope of applying to work at American or Canadian universi-
ties later on. Anna Fischer was soon my favourite. She didn't
need much help when it came to spoken English, but she
wanted me to help polish her written work. She was doing
her dissertation on Helmut Newton, the German photographer especially famous for his nudes. I knew a little bit about
the photographs, but Anna was a fanatic.

'There is always such strength in his models,' she assured
me. 'I like that. The women in *Big Nudes* are Amazons. But
he also picked women off the street. He chose models that no
traditional fashion photographer would use. He could find
the beauty in anyone.'

She showed me a couple of her own pictures. Self-portraits
in Newton's style.

'I try to be like one of Helmut's models every day. I'm not
going to hide. If people don't like the way I look, that's their
problem.'

She had blue-dyed hair but as far as I could see, Anna
Fischer didn't have any reason to hide herself away. She was
beautiful on anybody's scale.

'But your exterior reflects your interior,' she said. 'You're happy. You look it. You're mean. You look that way too. Or so we think. Not looking normal,' she made inverted commas around the word, 'can be a life sentence.'

She packed her photographs away. The bell rang and she was gone.

That evening, I got back to my building on the Hufelandstrasse at around six o'clock. Herr Schmidt had his window open and, as usual, classical music drifted out. Not Chopin this time but Schubert. His piano sonata in D major. A very mournful piece. Anyway, Herr Schmidt must have seen me pass his window on my way to the front door because by the time I let myself into the hall, he'd stopped playing and was coming out of the door to his apartment.

'Good evening, Fräulein Thomson,' he said.

'Good evening, Herr Schmidt.' I gave a little nod. Sometimes it was all I could do not to curtsey to my distinguished landlord.

'I am wondering if you are finding your accommodations comfortable?' he asked, in his curious, mannered English.

'Oh yes,' I assured him. 'Everything is just perfect. I'm very happy indeed.'

'I wonder also,' he asked, looking a little embarrassed this time, 'if I might ask you for a favour.'

'Of course,' I said. 'How can I help you?'

'My Internet does not seem to be working correctly,' he said. 'But perhaps it is I who do not know how to make it work correctly. Would you please take a look and see if you know how to restart it?'

I followed Herr Schmidt into his flat. The smart new laptop his great-nephew had bought for him was on the table in the dining room. I set about checking the laptop's settings.

Everything seemed to be in order. I got down on my hands and knees and looked for the wireless modem hidden beneath the stiff-backed sofa. Of course, there was no dust under there. A cleaner came three times a week. I pulled the modem out. The light that should have indicated that broadband was available was red rather than blue.

'I think it may be a problem with the supplier rather than with your machine,' I informed Herr Schmidt. I went upstairs to check my own modem. Same red lights. Same problem. I came back downstairs. 'Hopefully, it will come back on soon enough, but if not, you'll have to telephone customer support. I'd do it for you but I'm afraid my German isn't up to it.'

'Your German is already much improved,' said Herr Schmidt.

'Thank you,' I said, though I thought he was being generous.

'Well, I . . .' I turned to go back upstairs to my own room.

'Will you join me for some supper?' Herr Schmidt asked. 'I have made too much.'

'Why not?' I said. I had planned to spend the evening watching British TV streamed over my laptop. That wasn't going to happen while the Internet was down.

'I have cooked some *sauerbraten*,' he said.

I racked my brains for a translation. Was that cabbage? I couldn't smell cabbage.

'Beef. A pot roast,' he helped me out.

Herr Schmidt was a good cook and he was also very interesting company. He had a wide knowledge of current affairs. What he knew about British politics put me to shame. I wasn't half as interested as he seemed to be in what went on in Westminster. I definitely wasn't as interested in Brussels and the EU. When I saw reports on the economic crisis, my response was to stick my fingers in my ears and go 'la la la'.

'You must pay more attention,' Herr Schmidt admonished me gently. 'The decisions these people make affect real lives. Yours and mine.'

He also asked me lots of questions about my work. Fortunately, this was a topic on which I could hold my own. I told him how I had been getting on so far in the vast archives of the university.

'But this subject has been covered so many times before,' I said. 'I'm hoping to find something new. Something that really brings the period to life. Like a diary written at the time, rather than a memoir. Memoir is so different, you see. When people look back after any significant period of time has passed, they try to find meaning in everything that happened and imbue it with a proper narrative. Fiction can't help but creep in. With a diary, written as events unfold, the writer doesn't know how it will all end and so they don't try to make the facts fit. You get a much truer representation.'

Herr Schmidt looked deep in thought for a moment. I wondered what I'd said to make him so.

'I think I may have something for you,' he said. 'Please, wait there.'

I remained at the table, with my fingers curled around the small glass of red wine I had been nursing throughout dinner. While Herr Schmidt was out of the room, I gazed around his elegant home, so oddly frozen in time. I tried to guess the age of the furniture. Perhaps it was as old as nineteen-thirties. The piano was even older: an upright carved out of oak stained so dark it was almost black. My attempts to guess Herr Schmidt's age continued. Listening to some of his memories, it seemed he was possibly closer to a hundred than ninety years old. I hoped I would be half as energetic if I got to such an age.

Herr Schmidt returned. 'Here it is.' He had in his hands a

shoebox, which was held shut by a number of elastic bands. He told me the story of how it came to be in his possession.

'I was injured at the beginning of the Second World War. I couldn't go back to the front so I spent the duration of the war here in Berlin, firefighting and clearing the rubble after the Allied air attacks. I found this in the remains of a burnt-out hotel just off the Ku'damm. The Kurfürstendamm, that is.'

He set the box in the centre of the table.

I reached for it.

'Please, take it up to your room,' he said. 'I don't need to see what is inside again. It mocks me after all this time. I shouldn't have kept it. I think it is self-explanatory. Once you have read it, perhaps you could find a way for it to be returned to the owner. Or to her family, if she is no longer alive. I think you will know better how to find them than I.'

I nodded again. 'I'll do my best.'

'It's getting late. I'm afraid I'm suddenly rather tired,' said Herr Schmidt.

'Then I'll say goodnight.'

I tried not to look too eager to take my new treasure upstairs.

When I got to my room, the Internet connection had still not been restored, so there was nothing to distract me from opening the shoebox Herr Schmidt had rescued from the burnt-out hotel. Why had he picked this up when there must have been so many treasures left in the rubble? I wondered if he had attributed some significance to it precisely because it hadn't gone up in flames. It wasn't even slightly singed. But the first thing I noticed – perhaps the thing that had caught Herr Schmidt's eye too – was that this was an English shoebox. I didn't recognise the name of the store marked on it, however; it was probably long since defunct.

I was careful as I took off the elastic bands, but they were old and perished and they crumbled in my hands. The box couldn't have been opened for years. I thought of Herr Schmidt's words, 'It mocks me after all this time', and wondered why he hadn't tried to find the owner himself. Perhaps he had. It wouldn't necessarily have been easy before the Internet became part of everyone's life. Even with the Internet it could sometimes be hard to track someone down. Not many people who'd been alive in the 1930s bothered to have a profile on Facebook.

The box smelled musty and damp, as though it had been kept in an attic or a cellar. As I opened it, I imagined a wisp of long-dead spirit smoking out into the air, filling my lungs with the past. I instinctively held my breath.

Inside the box was a treasure trove. There was a small Steiff teddy bear whose nose was worn bald by kissing. There was a handkerchief embroidered with the initials KH. There were several letters, bundled together with a piece of ribbon in Fortnum and Mason's distinctive pale green. There were also two diaries, one from 1932 and another from 1933. The diary from 1932 was English. It was made by Smythson, still one of Britain's best stationers in the twenty-first century. It was bound in red leather and embossed in gold with the same initials as the handkerchief. The 1933 diary was German in make. It was cheaper in construction and had a simple black leather cover. It was not embossed. The writing inside both was English and in the same girlish, neat hand using a fountain pen and blue ink, which had faded over the years.

Feeling a little like a thief, I opened the first diary and began to read.

II

Dear Diary,

Happy New Year! Ha ha ha! If only this New Year were happy. What a terrible New Year's Eve I had. I can only hope it doesn't set the tone for the rest of 1932.

As usual, we were asked to join Bettina and her family at their annual New Year's party at the Grange. It's always a fabulous affair. They give their terrible cook a night off, get proper caterers in and hire a band. Everyone in the village is invited. Like me, Mummy always wants to get dressed up and join in the fun. And every year Papa says he can't stand Bettina's braying parents and all the nouveau showing off and wouldn't it be much nicer to stay home instead? Well, I certainly wish he had stayed home last night. I wish we all had.

The party started at seven for the benefit of the old folk who might not make it all the way till midnight. I wore my new dress: the red silk one cut on the bias that Mummy made from a McCall's pattern. It's really rather lovely, even if it is home-made. Of course, Bettina's dress was a Norman Hartnell picked up on a trip to London,

74

but, if you ask me, it made her look a little old. Especially since she has started curling her hair.

Anyway, the moment I walked into the New Year's party, she grabbed me by the arm and pulled me out into the garden for a gasper. She shoved her lighter and cigarettes in my handbag for safe keeping in case any member of her family should appear.

'I swear,' she said, 'I will not make it to 1932. My mother has been driving me absolutely mad all day long. Until you turned up I was this close to throwing myself out of a window. Or her. I was ready to hoist her over the windowsill to oblivion. One of us has to go.'

Bettina's mother, Mrs Spencer, always gets rather overwrought in the run-up to the family's New Year party. Everything has to be perfect. This year, it was truer than ever because Bettina's brother Matthew was home.

'Have you seen him?' Bettina asked. 'Strutting around like a big fat turkey cock in his uniform? Anyone would think he was back from a year in the trenches instead of twelve months in an office just outside Torquay.'

Matthew was on leave from the army. I hadn't seen him but I couldn't wait to. I especially couldn't wait to see him in his uniform. As Mummy always says, there isn't a man in the world who doesn't look better in khaki.

Not that Matthew needs much help to look good. He's always been horribly handsome. I remember the very first time I met him, when Bettina invited me home to her house for tea. We were nine, which means that Matthew must have been fourteen. He seemed so worldly-wise compared to us girls. He was already six feet tall and played for his school's first rugby team. I forgot about my crush on Douglas Fairbanks at once.

After that, I would see Matthew just a couple of times a year, when he was home from boarding school or university. He didn't ever take much notice of me. I was just his sister's spotty little friend. Until last summer. Last summer he definitely noticed.

Back in June, Bettina had invited me over to swim in the Spencers' new swimming pool.

'Terribly naff to have a swimming pool in this climate,' said Papa.

But I was excited. I rolled up my costume in a stripy towel and walked down the lane to the Grange just after lunchtime. When I arrived, Bettina was already sunning herself, alongside Matthew who was wearing nothing but a pair of tight black bathers. I hadn't known he'd be there. The sight of him made me quite light-headed.

I didn't dare disrobe in front of him, so I changed in Bettina's bedroom and then spent the next hour by the pool sweating in a towelling robe, while claiming I was too cold to strip off. It was sweltering in the sunshine. I was almost relieved when Matthew announced that he had an appointment to keep and was going to leave us girls to it.

Bettina looked immediately suspicious.

'I know exactly where he's going,' she said. 'Come with me.'

Having quickly pulled on some clothes, we left the Spencers' manicured garden and headed for the farm attached to the house. Bettina bade me stay close to the wall as we entered the farmyard and made for the enormous loft, already full to the rafters with that year's hay. I was very glad I had my proper clothes on as I followed Bettina up a ladder and we hid with an eye on the doors. Hay is terribly scratchy.

'This is where he always brings them,' Bettina said.

'Brings who?'

'Ssssh!'

She clamped her hand over my mouth, just as Matthew came in. He was leading a village girl by the hand. I'd seen her before. We were a similar age but we weren't friends. Mummy and Papa didn't like me to mix with her sort.

'You'll get into all kinds of trouble,' they said.

The village girl certainly looked ready for trouble right then. She grinned widely as Matthew wrapped his arms round her waist and pulled her close. She protested in a most feeble fashion when he went to kiss her, and soon they were rolling around on the floor with absolute abandon. Matthew had his hands everywhere. Down the front of her dress. Up her skirt. Inside her knickers! And the things she was doing to him!

Both Bettina and I kept our mouths firmly covered and our eyes fixed on the action below. I was completely horrified by what they got up to. This was sex? It was nothing like the scenes I'd read in Mummy's novels.

In fact, it looked absolutely awful. So very messy and rather painful. And all that grunting too! But Matthew and the village girl seemed to enjoy it. So much so that afterwards, she tried to persuade him to do it all again. That was a bit of a worry for Bettina and me since we were expected for tea at four o'clock and there was no way we could get out of the hayloft without being spotted if Matthew and his girl didn't leave first.

Fortunately, Matthew claimed that he was having tea at quarter to – the rotten liar. He left the village girl pouting. She spent a couple of moments tidying herself up, then skipped out of the barn.

'Probably going back to her fiancé,' said Bettina. The village girl was engaged to be married to one of the farmhands. 'The slattern.'

It was later that same evening that Matthew caught me alone. I had been invited to stay at the Spencers' for supper. While I was carrying plates into the kitchen (Cook had the evening off), he grabbed me by the arm and pulled me into the pantry.

'I know you were watching,' he said.

'Watching what?'

'Me and that girl. From the hayloft.'

I shook my head and tried to deny it.

'You can't fool me, Kitty Hazleton. I heard you. And,' he reached for something just behind my ear, 'you've still got straw in your hair.'

I blushed furiously.

'But it's OK. I don't mind you watching. I suppose you must be curious, stuck in that boarding school of yours with no man to look at from week to week except that red-nosed bursar. Do you want a closer look at me?'

I'm afraid to say I nodded.

Matthew told Bettina and his parents he was going to walk me home. He did walk me home, but not before he had taken me back to the barn, where he had lain with the village girl only a few hours before. He pulled a blanket out of a secret hiding place – he hadn't bothered for the village girl – and laid me down upon it.

Matthew was a god to me. I would have done anything he asked. And I did. He opened the front of his trousers and encouraged me to put my hand inside. My eyes widened.

'What do you think?' he asked me.

'I don't know. It feels . . . What am I supposed to do with it?'

'Wrap your hand around it? Gently!' he winced when I held him too tightly. 'Gently. Hold on. Let's start again. It will be easier with my trousers down.'

That was the first time I saw a penis up close. What a curious thing it turned out to be. How quickly it grew with a little bit of encouragement. Knowing as I did from biology lessons that all the stiffness was achieved through sheer volume of blood, I looked at Matthew's enormous piece and began to worry that he'd faint. He didn't faint. Far from it. He made me tug his foreskin backwards and forwards until my arm ached like I'd played an afternoon's tennis. When I started to flag, he yelled at me not to stop or he'd kill me. Seconds later, a jet of gluey sperm arced high into the air.

Afterwards, Matthew's willy lay curled in my hand like a small baby mouse: hairless, pink and blind. I thanked Matthew for having been so kind as to let me see it. I didn't tell Bettina, of course.

Anyway, last night was the first time I'd seen Matthew since that day in the summer. Of course, I was thinking of him when I put on my red dress and begged my mother to allow me just one swipe of her lipstick. Enough to make me look my sixteen years and remind Matthew that I am quite old enough to be kissed. Heavens, I'm old enough to be married! With my parents' permission. Gah!

Matthew was in the kitchen when Bettina and I went back inside after our gasper. He sauntered out into the dining room. He was just as handsome as I remembered, especially in his uniform. He looked like such a man compared with the boys from the village who had been invited to swell the party numbers. He seemed even taller than I remembered.

We chatted for a while. He asked me about school. I reminded him that I was nearly finished with all that. I asked him about the army. What exactly was it he was doing? He smiled enigmatically and told me it was top secret. I decided that meant he must be in training to be a spy.

Shortly before ten o'clock, we danced. It was a slow dance. Matthew held me close and whispered in my ear, 'You're driving me crazy in that lovely red dress. I'll meet you in the outhouse in ten minutes. Tell your mother you need to get some air.'

I did exactly as he told me. I was so excited.

It was frigid outside and I wished I had taken my wrap, but I couldn't go back in to get it – I would risk getting stuck with the other guests – so I crept down the garden path, shivering all the way, taking care not to sink into the mud. I daren't use Bettina's lighter as a torch in case it drew attention.

Matthew was there waiting. He already had his trousers undone and was stroking the soft mouse of a penis I remembered from earlier in the summer.

'He'll start to wake up now you're here,' Matthew said as he guided my hand to his open flies. His willy jumped straight to attention.

This time he kissed me. It was absolutely swoonsome. I felt my insides turn to jelly as his hands sneaked to my breasts.

'You've got lovely tits, Hazleton,' he told me.

'Thank you,' I said. 'You've got a lovely . . .'

'Cock,' he said. 'Come on. Say it! I've been fantasising about you touching it since that night back in the summer. How does that feel? What's it like to know that you're helping a poor soldier get through the dull days of his service with the thought of your beautiful body?'

It felt very good indeed. As did Matthew's fingers inside my bodice as he groped to find a nipple to squeeze.

No one had ever touched my breasts before. The feeling was sensational. My most private parts shivered, just as I'd read in a novel. I felt myself opening up, in a funny sort of way. I was ready to give Matthew everything. He only had to ask.

But then it all went horribly wrong.

Who should come into the shed but Bettina's mother and Mr Rhys Blanchard, the local member of Parliament! Mrs Spencer was carrying a torch and shone it straight on my bottom, which was all but bare because Matthew had hoiked up my skirt. The horror on Mrs Spencer's face was absolute. She started shouting right away. She called me all sorts of names and none of them were Christian.

Matthew did little to defend me, though he did ask his mother why she was in the outhouse in any case. Had she been intending to have a tryst of her own? That earned Matthew a horrible slap. How dare he suggest such a thing! Mrs Spencer said that she had asked Mr Rhys Blanchard to accompany her because she thought there might be an intruder. Mr Rhys Blanchard hurriedly agreed that was exactly why he was there. The last thing he wanted was for us to get the wrong idea about that. He was an upstanding member of the Conservative Party, after all.

Then Mrs Spencer grabbed me by the arm – unnecessarily hard – and marched me back into the house. She interrupted my parents in the middle of their once-a-year slow dance and told them what she thought she had seen.

'Your daughter. Corrupting my son. In the outhouse.'

We didn't celebrate midnight at all. Everyone was far too busy shouting. We left at three minutes past.

All day today, I could hear Mummy and Papa arguing over what's to be done with me. The only thing they seemed to agree on is that Matthew and Bettina Spencer have always been a terrible influence and we must be kept apart. In the end, I got fed up listening and buried myself in my new book instead. But when the time came for us all to sit down for supper, it seemed they were ready to present a united front. And they were very much united against me! Papa glared at me across his mutton. He would not say a word. It was Mummy who told me that a decision had been made. They are sending me to finishing school. In Munich!

Munich! At least if it had been Switzerland, I should have known other girls there. But Munich! Nobody worth knowing goes to Germany.

'That is exactly the point,' said Papa. 'It will do you good to spend less time with fast girls like that Bettina Spencer.'

They are going to talk to one Frau Kluge of the Munich School of Womanly Grace and Charm tomorrow. Please, God, I beg you, don't let her have any places left this year. I can't stand the thought of going to Germany. They eat nothing but sausages. I shall come home oinking like a pig and no doubt looking like one too from all the horrid potatoes. And I'll be so far away from Bettina and everyone who makes life worth living. I can't bear it! If they insist on sending me there, I will run away at the first possible chance I get.

Surrey,
Saturday 2nd January 1932

Dear Diary,

I am doomed. Frau Kluge said she would be delighted to have me. Papa has agreed to wire a year's fees in the morning. Mummy has been doing much sobbing. It seems she was hoping, just as much as I, that Frau Kluge's horrible school would be full. All the same, she will not stand up for me against Papa. She says that I have really cooked my goose this time and it is probably for the best that I am far away from Surrey until the gossip has died down.

How long will that take? The people of this village have nothing to do but gossip. They could keep the story of my disgrace in the outhouse going for months! The only possible way I will cease to be of interest any time soon is if Bettina should do something worse.

I have tried everything I can think of to persuade Papa to let me stay home. I even said that I was worried we might go to war against Germany again and I would be stuck on the wrong side of the Channel when the declaration was made. Papa snorted and told me not to be ridiculous. We are never going to have a war in Europe again, he said. Not after last time. We should all have learned a lesson from that. On the contrary, it would be a damn good thing if I learned to speak German properly so that I am prepared for the day when Europe becomes fully integrated and we work together as one big happy economic family.

In that case, I then asked him, how would he feel if I fell in love with a German man and never came home at all? Papa says that is fine with him, so long as the German in question is solvent and I make sure I get an engagement ring before I follow him into any outhouse. The beast!

And now Mummy has just poked her head round the bedroom door and told me to stop writing. Apparently, I have to be up early tomorrow morning to start packing. Papa's secretary has arranged his diary so that he can take me to Munich himself on Monday.

Munich,
Thursday 7th January 1932

Charm school! What a horrible joke. If Frau Kluge knows the first thing about charm, then I am a monkey's uncle. Papa has just left. I can't believe he didn't take one look at this dump and insist I go back home with him. This place is less a finishing school than a prison. It's a horrible old building. Full of nasty brown furniture and horrible paintings of women who look like bulldogs. I am sharing an attic room with Miranda, a cross-eyed girl from Hampshire, who is here because she failed her final exams.

The food is too awful. I barely ate a thing at dinner tonight. The bread is almost black and the meat is so overcooked you can't tell whether it's pork or beef or the remains of the last girl who tried to escape. The only vegetable is cabbage. Cabbage, cabbage, cabbage. The smell of flatulence permeates every corner of this place.

It's only going to get worse, I know it. Frau Kluge has given me a timetable that includes swimming every morning. When I asked her where the swimming pool is, she just laughed. We have to swim in the lake! In the lake! When it's so cold that I am wearing a bobble hat in bed and I swear my bedtime cup of cocoa was iced over before I could drink it!

I cannot possibly stick it out here. I will die if they really make me swim in a pond. I'll have to pray that when he gets home to Surrey and thinks about it properly, Papa will turn round and come straight back to rescue me. Mummy will not hear of me living in such terrible conditions. She wouldn't let me go out without crampons in snow like they have here, let alone expect me to jog across the lawn in bare feet. I have already written to tell her just how terrible it is. Please God, let her insist that Papa fetches me home at once.

Munich,
Saturday 16th January 1932

Dear Diary,

Today we put on our snowshoes and trekked into town for an evening of 'musical entertainment'. All wind instruments, of course. Papa makes more entertaining music after he's eaten baked beans. But there was some dancing, which is good. All rather exciting. A little bit hectic. More like Scottish reeling than the sort of stuff they're doing in the dance halls in London these days. But I ended the evening in the arms of a fellow called Cord Von Cord, who is Frau Kluge's nephew.

He is so handsome! All the girls were swooning with desire for him but he chose to dance with me from the start. He told me as we danced that I was quite the most beautiful English woman he had ever seen and I gave the lie to the perception that English women are all whey-faced with big backsides and ankles like the horses we send down the mines. I know, Diary. He's not exactly a charmer, but I think it's just that we're communicating in different languages. When we are communicating through the language of dance, he has no trouble making himself understood at all.

How could I ever have been interested in Bettina's

oafish brother Matthew? What a lucky break I had when Bettina's mother found us in the outhouse. Not only did she save me from throwing my virginity away on someone who definitely wouldn't have deserved it, I wound up in just enough disgrace to be sent here to meet someone truly special.

I have written to Mummy and told her that she is not to worry about me after all. In just three days I have become quite accustomed to the cold and my room-mate Miranda is wonderful company. Her snoring hardly bothers me at all. No, I will be quite happy to spend the rest of the year here. Munich has become almost like home.

12

Venice, last September

One more try. Give it one more try. Marco heard the words as he woke from another deep slumber. He wasn't sure where they were coming from. Were they inside his head or had Silvio said them? Silvio was in the room, pulling back the curtains. Marco's early-morning cup of coffee was on the bedside table.

Marco sat up abruptly. He didn't like to be in bed when Silvio started work in the morning. It was especially embarrassing to be caught asleep when he knew his most loyal employee would have been up for hours already. Having opened the window, Silvio turned towards him and nodded as he always did: a greeting that felt intimate but not intrusive. Marco struggled to sit up against the pure white pillows. He felt so jaded. He wasn't sure why.

Silvio left the room, leaving Marco to prepare himself for the day ahead. But what was there to get up for? Marco continued to sit in bed, looking at the patterns on the wall made by sunlight streaming in through the windows. The ever-moving light of Venice, bounced in a thousand different directions by the water that weaved its way through the city's veins.

Marco had dreamed about Sarah again.

She had been in this room with him. In this bed. In his mind's eye, he could still see her on the pillow beside him.

Her long brown hair made a beautiful contrast with the white sheets, which had slipped to her waist, leaving her perfect back exposed. Marco coveted her body. He made an inventory of every corner, every curve. He stared at the pink petals of her lips. He even envied her eyelashes for touching her cheeks as she slept.

He felt unworthy of her and yet he could not keep from touching her with his sinner's hands. As she dreamed, he ran a finger along her long, lean lines. When she didn't stir, he dared to kiss her pale shoulder. The scent of her skin was such an aphrodisiac to him. It made him hungry for her. Greedy.

Slowly, she stirred. She opened her grey-blue eyes, blue like a pair of old Levis, and looked at him. A smile spread over her face. She reached up and cupped his cheek and brought his lips down to meet hers.

'I was having the most wonderful dream,' she said. 'I dreamed that you were making love to me.'

'Would you like me to make it a reality?' he asked.

She nodded and pulled him down to kiss her again. Slowly and seductively, she wriggled her tongue into his mouth. Her kiss filled his whole body with warmth. When she let him go, Marco planted kisses all over her, from her neck to her nipples. And as he worshipped her fragrant skin with his mouth, he slipped his hand down between her legs and stroked her clitoris. She arched against the mattress, pressing her body into his hand to increase the pressure. And the pleasure. A sigh of delight escaped her lips.

He slipped a finger inside her to find that she was wet already. Slowly he moved his finger in and out of her. Her eyes were closed in ecstasy. Her cheeks grew pinker and her lips more rubious as the blood rushed to show how good he was making her feel.

'Don't stop,' she begged him.

He felt the early ripples of arousal. Her skin grew warm. He kissed her on the mouth again. He couldn't get enough.

She reached for his penis. She wrapped her hand around him and caressed him into an erection. She continued to press her body against his, signalling her desire for him with every part of her. With her body, with her murmurs, with the fluttering of her lashes upon her cheeks as he set her tingling with his fingers. The very thought that he made her so greedy for him made him hard.

Reverently he entered her. He felt a sense of completion as he pushed all the way in so that he filled her completely. Her body moulded itself to him. The warmth and the wetness of her made him harder still. He moved slowly to begin with, relishing every stroke, driving himself and her crazy until . . .

She wanted to be on top, she told him. He acquiesced.

Using all her strength to tip him over onto the mattress, she took control. She rode him majestically. Her hair streamed around her shoulders. She was like a beautiful warrior princess. He put his hands on her waist to help her move up and down and to attempt to control her speed. She was moving too fast for him and he wanted this moment to last longer. For ever. But she wouldn't slow down. She moved faster and faster, as eager to reach her own climax as he was to prolong the arrival of his.

She was too much for him. He couldn't hold it in. He bellowed as his orgasm was ripped from his shaking body. Sarah looked down on him in triumph. She ran her finger down his cheek, then she got up from the bed and was gone. He called out for her to come back. His words echoed in the silence. Then . . .

'One more try?'

Who had said that? If it wasn't Silvio then perhaps it had been Sarah. Yes. It was a woman's voice.

Marco finally got out of bed. He washed without looking in the mirror and shaved in the same way. He no longer cut himself accidentally; he knew his scar tissue very well. But this time, when he had finished shaving he found his hands drifting back to his face, feeling his damaged skin with the tenderness of a lover. Was this what it would feel like if Sarah touched his face?

'One more try,' he said to himself.

He dressed and went to his office, opened up his computer and began to write.

13

Berlin, last September

Katherine Hazleton's diary kept me up until the early hours. When I went up to my bedroom after supper with Herr Schmidt, it was about ten o'clock. When I next looked at the clock, it was two in the morning. I had read as far as May. Katherine – Kitty as I had come to think of her, just as her friends did – had escaped the monstrous finishing school at last, sneaking out in the middle of the night to catch a train to meet her lover in Berlin. Her cross-eyed room-mate Miranda kept watch while Kitty shinned her way down a drainpipe. All the girls at the school came to their windows to silently cheer Kitty on her way.

As I closed the diary, Kitty had just arrived in Berlin. She had found herself a room at the Hotel Adlon and sent word to Cord Von Cord that he should meet her there. I had the feeling it would not go well but I also had the feeling that it wouldn't matter if it didn't. Kitty Hazleton was clearly a girl of some spirit. As I walked past the Adlon the following morning, I imagined Kitty holed up inside, waiting for her dashing German lover to arrive and relieve her of the heavy burden of her virginity.

When Anna Fischer came for her English lesson, I told her about Kitty's adventures.

'My sister stayed at the Adlon once,' she told me. 'She was also with an unsuitable boy.'

As I arrived home from a day in the library, I tapped on Herr Schmidt's door in passing.

'Thank you,' I said. 'For giving me those diaries. I'm half-way through the first one. It's really rather funny, don't you think?'

'I don't know,' said Herr Schmidt, somewhat abruptly. 'I haven't read it.'

'Really?'

'I don't read English as well as I speak it and the handwriting is quite untidy.'

'I suppose it is,' I said. It was a good job Herr Schmidt had never tried to decipher a page of my own writing, which was legendarily bad.

'Do you think you can find the owner?' he asked.

'Well, her name is on the outside of the letters in the box. It's not very common. Hazleton. I'm sure I'll track her down. You can find most people on the Internet these days.'

'Good,' he said.

I almost pointed out to him that Kitty would probably be dead by now. Though not necessarily; plenty of people lived to a hundred. Perhaps he already had.

'If you'd like me to translate the diary for you, I'd be very happy. My German isn't wonderful, as you know, but between us, we could get the gist. If you'd like to hear what Kitty got up to . . .'

'There's no need,' he said. 'I don't need to know what the diaries say.'

'But . . .'

He shook his head. 'I'd just like to reunite her with her belongings.' Herr Schmidt didn't seem so keen to chat that evening. In fact, he looked a little tired. I bade him goodnight and made my way upstairs.

When I got to my study I discovered that the Internet was working again so I was able to get online and check my private email account. I'd been avoiding doing so at the office because I wasn't sure whether such things were frowned upon. I scrolled through the usual spam. Bea in Venice had sent me a link to a funny video of a kitten. My mother had sent an email reminding me my sister's birthday was coming up.

The last thing I was expecting was an email from him. It came in while I was replying to Bea.

Just seeing his name was still enough to make me feel as though I had reached the top of a roller-coaster and was plummeting down through a second of zero gravity, while all my internal organs raced to catch up. I stared at his name, bracing myself for the disappointment that would inevitably follow. Then, when I could wait no longer, I clicked the open button.

Dear Sarah,

I don't know if you ever expected to hear from me again or if this email will be welcome. I am only sorry that I have to get in contact with you in this terribly impersonal way. I would far rather have written a letter. Putting pen to paper feels so much more intimate than this electronic method of communicating, but right now I don't know where you are and I didn't want to contact you via your old university friends.

So, forgive me for this and trust that while this may seem like a lazy way of reaching out, I have certainly not written to you quickly or lightly.

I think I owe you an apology. That afternoon in Venice, when you took me by surprise, I said some terrible things and not all of them were true. None of them, in fact. You have every right to decide to cut me out of your life, just as I asked you to, but if, by some chance, you were still willing to be in contact with me, I would consider myself to be a very lucky man.

With fondest wishes,

Marco.

I couldn't believe what I was reading. He wanted to be back in touch with me.

I didn't know how to respond. In so many ways, this was the email I had been waiting for, yet now that it had arrived, it suddenly seemed too little, too late. It was bloodless and formal. So very Marco. And it was a very easy, lazy way to test the waters. I had put everything on the line when I flew to Venice to confront him in person. He had typed a couple of paragraphs and pressed send. If it mattered so much to him to make a good impression on me, then surely he would have found a way to talk to Nick or Bea. He knew I was going to be in Germany; I had told him about it months ago. He might have called the university or sent a letter in its care.

It was not enough. It did not touch me half as much as it should have done. Something about the tone still suggested that an overreaction on my part had led to our estrangement. He said he 'thought' he owed me an apology. I found my eyes stinging as I thought about that last trip to Venice. I remembered the moment when he told me to go and I had to walk out past Silvio, feeling like a fool who had misinterpreted mere friendliness as love.

No. I'd had enough of humiliation.

I decided I would not reply. I went so far as to press delete so I could not even be tempted. Marco was no longer in my address book, I told myself. Oh, as though I didn't know his email address by heart. But I had to stay strong. No more fantasies. I picked up Kitty's diary again and forced myself to read on.

14

Berlin,
Saturday 2nd July 1932

Dear Diary,
I hardly slept a wink after Otto kissed me. I lay on top of the
scratchy blankets and remembered the moment again and
again and again. When I put my fingers to my face, I could
smell the scent of Otto's hand on mine. He uses a delicious
sandalwood soap. Today I'm going to buy a bar so I can
sniff it when he's not around.

Berlin,
Saturday 2nd July 1932
The very early hours!

Dear Diary,
   I've just got back from work. I had the most wonderful
evening.
   'You're early,' said Marlene, when I turned up. 'And
you don't look in the least bit tired, which means he
didn't keep you up. What happened? Did he only want to
walk you home so you could gossip? Did he tell you that
he's actually in love with Isadora?'

'No!' I protested. I was about to tell Marlene about the kiss when Otto walked in. Everything happened exactly as it does in all the best novels. My stomach actually flipped. I saw stars. He kissed Marlene 'hello' as is his custom. Then he did the same to me. But this was no ordinary kiss of greeting. His lips lingered on my cheek. I felt myself turn crimson.

'I'll walk you home again tonight,' he said.

'Yes, yes,' I said. 'Yes, please!' I couldn't wait for my shift to be over.

Nothing could spoil my mood. The boorish customers who would ordinarily have made me want to drop sauer-kraut in their laps seemed sweet and kindly this evening. I had a smile for everyone. No wonder my tips went up.

When I had my break, I spent it at the side of the stage, watching Otto play the piano. I could watch him for days. He is so beautiful to me. I love everything about him. I love the shape of his head as he bends over the keys. I love his big hands and his strong fingers as they wring wonderful music out of the battered old piano that is never quite in tune. I love how serious his face looks when he's giving the rest of the band their cues. Of course, my imagination is already in love with the bits of him I haven't yet seen as well!

So, he walked me home again. This time, we didn't wait until we were outside the Hotel Frankfort before we kissed. Instead we chose a far more romantic spot, just under the railway bridge. We kissed for ages. My lips are quite chapped and sore. We only stopped when the church bell sounded three and Otto said his mother would be worried that he hadn't yet come home.

We hurried the rest of the way and outside the hotel is when he asked me.

'I was wondering,' he began.

'Whatever it is, I'll say yes,' I interrupted him.

'I was hoping you'd say that.' He grinned.

'Now you'd better tell me what you're proposing.'

'Tuesday is your night off, yes? I have asked Schluter if I may have a night off too. He has agreed. And since we both have a night off, I wonder whether I might take you to the Haus Vaterland?'

I clapped my hands together in joy. I have heard great things about the Haus Vaterland. It's an enormous palace of entertainment on the Potsdamer Platz, bigger and more amazing than anything they have even in New York. I have been itching to see inside. Though I wonder how Otto can possibly afford it. Schluter is a kind man but he certainly doesn't overpay us. Still, I decided that was a question that would have to go unanswered. Otto wants to take me out and he wants to take me somewhere wonderful. I feel I can be sure now that the kiss was not one of those spur-of-the-moment things that turned out to mean nothing very much. Otto really, really likes me.

Berlin,
Tuesday 5th July 1932

Our night at the Haus Vaterland was everything I had imagined and more. We had Schluter to thank for that;

he knows several of the staff at the Haus. Some of them used to work at the Boom Boom. They all remember Schluter fondly and so they were more than happy to be of service when he asked if they could make sure our evening was special.

If the building looked amazing on the outside, it was like something from a dream once you stepped through the doors. The different floors were arranged according to theme. There was a Wild West bar with cowboys and Indians and a Bavarian beer garden with an artificial lake. But Schluter had made sure that Otto and I would experience the most spectacular show the Haus had to offer.

We made our way to the Rhine room. I had heard people talk about it, of course. It was the stuff of Berlin legend. But I was still so surprised when I walked in to see an actual river. A river! Almost as wide as the Rhine itself. On one side of it was a model of a ruined castle. There were even little boats!

A waiter, dressed in the traditional clothes of the region, showed us to our table on the riverbank.

'My father would love this,' I said. 'He's a keen fisherman.'

'I don't think there are any fish in there,' said Otto. 'But I wouldn't be surprised.'

I wouldn't have been surprised either. The attention to detail was astonishing. I was agog. I wondered how long it had taken them to recreate the Rhine in this corner of the city. Trees grew out of the floor. From time to time we heard cowbells. I was certain I even heard birds tweeting.

The only things that reminded us we weren't actually on the banks of a real river were the beautifully laid tables and the elegantly dressed customers who sat at them. I was wearing my 'one and only'. That is to say the 'one and only' serviceable evening dress I have since I left so much behind in Munich. For jewellery I only have my crucifix. I felt a little dowdy surrounded by Berlin's most fashionable fräuleins, in their silks and their furs and their glittering diamonds.

Perhaps sensing I was feeling slightly provincial in the presence of so many exotically dressed women, Otto took my hand across the table and squeezed it tightly. 'You are the most beautiful woman here tonight.'

And I knew that even if it wasn't true, Otto believed it. That was enough for me. He was certainly the most handsome man. Oh his eyes. His eyes! I wish I could dive in and go for a swim in those deep sea-blues.

While Otto was talking to a waiter who had previously worked at the Boom Boom, I cast my eye around the room again. I had not noticed before that each of the exotic beauties in the restaurant that evening had accessorised her outfit with an umbrella. Most strange, I thought. The weather had been magnificent all week. It was so sunny and warm, in fact, that there had been murmurings of forest fires outside the city. But every single one of the women had an umbrella next to her chair.

I soon found out why. The Rhine room was so realistic it was as though there was no roof above us, only the vast blue sky. Well, the painted firmament suddenly darkened. The cowbells were silenced and in their place came a rumble of thunder. I looked at Otto in confusion. His eyes were crinkling in amusement.

'What's going on?' I asked, as a drop of water darkened a spot on my napkin.

'Now!' someone shouted. And suddenly a hundred umbrellas were unfurled. I opened my mouth in horror as the rain began to fall. But Otto was right beside me, opening an umbrella over my head.

The delighted customers whooped and cheered as the rain came down. The waiters, now garbed in waterproofs, continued to serve drinks and entrées. It rained for a full five minutes.

'Do you like it?' Otto asked.

'It's amazing,' I told him.

'Good. Because it happens three times a night. It's incredibly popular. It's a guaranteed way to get close to your girl. When the rain falls and she has to share your umbrella. A great excuse.'

Otto sneaked his arm round my back.

'You don't need an excuse,' I said. 'I want to be close to you all the time.'

As we kissed beneath the umbrella, the rain stopped. Just a few drips dropped onto our table and into our wine. The lighting changed so that it appeared as though the sun was coming out again and the band started to play 'Blue Skies'.

I sang along.

'I didn't know you were a singer,' said Otto.

'You make me feel like singing,' I said.

'Then sing. Sing some more.'

I belted out another little snatch of 'Blue Skies', which

was a song my mother used to sing to me when I was small and refusing to sleep. It was one of her favourites.

'You shouldn't be waiting tables at the Boom Boom,' said Otto. 'You should be on stage.'

I blushed.

'I couldn't,' I said. 'I haven't the courage.'

'You had the courage to come to Berlin all on your own. I don't believe for one moment that you don't have the courage to get up on stage at the club.'

'After a star like Marlene?'

'I would like to see you in the spotlight,' said Otto, kissing me again. 'Though at the same time, the thought of all those men seeing you up there and realising how beautiful you are? It would drive me mad with jealousy.'

'I'll never make you jealous,' I promised.

He continued to kiss me until the waiter, who had just appeared with our dinner, cleared his throat to draw our attention to his presence. We broke apart, laughing.

Though it had been hot and sunny all day, when we came out of the Haus Vaterland, we discovered that it had clouded over and the air was heavy with the crackling feeling that foretold a real summer storm. I held on tight to Otto as he guided me through the streets. As I suspected, our trip to the Haus had wiped him out. We didn't have enough between us to get a taxi and neither of us wanted to push our way onto a tram with all the other sweaty punters making their way home. Instead, we walked. I didn't mind. I preferred it and I relished the opportunity to spend a little more time with my love.

As we walked, we talked. He told me more about

himself. He told me about his ambitions. He had embarked upon his training as a lawyer not so much because he had a passion for the law but because it was the best-paid job he was qualified for and he needed to earn as much money as possible to support his mother and his sister now that his father was dead.

'But,' Otto continued, 'I found that when I actually started my studies, I was fascinated. I want to be a lawyer for people who cannot afford to pay for representation. I want to help society's lowest to get the justice they deserve.'

'You're very noble, Otto,' I said. 'And very handsome too. If I were on a jury, I would believe whatever you said.'

'My dear heart, I hope you would only believe the truth.'

Otto is unlike any English boy I've met. Perhaps it is his being German that makes him so serious. Perhaps it is that he has lost his father. Whatever the reason, I find his seriousness quite refreshing. He has integrity and I trust him absolutely. I feel safe whenever he is around.

We kissed again at the door of the hotel, of course. My insides were positively molten with desire for him but I knew he would not come in if I asked him. And I know I should be patient, like a good girl, and enjoy the kisses without wanting anything more. But oh! This is worse than a month of Christmas Eves!

15

Berlin, last October

How much Berlin has changed. After reading about Kitty's evening at the Haus Vaterland, I decided I ought to go and see where the Vegas-style palace of fun once stood. It was on the Potsdamer Platz. The address still existed, but how different it was eighty years later. There was no sign of the Kempinski-owned nightclub. It had long since been destroyed. In its place were a variety of buildings that owed nothing to history. They were as modern as it is possible to be, like a little corner of Tokyo in Germany.

Kitty had mentioned a couple of other clubs too. Heaven and Hell, where once doormen dressed as St Peter and Satan had prodded revellers in the direction of their tables and their fate for the evening, was now a branch of H & M. Where once stood the Kakadu – the glamorous Kakadu, Berlin's own little piece of the South Pacific – was now a branch of Subway, the sandwich chain. Seeing tourists stuffing their faces with soggy bread rolls, it was very hard to believe that the Ku'damm had once been the centre of Berlin's vibrant and decadent nightlife. You needed a very creative imagination to be able to dream up a Saturday night in 1932. It made me feel more than a little sad. Doubtless far more important things had been lost since, but I wondered what Kitty would think were she suddenly to find herself teleported into this desert of grey sixties buildings and international retail chains.

Kitty would probably need a drink. Fortunately, that was on my agenda.

I was meeting Clare and Harry in a beer garden by the zoo, but since I had a little time to myself, I decided to drop into the nearby memorial church with its broken spire. I had read about the cross of nails, the symbol of forgiveness that originated when someone created a cross of nails in the ruins of Coventry Cathedral. Since then it had spread around the world, including to Berlin, a city equally broken by Hitler's ambition. It struck me that the constant message that beat from the heart of Berlin was one of forgiveness. Forgive the past. Forgive them. Forgive me.

I thought about Marco's last letter to me, in which he asked me not only to forget him but to forgive him too. And then I thought about his email. His chilly, lazy email. 'I think I owe you an apology.' Think harder, I thought. Tell me something I don't know.

I crossed the ugly courtyard to the new church. An octagonal monstrosity from the outside, inside it was a magical place, with the sunlight streaming in through the blue glass windows making it seem as though you were under the ocean when you stepped through the doors.

Though I have never considered myself to be especially religious, I felt the urge to light a candle. I exchanged a euro for a votive in a plastic cup printed with an apple – the emblem of the new church. My mind was still on Marco. I could have forgiven him anything. I still would. But in truth, I wasn't sure that would make any difference. Not unless Marco was prepared to forgive himself first. Until he did that, we could only continue to dance around one another, with him drawing closer and running away according to how he was feeling about himself in that moment. I wanted an end to that, one way or another. That was what I prayed for. That Marco would make peace with whatever was troubling his heart and that my heart at last could be free.

I bumped into Harry as I was coming out of the church.

'What were you doing in there?' he asked. 'Praying for God to send you a man?'

'Something like that,' I told him.

Harry didn't pry any further, thank goodness. He was too excited at the prospect of telling me about the answer to his own prayers. A couple of nights earlier, he had picked up a new man of his own. His animated retelling of the way it had happened reminded me of Kitty Hazleton, writing in her diaries, breathless with excitement every time a young man paid her some attention. First Matthew Spencer, then Cord Von Cord, now Otto. I hoped that, as I continued to read her diaries, her enthusiasm for Otto would not turn out to be misplaced.

Clare was waiting for us by the beer garden. We three linked arms and walked on in. When Clare greeted me and told me that I looked a little preoccupied, I half wished that I was meeting only her that evening. Perhaps I would have told her about Marco's email. Perhaps she might have had some useful advice. As it was, there was no chance that anyone would be able to get a word in edgeways until Harry was tired of telling his tale. Clare and I made all the right noises, though when Harry went to fetch the first round of drinks, Clare commented, 'I'd be amazed if it lasts more than a week. Every new guy he meets, he is convinced he's in love.'

The atmosphere in the beer garden was raucous. Unlike Harry and Clare, who had been in training for years, I was completely unable to drink more than one stein of the heavy German beer before it started to affect my perception.

Under the autumn canopy, saying goodbye to the last of summer, I found myself imagining Kitty at the Haus Vaterland, dancing in the arms of her beau. I was back in time, when the horror of the First World War was almost forgotten and the idea of a second world war seemed impossible and everyone lived as fast as they could in honour of those who had died. I thought about the bench in the Peggy Guggenheim museum in Venice, with its inscription: 'Savor kindness because cruelty is always possible later.'

Was I being cruel to Marco by leaving his message unanswered? Had he meant to be cruel to me by sending his half-hearted apology?

I got back to my rooms around one o'clock in the morning. The house was dark; Herr Schmidt had already gone to bed. I opened my laptop. Marco had written again. I did not open his email right away. I made some tea and sat by the bedroom window, watching the street below, but I was just torturing myself. I held out for three minutes before I returned to my laptop and opened his new note.

Sarah,

I hoped I might have heard from you before now. Please at least let me know that you have received my email. As long as I don't know that you have read it, I will be in torment, wondering if I will ever track you down again. But if you have read it and decided that you no longer want to hear from me, just say. That way I can give up on you altogether and continue my solitary life.

Marco

That last line made me angry. I barely hesitated before I pressed reply and began to write my response. The fury

Marco had aroused in me made me type quickly and passionately. Everything I said came straight from my heart.

> Give up on me? It is you who has given up. On yourself.
> Unless that's changed, I don't have time to listen to your
> self-pity. There are people in the world with far greater
> reason to feel angry than you have. Far greater reason to
> believe that the only way to survive is to cut themselves off
> from the rest of humanity.
>
> You know what? When I first looked at those
> photographs of you online, I didn't just see a handsome
> young man, I saw a spoilt young man who never had to
> work for what he wanted. I saw a young man with all the
> advantages Mother Nature and rich parents can bestow.
> Your decision to cut yourself off is just another symptom
> of how far your privilege has warped you. You don't have
> to engage with the world because you can afford not to.
> You can send your manservant out there instead. Your
> reclusive lifestyle is just another luxury choice.
>
> Your body is damaged, Marco, but you are still alive.
> How can you choose not to make the most of every day
> you have left to you when the other guy in your car doesn't
> have that choice? If you don't want to help yourself, I
> certainly can't help you. You can't make me responsible for
> this decision. And you can't expect me to entertain you in
> your self-made cage. I've had enough.

I felt sick as I read my email back to myself. Who was I to tell
Marco that he was being self-indulgent? On the other hand,
who was he to keep yanking my chain? It was as though he
could sense me moving away from him and every time I did
he reached out to me again. Enough.

But my subconscious did not seem to think that was

enough at all. I went to bed. Of course, I dreamed that I was in Venice again.

I was in the library, sitting at the desk where I had spent so many hours. In front of me was a diary. I didn't recognise it. It wasn't Luciana's. It wasn't Augustine's. It wasn't Kitty's. The writing was familiar, however and I turned the pages quickly as though I knew what I was looking for. Eventually, I came to the place I wanted but when I tried to read what was written there, the words swam in front of my eyes, rear-ranging themselves into incomprehensible patterns of squiggles and swirls. I stared and stared but the words would make no sense to me. I turned over more pages. Not only were the words moving, they were starting to disappear. They were fading even as I watched them, until at last, all the pages in this diary that was clearly so important to me were suddenly completely blank.

What did it mean? In my dream, my eyes swam with tears as though I knew that what was lost had huge importance. I seemed to understand that the diary had held the key to something. And now its secrets were gone for ever. I would never get them back.

While I was still staring at the blank pages, as though sheer force of will might cause the swirling ink to reappear, I heard footsteps in the room behind me. I turned to see who was there.

It was the man in the mask. My dream Marco, his face half-covered by the unchanging white carapace. I stared into his eyes. They were as impenetrable and powerful as ever.

He drew closer. I didn't want him to touch me. He reached for my arm but I shook him off with a snarl. However, he would not take no for an answer. As I tried to leave the library, he prevented me. He stepped in front of me and physically blocked my way. He seemed taller and stronger than I remembered. Almost superhuman. He put his hands on my shoulders and walked me backwards into the centre of the room.

'You have to let me go,' I told him.

'I don't want to,' he said. 'You don't want me to.'

He pulled me to him and silenced my protestations with a kiss. I felt small and weak in his arms, like a rabbit giving up in the coils of a python. When he stopped kissing me for a moment, I found all I could do was look into his eyes. Dark eyes. Animal. Kind and hurt and dangerous all at the same time.

Marco continued to walk me backwards until, suddenly, we were against a bookshelf. The sharp corners of the books pressed into my skin as Marco leaned heavily against me. He devoured me with kisses. He touched me roughly, pushing up my shirt and squeezing my breasts. He wouldn't rape me, I knew. I was certain I could make him stop. But I didn't want to. Part of me – a strong and vocal part – wanted him more than ever. I started to kiss him back, every bit as violently.

We made love angrily, pinching and twisting flesh and pulling each other's hair. And yet there was still love in there, beneath all the fury. We both knew that. It was as though we were each trying to force the other to see our point of view with those harsh, almost painful kisses and unforgiving thrusts that filled me with molten desire. Still joined, we stumbled towards the fireplace and sank down onto the rug.

He pounded into me and I pushed up against him. The sex was crazy. Frenzied. We were unstoppable force and immoveable object. Which one of us would give in first?

I came with tremendous force, crying out and writhing in the flickering light. I thought it would never stop. He yelled out as he pounded into me, flooding me with the ecstasy of his own orgasm. We clung together. My fingernails dug into his back. It was as though gravity had ceased to exist and we had to hang on to each other or risk flying away.

Afterwards, however, it was as though someone had thrown a blanket over a fire. The flames were out. We were exhausted but calm. I rolled over to take Marco's hand. I wanted to look into his eyes and find out what he really needed from me. But he had rolled away to face the wall.

'You don't understand,' he said. 'You have to understand.'

16

Dear Diary,

Otto is still being wonderful. Everything is exactly as it should be. It's clear to me that our relationship is not just a fling to him. He wasn't at work this evening – he had a paper to write – so I was able to corner Marlene and ask her for the gory details at last. She said that in the three years Otto has been playing at the club, she has never known him flirt with anyone. Not a staff member. Not a dancing girl. Not a customer. And it isn't as though he doesn't have his fans. There are often tables full of young women making moon eyes at Otto across the dancefloor. He never seems to notice them at all.

'It was different when you arrived,' Marlene said. 'I could see the instant connection. He could not take his eyes off you. I'm not in the least bit surprised you've managed to bag him. But he is a good boy, Kitty. He's a romantic. All I ask is that you don't break his heart.'

'I have no intention of breaking his heart!' I protested. 'Marlene,' I dropped my voice low, 'I think I may be in love with him.'

Marlene grinned. 'That's just marvellous, because the feeling is so obviously mutual.'

How could any girl not fall in love with Otto Schmidt? Every day I learn something new about him and every time it is something that fills me with delight and makes my heart expand a little more. Yesterday, he was unable to join me at lunchtime because he had to go shopping for an invalided neighbour. Can you imagine? He is handsome, he's clever, he's kind AND he dances like a dream. I am definitely hanging on to this one.

Berlin,
Wednesday 27th July 1932

Last night, Otto told Schluter about my singing voice.

'Let's hear it,' Schluter demanded.

'Oh no,' I protested. 'I'm not really any good at all.'

Otto gave me a stern sort of look. 'Don't hide your bushel,' he said.

'It's "don't hide your light behind a bushel",' I corrected him.

'All the same.'

'Don't hide your bushel either,' Marlene laughed. 'Come on Kitty. We want to hear you sing. You can't be any worse than the people who come here on amateur night.'

'I wouldn't bet on it,' I told them.

Otto had already opened the piano. 'What will it be?'

'This is silly,' I said. 'It's so embarrassing and you'll wish you hadn't asked.'

'Let us be the judge of that,' said Schluter. 'Get up there.'

Reluctantly, I climbed up onto the stage, feeling like a proper fool. I wasn't sure if I felt better or worse when Young Hans turned on a spotlight. It meant I couldn't see my audience, only Otto at the piano. Perhaps if I imagined I was singing only for him. He started to play. 'Join in whenever you want.'

I sang 'I'm Good For Nothing But Love'. I made a terrible start. My voice was all over the place. Darling Otto did his usual trick and changed key in an attempt to make me sound vaguely in tune. But once I got going, things were better. Eventually I was almost enjoying myself. When 'I'm Good For Nothing' finished, Otto kept playing so that I had to segue straight into 'I Got Rhythm'. I ended up singing three songs. The last – 'Love Me Tonight' – was all but perfect.

Marlene pursed her lips and nodded. 'She's not bad.'

'Not bad at all,' said Schluter.

'But you need a dance to go with it,' said Marlene. 'You can't just stand there like a shop dummy.'

'Oh, I don't really dance,' I said. 'Except for Scottish reels.'

'I'll do the choreography,' Marlene assured me. 'Thursday night?' she suggested to Schluter.

'Great,' he said. 'And if Kitty isn't waitressing, it will save me a fortune in broken crockery.'

'See?' said Otto, when we were alone together later on. 'You have a true talent. You're going to be a star.'

'Whatever will your mother think? You with a dancing girl?'

'She will love you because I love you. Even if you were a dancing bear.'

'Did you just say you love me?' I interrupted. Otto blushed.

'I think I did,' he said.

'Oh, then say it again,' I begged him. 'Assuming you mean it, that is.'

'I definitely mean it,' he told me. 'I love you, Kitty Hazleton.'

I threw my arms around his neck and we kissed more deeply than ever before. My heart was beating fit to burst. When I placed my hand on his chest, I could feel his heart pounding too. I pressed myself against him and felt his hardness against my thigh. It was reassuringly long and substantial.

'Otto,' I murmured. 'I love you too. Perhaps . . . tonight . . .'

'You should go inside,' he said, putting me away from him. 'You need to be ready for your first practice tomorrow, Miss Star.'

I had the feeling that he was struggling to control himself. I decided I had better not tempt him. Instead, I kissed him on the end of the nose.

'Even when I'm famous,' I said, 'I will only have eyes for you.'

Friday 26th August 1932

I'm officially an artiste! Tonight my name will be on the Boom Boom's hoarding. Well, not my real name, of course, but my stage name. We've decided on 'Kitty Katkin'. It took ages to make it up. I quite fancied something like 'LouLou Lamora', but Marlene said that my role at the club is to provide light relief. I must be playful, not too sexy and LouLou Lamora sounds like a slut.

'Perhaps when you're older,' she said.

'How about when I'm seventeen?' I asked her. Everybody laughed because I'm seventeen today. Happy Birthday to me! When I went down to breakfast this morning, Enno brought me two fried eggs on toast instead of the usual one. What's more, they were almost edible. He also brought a handful of cards and a present. The cards were from Enno and everyone at the club. The present was best of all. Apparently Otto secretly dropped it off last night because he wanted me to have it first thing. It's a little Steiff teddy bear with a very fierce face and perfect button eyes. I love him. Almost as much as I love Otto. I have called him 'Little Adolf'.

I was upset of course that there was nothing from Mummy and Papa but I have just about given up on them. They'd certainly give up on me if they knew I'd become a dancing girl. But needs must. Schluter has upped my wages by 100% and, what's more, I'm having fun. I love spending my days practising the dance routines. Marlene and I have just created a wonderful dance in which we play twin sisters, in matching dresses and wigs with only a height difference of fifteen inches to help the audience tell us apart. It's terribly funny. I think it will bring the house down when we debut it tonight.

And after the show tonight, Marlene says she's

throwing me a birthday party. Otto will be there of course. A very Happy Birthday to me!

Monday 29th August 1932

Dear Diary,

Something has happened which makes me absolutely certain of Otto's intentions towards me. He has invited me to join him on Sunday. At his family home! He said he has told his mother all about me and she is very keen to see me in person. Can you believe it? It's proof. You don't just take any old girl home to meet the family, do you? We're in love! We're in love! We're in love!

Sunday 4th September 1932

Dear Diary,

It took me a very long time to get ready for my lunch with Otto's mother. What on earth should I wear? I've become very sensitive to the meaning of clothes since my awful experience in the café. Those green boots were definitely not going to be part of the ensemble.

In the end, I put on my most sober dress. It's one I haven't worn since Munich. It's a little heavy for the weather and too dark in colour but it has a high collar and long sleeves. I did my hair in the most sensible fashion I could think of.

Enno smiled his approval.

'You look wonderful. You could have tea with the King of England in that get-up.'

Otto too seemed pleased.

'You look beautiful,' he said. 'My mother will be very happy to see I've made such a catch. Though I think I prefer it when your hair is not quite so severe.'

'Me too,' said Enno. I reminded them both that I wasn't dressing with them in mind.

Otto and I caught the tram towards Prenzlauer Berg. It's quite a nice area. The house, which is very close to an enormous park, is tall and white, elegant and imposing just like the boy who lives there. The Schmidt family have been there for years apparently. Otto's grandfather bought the house and Otto was actually born there, twenty years ago this month.

Otto's mother is exactly as I imagined. She is warm and kindly but she also has a sense of humour. At least, I think she has a sense of humour. She speaks only German and my German is nowhere good enough to get all the nuances of her speech. Otto and his younger sister translated, thank goodness.

Oh, his sister Helga is a delight! She is so pretty. Like a feminine version of Otto. She has his startling blue eyes. She is obviously very bright. She told me she wants to become a doctor and move to London when she has finished her training. She asked me lots of questions about life in England and much admired my dress. I told her that she can have one just like it. I'll get Mother to send the pattern over from Surrey. If she ever writes to me again. Mentioning my mother made me just a little sad. Still no sign of a birthday card. They really must have cut me off.

Later Otto's mother told me that she likes my pretty hair.

'But you should wear it a little looser,' she said.

All in all, I think the meeting was a terrific success. Only Otto's brother seemed reluctant to be charmed. He was not at the table for lunch. He joined us later. Having made such a hit with Otto's mother and sister, I was very much looking forward to meeting Gerd, the middle child. Otto's mother talked very proudly of her son. She said that, like Otto, Gerd had excelled at school. He was also an excellent sportsman. He took after his father in that respect.

'Whereas Otto takes after his grandfather on my side,' she said. 'With his musical talent.'

We all cooed over Otto's musical talent for a while.

'Gerd's not such a bad musician either,' Otto said to deflect some of the gushing praise, which he seemed to find embarrassing.

'Play something for us,' Helga insisted. Otto treated us to small burst of Chopin on the family's upright piano. I will never tire of his playing.

Then Frau Schmidt told a tale to illustrate Gerd's physical prowess. Apparently, when Otto was fourteen and Gerd was just twelve years old, they went with their father to fish at a lake out in the country. It was a cold day and the lake was partially frozen over. Some children on the opposite bank were larking about on the ice. The fish weren't biting and Otto's father decided it was time to pack up and go home.

'Via the market,' Otto's mother said. 'My husband would often try to pass off some market fish as something he'd caught himself. I never told him I knew the difference between a seawater fish and a freshwater one. Anyway . . .'

The Schmidt men were packed up and ready to go home when they heard the ominous sound of cracking ice. While they'd been fishing, the children on the opposite bank had been staying very close to the shore, but one of them had ventured further out and now he was in the freezing water.

Gerd did not hesitate. He ran all the way round the lake, to be closer to where the child had fallen in. The child's friends were trying to haul him out with a dead branch from a tree, but the wood was so rotten that every time the poor boy in the pond made a grab for it, a section broke off in his hand. He was drifting further from the shore and he was getting tired and dangerously cold.

'I am so glad I was not there,' said Otto's mother. 'Because I would have done my very best to prevent what happened next.'

'Gerd jumped into the water!' said Helga, breathlessly. 'He took off his jacket and his boots and he jumped straight in. He didn't care about the ice.'

'He was always a strong swimmer,' said Frau Schmidt.

Helga took up the story again. 'The boy was sinking. Gerd dived under the surface and brought the poor child up for air. He held him clear of the water so he could breathe and kept him there until our father arrived and was able to haul them both to safety.'

'The young boy was saved. It turned out that his father was the local mayor. He was so grateful he invited our whole family to his house,' said Frau Schmidt.

'And that was where the trouble began,' said Otto darkly.

His mother and sister looked at him with expressions of slight confusion but Otto smiled and Helga continued with the story.

'Gerd was treated like a hero. The mayor offered him a financial reward but Gerd refused to take it. He said that the mayor should give the money to the war widows instead.'

'Such a kind heart,' said Otto's mother. 'So patriotic. And it was the right thing to do, because after my husband died, the mayor who had been so impressed by Gerd's self-sacrifice offered to finish putting the boys through school.'

'He said that now we had no father, we should consider him to be our father instead,' Helga explained. 'He said any man would be proud to have Gerd as his son.'

The more they talked, the more I was looking forward to meeting the public-spirited, kind-hearted family hero.

'And what's he doing now?' I asked. 'Is Gerd studying like his brother?'

Otto and his sister shared a look.

'No. He is not studying. He is in the SA,' said Otto's mother.

I looked to Otto for an explanation of the abbreviation. There wasn't time for him to elaborate. We all turned at the sound of a key in the front door.

'And here he is!'

Otto's mother and sister got to their feet. I followed their example. Only Otto remained seated at the table.

Gerd Schmidt appeared in the dining-room doorway. He was almost the spitting image of his brother, but though it was a Sunday, he was wearing a pale-brown uniform. The SA, I understood then, was short for the Sturmabteilung. The Nationalist Socialists' paramilitary branch. Cord Von Cord had been much in awe of them as they marched around Munich.

'*Heil Hitler*,' said Gerd as he flipped us that strange salute and clicked his heels together.

Gerd Schmidt is a very serious young man. He sat down at the table while his mother and sister immediately flew into action, bringing his meal from the oven where it had been keeping warm. He ate quickly and without taking much notice of social niceties. He didn't seem terribly interested in who I was. Eventually, Otto drew his brother's attention to the fact that the family had a guest.

'Miss Katherine Hazleton from England.'

'Ah, England,' said Gerd. 'And what do you think of your chancellor?'

I had to admit I hadn't given him much thought.

'Politics aren't really my thing,' I said.

'Well, they should be,' Gerd admonished me. 'There is no excuse for ignorance. That is how the wool is pulled over our eyes. And where did you meet my brother?'

'In the club,' I said. 'I've been working there.'

Gerd didn't try to keep the disapproval from his face. His mouth tightened. 'You work at the club? I see.'

123

Otto's mother tried to defuse the tension of the moment by asking her son what he had been doing that morning, but his answers made the atmosphere even darker. Otto kept rolling his eyes. It was clear that the Schmidt brothers were no longer the close friends they had been as children. Perhaps they still teased each other, but there was a distinct edge to that teasing. I wished I could get to the bottom of it.

We left about an hour after Gerd arrived.

'Thank you, Otto, for taking me to meet your lovely family,' I said as he walked me home. 'Your mother and your sister were absolutely charming.'

'And my brother? I can't believe he was so rude to you.'

'He wasn't rude,' I said soothingly. 'Some people find it difficult to meet someone new for the first time. He was as nervous of meeting me as I was of meeting him. That's all. I'm sure that we'll all become great friends in time. He's your brother, Otto. That's all I need to know to love him.'

'If he weren't my brother, I would walk past him in the street.'

'Don't say that,' I told him. 'I have spent my whole life wishing I had a brother or a sister. I wouldn't care how annoying they were. When did Gerd become a soldier?' I asked.

'Just last year, but he's wanted to sign up for a long time. Ever since he dragged that wretched boy out of the ice pond and the mayor decided to try to make us his second family. The mayor is a National Socialist. Gerd believes everything he says. My brother saved that man's son and in return for Gerd's kindness he stole him away from us. Our father would never have let Gerd join the Party. Never.'

With that, Otto thumped his fist against a wall.

I didn't know what to say. I had never seen him quite so agitated. I sensed that since I couldn't think of anything especially sensible, it was best if I said nothing at all. Instead, I wrapped my arms around Otto and started to kiss him. I took his sore fist and kissed that too. That soon chased his bad mood away.

'Why don't you come up to my room?' I said. 'It's still daylight. No one can possibly disapprove of you coming into the hotel during the afternoon. Even if it is a Sunday.'

This time, Otto nodded.

Oh, Otto is driving me crazy with desire. When my mother first told me about the birds and the bees, she warned me that boys would try anything to get me into bed with my clothes off. She didn't warn me that I would feel just as full of raging lust myself. When it comes to me and Otto, he is the one who is in danger! I am lucky, I suppose, that he is such a gentleman, because if the crazy creature inside me had her way, I would strip all my clothes off the moment I saw him, whether we were in my bedroom or the middle of the street! For how long should a good girl hold out?

I know I should stop complaining. Otto has great respect for me, which is more than Matthew Spencer or Cord Von Cord ever had. When the time is right, I am sure he will make love to me properly. In the meantime, I must be patient though my heart says 'Tonight, tonight, TONIGHT!!!'

17

Venice, early last October

As the seemingly endless summer weather began to stutter and rain showers threatened the perfect days, Silvio could not help but notice that it felt as though winter had already arrived at the Palazzo Donato.

When there was no one in the house but Silvio, Marco would not, of course, confine himself to his secret office. He would sit in the armchair by the fire in the library. He would walk round the courtyard garden or simply sit in the sun there, making plans for the next year's planting. When he'd told Bea that he was the palazzo's gardener, Marco was not being entirely untruthful. The garden was indeed his domain. Silvio may have swept the paths clean on a daily basis, but it was Marco who had chosen and tended the plants. He did everything from potting to pruning. It was a way of keeping fit now that he would not step outside the palazzo's grounds. There was a small gym too, with a running machine and a static bicycle. Marco had once explained that while he was content to hide himself away, he did not want to wither away at the same time. He had no intention of making Silvio a nursemaid.

But that seemed to have changed. Marco had not been into the garden for a week. He had been into the library, but when Silvio put his head round the door to announce that the mail had arrived or to ask whether Marco wanted coffee, he found his master not reading but staring into space. It was as though they had slipped back in time to the early years after the accident, when Marco seemed every bit as dead as the other passenger in the car. Silvio had done his best to bring him back to life then. He had made sure that Marco ate. He'd stopped him from becoming a hobo by shaving him each morning and ensuring that he changed his clothes. It had taken a colossal effort to bring Marco back to the point where he was willing at least to dress and feed himself. Now he was slipping backwards again.

It was worrying.

Silvio was an honest man. When Marco inherited the palazzo and Silvio along with it, Marco had made him promise that what went on inside the palazzo from then on was entirely private. Silvio should never speak of his employer outside his four walls. He should not ask questions. He should just continue to do as he had always done. Tend the house. Tend the valuable antiques inside it. Tend the beautiful boat that had belonged to Marco's grandfather.

Silvio sometimes wondered if he should not wear a *servetta muta*. But his discretion did not mean that he did not care what went on behind the Palazzo Donato's closed doors. It did not mean that he hadn't grown to care very much about the young man who employed him. Silvio's heart had blazed with happiness when Marco announced that he wanted to host a Martedì Grasso ball in honour of the English girl. He thought that it was the beginning of something. It was obvious the girl felt the same. And while the ball had been a disaster for Marco, the girl had come back again after that. And again. She was tenacious in her love for him. Was she still trying to get through to him or was she behind the way things had taken a turn for the worse?

*   *   *

One night in early October – it was a full moon – Silvio decided to act. Marco was in his bedroom. He was going to bed earlier and sleeping longer these days. Plus, even if Marco did wake and decide to roam the palazzo by night, Silvio would hear him coming. In his long service at the palazzo, Silvio had come to know the house as intimately as a lover's body. He knew her sighs as she settled down for the night and her squeaks of indignation if someone stepped on the wrong floorboard. The house was in cahoots with Silvio. She would let him know if he was in danger of being found out.

Silvio knew about the secret office, of course. Apart from the Donato family, he was one of the few people who had ever seen inside it. He knew it had been installed by Marco's distant ancestor Ernesta so that she had somewhere to hide if she found herself caught unawares by an unexpected visitor she didn't wish to entertain for any amount of jewels.

Ernesta had used her hideaway when Napoleon and his troops ransacked the city. It had probably saved her life. It had probably saved the life of Marco's father too, as he hid his mistresses in there whenever his wife came home unexpectedly. The things that room had seen . . . The things *Silvio* had seen in that room. His mind flashed to his discovery of a drawing of the English girl, sitting at the desk with her shoes kicked off. That wasn't what he had come for.

Silvio wasn't sure whether the thing he was looking for still existed, but he felt sure that something would guide him to its hiding place if it did. As he passed her portrait, he had the feeling that the spirit of Ernesta was looking down on him. He felt she would approve.

Inside the secret office, Silvio stood over the desk and looked at the jumble of papers on it. He rifled through them, just as Sarah had done all those months before. He came across another drawing of the English girl sitting in the library. Yes, there was no doubt that the English girl had touched his master's heart. But this drawing was not what he needed either. Moving quickly, he opened the desk drawers. Nothing there.

He saw the Buddha on the plinth by the window. Its smiling face had drawn his attention. It was resting on a pile of books. A pile of diaries to be precise. And there it was. Right in the middle.

Like the ultimate cat burglar, Silvio slid his prize out of the tower by replacing it with another almost identical volume. He flicked through the first few pages. It was the right one. The words brought tears to his eyes just as they had done when he saw them for the first time more than ten years earlier, when he had found the book on the floor next to Marco's bed on the terrible day when they thought they might have lost him for ever.

There must be no repeat of that day. Silvio was determined. He put the book into a carrier bag and slipped out of the secret office, leaving it almost exactly as he had found it.

18

Berlin, last October

The day after I sent Marco that email telling him enough was enough and he was a self-indulgent idiot, I was surprised to note that I felt a little better. A little lighter in the heart.

I went with Clare and Harry to the recreation of the Boom Boom Club to celebrate Clare's birthday. Deep as I was into Kitty's diaries, I couldn't wait to see the place where she had found her great love. At least, I couldn't wait to see the club's reincarnation. I wondered what Kitty would have thought. Would it seem authentic?

There was quite a crowd outside waiting to go in when we arrived. The punters had made a real effort. I felt as though I hadn't tried hard enough, in my jeans. But Harry told me not to worry. He said he needed some dowdy females – aka me and Clare – to properly set off his peacock perfection. Harry grumbled at the long wait to get in but I was quite happy to stand in the queue for a while. The glass poster-cabinet outside the entrance contained some very interesting posters, which appeared to date from the club's first life. I was delighted to see them and hoped for a picture of Kitty. There was none, alas, but the redheaded siren on one of the posters could only be Marlene. It was a striking portrait. Her feminine coiffure was offset by a tremendously square jaw. She might have been carved by Epstein. I pointed the poster out to Clare and told her about the diary connection. I also told her about my increasing suspicion that Herr Schmidt had not in fact found the diaries in the ruins of a hotel.

'It's a hell of a coincidence, isn't it? Him being a Schmidt and her falling for one. The Prenzlauer Berg connection. And all that stuff about his eyes! Herr Schmidt's eyes are a very strange blue. Kitty is always writing about Otto's blue eyes.'

'Schmidt's an incredibly common name,' Clare pointed out. 'Besides, if he is the guy in the diary, wouldn't he know where to find its owner? Wouldn't he have told you he knew her?'

'Maybe you're right,' I said. 'He would have told me. It would be strange not to.'

Clare agreed.

We had reached the head of the queue and were greeted by the door staff: a bouncer as big as a tower block and a diminutive transvestite dressed as a dominatrix in lots of black leather and fishnet. She looked us up and down and for one awful moment, I thought she wasn't going to let us in. Then she uttered the damning phrase 'You'll do' and the velvet rope was moved aside. We were in.

There were eight of us altogether and we had a table near the stage. We ordered champagne. Clare, who knew about such things, pronounced it awful. We drank it all the same.

The club quickly filled up and the band took their places. You could feel the excitement crackling in the air as the audience settled in their seats and began a slow handclap to encourage the swift raising of the curtain. When the curtains finally parted, the applause was riotous.

The show was opened by a fabulous mistress of ceremonies, who called herself Marlene, in tribute to the original. She was almost eight feet tall in her heels and had her red hair arranged on top of her head in the style that I imagined when Kitty described Marlene's do as 'profiteroles'. To get the audience warmed up, she did a little act of her own. She sang some old favourites from the film *Cabaret*, mixed in with some Lady Gaga. Her act was accompanied by a small troupe of dancers, who were every bit as good as you would have expected to see behind Madonna or Beyoncé. They were all dressed the same and wore identical wigs. It was hard to tell whether they were girls or boys, but they were definitely beautiful.

The amateurs who took to the stage that night were a mixed bunch, just as they had been in Kitty's day. Cross-dressing was a popular theme. Harry looked rather under-dressed compared to some of the other guys. I had never seen such flamboyant or beautiful transvestites. There were no comedy-act trannies here; every one of them was as elegant and beautiful as the dancers at the Crazy Horse.

'You've got some competition tonight,' Clare told Harry.

Not just from the other trannies, it turned out. After we had watched five men dressed as variations on Sally Bowles, the MC announced that it was time for something different.

'Something good,' she added. The audience roared. 'Let's have Anna!'

A young girl stood up.

I recognised her at once. It was Anna Fischer, my English-language student. I'd had no idea that she would be at the club that night. The mistress of ceremonies asked her what she was going to be singing. She said she was going to sing Tim Buckley's 'Song to the Siren'.

Clare nodded her approval. 'Great song.'

I agreed. I told Clare how I knew her.

'And as usual,' Anna added, 'I'm going to dedicate it to my sister. I wish she could be here tonight. I miss her every day.'

The mistress of ceremonies squeezed Anna's shoulder and

they shared a look that suggested the dedicatee had been special to both of them. The MC stepped down and let Anna take the stage. She climbed onto a high stool with her guitar and began to play.

Anna was amazing. Petite as she was and slightly scruffy, I never would have guessed that she was in possession of such an amazing voice. The nature of the song did not require that she belt out the lyrics, but she managed to reach every corner of the room while giving the impression that she had barely raised her voice above a whisper. She had the room in the palm of her hand. There was not a murmur as we watched with due reverence, definitely none of the heckling that had dogged the previous acts. A shiver passed through me at the magnificence of the sound she produced.

It was a wonderful song and she nailed it.

When she finished, it was a second before the applause started, as though everyone in the room was in shock. When I looked at Harry, he was actually wiping a tear from his eye.

'Well,' he said. 'I don't know how I'm supposed to follow that.'

As it was, Harry more than held his own on the stage. I think that after the intensity of Anna's song, the audience was glad of a moment of levity. The song Harry had chosen – 'Diamonds Are a Girl's Best Friend' – was an old favourite. He dedicated it to Clare. And his dancing was superb. When the mistress of ceremonies decided the evening's winner – she had announced that they would be chosen on the loudness of the cheers – she declared Harry joint second with a Liza Minnelli impressionist. Anna was the winner by a long way. Apparently, she was the winner pretty much every week. She proudly accepted the envelope containing the fifty-euro prize. I felt very happy to see her talent rewarded.

Before we left the club that evening, I sought Anna out.

'You didn't say you were a singer as well as a photographer,' I said.

Anna shrugged. 'Runs in the family. My mother sings and my sister was way better than both of us.'

I noticed the past tense but didn't pick her up on it. I was sure I would hear more in our conversation class. And now her friends wanted her to join them. Among them was the guy she had kissed under the street-lamp. He was obviously besotted and could hardly wait to spirit her off.

Anna embraced me and followed her man back into the crowd.

Back in my room, I looked for 'Song to the Siren' on YouTube and found a version by Elisabeth Fraser of the Cocteau Twins. I'd heard it before that night but didn't know it well. Listening to the lyrics more closely, I couldn't help but think about Marco. The singer asks whether they should give in to the siren's song and face an inevitable fate. The imagery of water and death was perfect for a Venetian recluse. And there was such love and longing in Fraser's voice.

The song inspired me to pick up a pen. I started to write a letter but I knew I wouldn't send it. After a while, I put my pen down again and picked up Kitty Hazleton's diary. I fell asleep with her diary in my hands.

The song must have affected me even more than I knew. I dreamed I was in Venice again, but this time I was not in the city itself; I was way out on the lagoon, near the Isola di San Michele, the cemetery island. I was standing at the prow of a gondola but there was no gondolier to help me steer it. I looked behind me to the felce, with its black velvet curtains. The boat was decked for a funeral, but there was no body to be seen.

As I stood there, with no oar, unable to take the boat in any direction, it drifted closer to the island on the tide. It was night-time, but a full moon reflected on the still water made it bright. There were no lights on San Michele. Its monastery made a shadow so dark, it seemed like a hole in the sky.

I stood there for what seemed like a long time, helpless to do anything as the boat drifted closer to the shore. I had a feeling of foreboding and yet, at the same time, I wasn't really afraid. The lagoon was all but silent. There was just the sound of the water lapping against my boat. The gentle rocking was calming. It was lulling me.

I was close enough to smell the scent of the cypress trees on the island when I made my decision. I thought I heard someone call out to me.

I took a deep breath and dived into the water.

The water of the lagoon was far deeper than I had imagined. As soon as I was beneath the waves, the bottom seemed to fall further and further away. I followed it down, holding my breath, moving further from safety with every kick of my legs. Yet I was not afraid. I seemed to know that something was waiting for me, if I could just swim far enough.

I saw her white arms first, snaking out of the bottomless darkness, beckoning me closer still. I followed her sema-phore. My cheeks were full and my lungs were bursting. I needed to breathe but I had to find her first.

Her face loomed out of the blackness, pale as the full moon in the sky above us. She was no fairytale mermaid. Her hair was not golden and long. She had no fish's tail. She was not streamlined like an eel and when she reached out her arms to bring me to her, there was no flash of silver scales. She was an ordinary woman, white and blue because of the water. Her face was kind but serious. It was familiar though unknown. There was something else about it that I could not articulate right away. Her mouth was twisted upwards even though I knew she wasn't smiling. Not yet.

As I stared, her cold hands wrapped themselves round my wrists and she pulled me to her. I floated above her, as though my body was still straining towards the light. Towards the air. With unusual strength she reeled me further in. My face hovered an inch away from hers. She looked into my eyes. Hers were dark, almost black, like a seal's. I could not tear my gaze away.

She was singing 'Song to the Siren'.

I could no longer resist. She enfolded me in her arms. She pressed her body against mine, like a greedy lover who would not be refused. Her hands roamed all over me. Her soft breasts seem to melt into my own. She wrapped her legs round me to hold me tighter still.

I struggled to get away but she pressed her lips to mine and forced them open with her tongue. I was too weak to stop her. She held the back of my head so that I could not pull away. My whole head was full of her. Her kiss had such power and determination in it, there was nothing I could do but acquiesce. And when I did . . .

Suddenly, I was able to take a breath. She pulled away for a moment and I emptied my lungs of carbon dioxide, feeling the tremendous burning inside me subside at once. I could breathe again. Or else I was dead. I looked at her in astonishment. This time, she really was smiling. She released her hold on me and swam into the blue-black distance. As she disappeared, this time I did see the silvery flash of a sea-creature turning tail.

I looked up to the surface glittering way above me and started to swim towards it. I still had some living to do.

*   *   *

I sent Clare and Harry a text the next morning, thanking them for a great night on the tiles. 'Weird dream,' I wrote. 'That champagne was strong stuff.' Harry texted back immediately, accusing me of being a lightweight. I certainly felt a little jaded as I got ready to leave for the library.

Herr Schmidt was already up when I left the house. That morning he was playing Ravel. 'Le Gibet' from *Gaspard de la Nuit*. Beautiful but sad. His door was ajar. I considered knocking on it to tell him how much I appreciated his playing but he looked utterly lost in the music. His noble head nodded as he found the chords. I wondered what he had looked like as a young man. His profile was classical. I had seen his smile but rarely, but it was a generous sort of smile. As I watched him play, he lifted his left hand to wipe away a tear. He achieved this small act without missing a beat of the music. I decided not to disturb him after all.

19

Dear Diary,

I am so much in love with Otto Schmidt. I have even been practising signing my name as his wife. Can you imagine me as a Frau? Frau Schmidt. Frau Kitty Schmidt. I rather like it. Much more exotic than a plain old Missus back in the Home Counties, even if Schmidt is more common than Smith. There are three Schmidt families on this street alone. Perhaps I would differentiate myself by being Katherine Schmidt Hazleton. Gosh that sounds grown-up.

Otto is a virgin. Can you believe it? I have to say, I was surprised when he admitted it. How could someone so gorgeous not have had a hundred girls queuing up to give themselves to him? I told him so. He said the queues had indeed been embarrassingly long but he has been waiting for the right girl. Then he looked at me in a very meaningful way. I went all hot and cold.

Thankfully, he did not move the conversation on to my own past. Thank goodness he's much too polite to ask such questions of a lady. Though lady I fear I am not. As he told me about himself, I was suddenly deeply ashamed

138

about the whole business with Cord. I had managed to stay pure for so long – though admittedly not through want of trying. After Matthew Spencer, I too had been determined to save myself for the right one. I still can't believe I ever thought Cord was the right one. His eyes were so close together.

How I wish I could turn back the clock to the night of that dance in Munich and tell Cord Von Cord that he should keep his wandering hands to himself! Why did I have to be taken in by his wanton whispering and his delicious cologne? A scent that I now find quite disgusting, by the way. A customer at the club was wearing it the other night and I swear I was almost sick on the spot.

Oh, how I wish I had been more careful. I love Otto so much. I want to be able to give him a gift worth more than all the gold in the world and I no longer have it to share with him.

Saturday 17th September 1932

Dear Diary,

I decided that I had to tell Otto the truth face to face. It would have been too awful if he found out some other way. He had already told me he wanted to lose his virginity to me and he must have been assuming that it would be a moment of mutual discovery. I didn't think he would be able to tell I'd already lost mine just from looking at me – Cord was very quick after all and there was no blood, despite Bettina's insistence that there would be great spurting gouts of it as my hymen was ripped to shreds

– but what if I moved in such a way that made it obvious I wasn't an absolute beginner?

It was the most awful thing I have ever had to do.

'Otto,' I said, quite meekly, 'I will understand if you decide you never want to see me again.'

But darling Otto took my hand, lifted it to his mouth and kissed it.

'My dear Kitty,' he said, 'you are the angel of my heart. Of course, I am disappointed that I won't be the first man to know you, but I knew when I met you that you were a woman who would always defy convention. You are an adventuress with an appetite for experience. That is a part of your character I adore.'

'Well,' I said, 'it was just the once so I'm practically good as new.'

'You're as good as *you*,' said Otto. 'And that's all I ever want you to be.'

It was the most marvellous thing I'd ever heard. Otto always says the right thing.

And then it happened. We did it! At last!

After Otto told me he still wanted me, I threw my arms round his neck and started to kiss him. Before long, we had fallen back on to my bed. Ordinarily, we would have just kissed but kept our clothes firmly in place. Sometimes Otto would not even put his hand up my skirt for fear of inflaming unstoppable lust. Today was different. Now that we had spoken honestly, the barriers to propriety had come down. For once we wanted our lust to be unstoppable.

As we kissed, I felt his hand move beneath my sweater.

I felt his fingers on the bare skin of my midriff. The slightest contact sent a sensation like electricity throughout my whole body. Every tiny hair on my skin stood on end.

Oh, I felt like a virgin in Otto's arms. I had never experienced such a rush of desire. I wanted him to be all over me and in me. I wanted him to fill all my senses. How I love the sight of him, the sound of his voice, the way his skin tastes when I kiss it. At the same time, I was incredibly nervous in a way I hadn't been with Cord at the Adlon. Of course, it was because this time it really mattered. I wanted it to be perfect. With Otto it could never be 'just sex'.

Otto undressed me so carefully. As he took off my skirt, he even went so far as to fold it before he put it on the back of the chair.

'For Heaven's sake,' I told him. 'I'm waiting to be ravished.'

He blushed in that way I adore and bounced straight back to the bed. He admired me in my underclothes.

'If I were a painter,' he said, as he pushed my silk slip up my thigh, 'I would stop and capture your beauty right now for all eternity.'

'Otto,' I said. 'Please don't stop for anything!' I pulled him towards me by his belt.

I unbuttoned his shirt. I was so excited I was actually trembling. He too seemed slightly shaky with the momentousness of the occasion. When I pretended I was going to fold his shirt, he pulled it from my hands and threw it into the air so that it landed on a lampshade.

'I am waiting to ravish you,' he said.

His body is so beautiful. Otto claims that he absolutely

hates sport, but you wouldn't know it to look at him. He is so muscular. I love to lie on his chest. It makes me feel so petite and feminine. I feel so very safe within his arms.

Without his shirt on, I saw for the first time that he has quite a hairy chest. As we lay down side by side, I ran my fingers through the soft fur. I followed a line right down his middle to the waistband of his underpants. His penis was already tenting the fabric there. The sight of his arousal made my heart skip.

I laid my hand upon it. I felt it twitch beneath my palm.

'Are you sure about this?' I asked. 'You don't want to save yourself for a worthier girl?'

He put a finger on my lips. 'You are all I want. You're all I've ever wanted. You're all I ever will want and I want you now!'

I helped him out of his underpants at once.

Suddenly we were as naked as Adam and Eve before the fall. When we realised that we were totally bare together for the first time, we both laughed. It was so wonderful and so natural. I pressed myself against him, revelling in the warmth of his skin. I massaged his penis until he begged me to stop out of fear he would have nothing to give me when the time came. Meanwhile, he touched me between my legs in the gentlest of ways. He carefully rubbed my clitoris, then he slipped a finger inside. I was thoroughly wet and ready. Total bliss!

'Shall we? Now?' I asked him.

He nodded. I arranged myself on the bed with my legs open wide. He positioned himself above me and closed his eyes tightly as he pushed his way inside.

*   *   *

We moved together so perfectly. It was as though our bodies had been made to find each other. It did not hurt in the least when he thrust into me. I was ready for him. I had felt that strange blossoming feeling from the moment he kissed me. He told me I felt warm and juicy. Juicy! I told him he felt strong and firm and I'd never been so happy in my life.

It did not take long before we both reached a climax.

Otto's face . . . I want to remember his expression for ever. At first he was a little shocked but soon his mouth spread in a wide, wide grin. He collapsed on top of me and we both dissolved into the giggles. When we'd finished laughing, Otto took my face in his hands and regarded me quite seriously.

'I love you,' he said.

'And I love you, Otto Schmidt.'

He was still inside me. His penis gave a little spasm as if it agreed with me.

'How was it?' I asked him afterwards. 'Was it like you imagined it would be?'

'It was so much better,' he said. 'I want to do it again and again.'

We managed another three times that day.

Before he left to go back to the Prenzlauer Berg, he sang me to sleep. The song I like best is called 'The Song is Ended'. It's by Irving Berlin and it's very romantic. It's the perfect tune for such a momentous occasion. I've decided it will be our song.

Oh Diary, I start and end each day by thanking God for bringing me and Otto together. It was worth it, the embarrassment of Matthew and the horribleness of Cord, because without them I would be back in Surrey and getting married to some horrible accountant. Now I have my darling Otto. I am the luckiest girl in the world.

Sunday 18th September 1932

Dear Diary,

We had dinner with Otto's mother and sister again last night. Gerd turned up late, as before. He was at one of his terribly important SA meetings. Oh, he takes himself so seriously. It makes me want to giggle. The horrible uniforms and the heel-clicking. It's all so very camp! Otto told me that there is a cabaret artist in one of the private gay clubs who dresses as one of the Sturmabteilung for a striptease, which he performs to the tune of the *Horst Wessel Lied*, the Nazi anthem. When the conversation hit a lull over dinner, I'm afraid I brought the subject up. Gerd was absolutely furious.

'There will come a day very soon when no one will dare laugh at the uniform of the Sturmabteilung,' he warned us all. He was full of portent. Then he burst into a rendition of the *Horst Wessel Lied* of his own. It wasn't a bad rendition. He is an excellent singer but his face was so very serious it was all I could do not to laugh.

20

Berlin, October last year

Kitty Hazleton's diaries would make the perfect basis for my research project, but, of course, I couldn't start writing about her without trying to find out whether she was still alive. Just as I had promised Herr Schmidt, I had to look for her. A quick online search had turned up nothing useful, but I had found a record of her birth, which at least helped me to narrow down the part of the country she had come from. I would be able to do more in London, where I could get easy access to marriage and death records at the National Records Office.

I would have a good reason to go back to London relatively soon. At the beginning of October, I got the news that I had been awarded my PhD for my work on Luciana Giordano. At the same time, I heard that the university press would be publishing my thesis. It was cause for great celebration. I immediately phoned Mum and Dad, who were thrilled by the news. It was a validation of all the time I had spent with my nose in a book.

'Does this mean we have to call you Doctor Thomson now?' my mother asked.

'Absolutely,' I told her. 'I will answer to nothing less.'

When I called Bea with the news, she burst into a rendition of the 'dottore' song that rang out from the beloved student bars of the Campo Santa Margherita whenever someone took their gown. It made me wistful for the other side of Venice, the raucous partying side that had been the counterpoint to my quiet days in the library. I wished that I might have been there in the bar by the Ponte dei Pugni, celebrating with a good Venetian spritz.

Instead I celebrated with Harry and Clare in the traditional German way. With lots of beer. It was such a relief to know that I had achieved my goal. Sticking those letters after my name would make it much easier to find respect in the academic community.

'You've got to get your credit cards changed to say "Dr",' Harry told me.

'I'm worried it's just a matter of time before someone has a medical emergency and expects me to be able to deal with it,' I said.

'They should probably make a first-aid course compulsory for a doctorate,' Clare agreed.

We had a wonderful evening celebrating my success, but I couldn't help but feel a little sad when I got back to my apartment that night. I had told so many people and received so many heartfelt congratulations. Earlier in the day, Herr Schmidt had shaken my hand and told me, with a twinkle in his eye, that he would have to put my rent up now that I was more highly qualified. Later, he pushed a congratulatory card under my door. It had a picture of a mountain scene beneath the word '*Glückwünsche*'. I was pleased to be able to add that word to my vocabulary.

So, I was being suitably well lauded, but there was still one person I didn't tell. One person I really wanted to know how I had done. Marco.

Was this the excuse I needed to contact him? It wouldn't be such a big deal. I could even just copy him in on an email to several people, as though he were an afterthought. But then I thought again about the last email I had sent him and further back to our meeting face to face. The words still stung.

I decided he would have to wait. If I ever told him at all. Perhaps when the thesis was published, I would send him a bound copy for his precious library, where it could gather dust along with his heart.

Perhaps because I had spent so much of the day thinking about Luciana Giordano, she came into my dreams that night. Her laughing face was so familiar. She was dressed in boy's clothes. It was the disguise she had used for her secret assignations with Casanova. I glimpsed her as she weaved across the Rialto bridge, with her hat pulled low to meet the mask that hid her eyes. She had not covered all her hair. I followed her through the city's rambling streets until she ducked down a narrow alleyway.

She stopped at the door of the house with the monkey's-head door-knocker. I caught up with her and we stood side by side. She smiled at me and nodded, as though we were old friends on a mutual mission. When I looked down at myself, I discovered that I was dressed as she was, in a boy's trousers and a shirt. Presently, the owner of the house opened the door. But it was not Casanova. It was Marco. And when I turned to express my surprise to Luciana, she was already gone.

Marco took my hand and quickly pulled me inside, as though there might be someone watching. I knew instinctively that like Luciana, I was not supposed to be there. I followed him up the stairs to the bedroom with the extravagantly carved four-poster I had come to know so well.

We did not speak. We started kissing right away. Like me, Marco was wearing a voluminous white shirt. My hands wandered inside that shirt, over his well-muscled chest and the soft hair that covered his perfectly designed pectorals. He was already untying my belt. The leather slipped easily from the well-worn brass buckle. He insinuated his hand inside the loose waistband of my trousers and I was momentarily embarrassed to discover that I wasn't wearing anything beneath. The feel of his fingers on my clit soon made me forget everything but how much I wanted him.

I stroked him into hardness. He groaned with pleasure at my attention and I gasped a little gasp of delight as he pushed one finger inside me to find me hot and wet. Locked together, we stumbled towards the bed. My boy's shirt and trousers were left on the back of the chair. It was cold outside, but I didn't feel the chill on my bare white skin. Marco towered over me with his penis in his hand. I was thrilled by the animality of his lust for me. I opened myself wide.

Our lovemaking was frantic and frenzied, as illicit sex is wont to be. The thought that someone might discover us was a fear and a thrill. We had to be fast. But eventually, we reached a point where we couldn't have stopped if we wanted to. I dug my fingers deep into Marco's buttocks as he jerked his body against mine. He put his full weight behind each thrust now, burying his face in my neck.

My orgasm ripped through my body, taking me by surprise with its force. I wrapped my legs and arms round him as though I would never let him go. He gripped me tightly in return. He moaned into my shoulder as he came.

Afterwards, I dressed quickly and headed for the door. I knew I had to be somewhere before the bells of the campanile struck midnight. Marco walked me back downstairs. Before I left, he grasped me to him and kissed me so hard I would still be able to feel his lips on mine when I was far from the little house, crossing the Rialto bridge, unrecognised in my cape and mask.

21

Venice, last October

Bea did not often feel unsafe in Venice. She had been living in the city for five years now and knew how to stay out of trouble. So she was surprised to feel a prickle of fear as she turned off the Campo Santa Margherita into the street where she lived. It was an unusually chilly night and there weren't many people around, but someone was definitely following her. She could feel it as keenly as a rabbit understands when the eye of a fox is upon it. Bea quickened her step. She was not far from her door. The important thing was not to be caught as she was letting herself into her home.

But the person behind her soon matched his speed to hers. With her door in sight, Bea took the decision to keep on walking right past. In her house, she would be alone and vulnerable. If she could get to the bar on the corner, she would be safe. She would wait until the danger had passed and get the owner to walk her home. But suddenly, the bar seemed so far away. The faster she walked, the faster her pursuer walked behind her. His footsteps were growing louder. He was definitely catching up. Bea was desperate. There was an alleyway to the left but if she ducked down that, she might only be putting herself in more danger. It was dark. It was a dead end. To her right was the canal, black as oil in the darkness. Should she jump straight in so that her assailant had to swim for her? She realised she had no idea how deep the water was or what lay beneath it. The canals of Venice were hardly the Cipriani swimming pool. Bea decided it was time to run.

'Wait! Wait!'

Bea took no notice.

'Wait! Please wait!'

Bea heard an unearthly groan from behind her.

That wasn't part of the usual nightmare script. Unable to ignore the sound of such human agony, Bea dared to pause and look. Her pursuer had collapsed in the circle of light beneath a street-lamp. The fierce rapist of her imagination was an old man. He was doubled over. He was breathing heavily. He didn't look as though he would be any trouble now, but what if this was a trick? She remained ready to run at any moment.

'Wait. Please. I need your help, Signorina. Please.'

Bea took one step towards him.

'Thank you,' said the old man. 'Thank you. You don't know how important this is. Take this, please. Take this.'

He handed Bea an envelope.

22

Saturday 8th October 1932

Dear Diary,

I can barely walk! Every minute Otto and I have to ourselves, we spend in my tiny narrow bed. Otto may have been an absolute beginner when he met me, but he's a very fast learner. He's so good, in fact, that there are moments when I wonder whether he didn't lie to me about having been a virgin that night three weeks ago.

Otto is magnificent. He is what I imagine those lady novelists mean when they refer to a 'generous lover'. He is always thinking of my pleasure. Bettina once told me that men like to put their penises in a girl's mouth – indeed that is exactly what Matthew had that girl do in the barn – but I had no idea that it ever happened the other way round! When Otto first tried to put his head between my legs, I was so shocked I tried to put a stop to it. Otto held me still and forced me to acquiesce. I'm glad he did. You can't imagine how strong is the sensation of his tongue upon my clitoris. I have to bite my knuckle most of the time. But it is wonderful. The first time he did it, when I started to orgasm, I thought I would never stop. I thought I might even die. And Otto was so pleased with himself for having made me wriggle and squeal.

Nothing is too disgraceful for him. Sometimes, when we get back from the club and I tell him that I'd like to have a wash, he actually stops me. He says he doesn't have the time to wait for me to bathe and he'd rather have me slightly grubby. He says he wants the taste of me – of my skin and my juices – and not the taste of the last bar of Pears soap I have left over from England.

I love the taste of him too. I never would have imagined it, but to take his manhood in my mouth really is the most erotic sensation. The skin on his penis is soft, like warm velvet. I have even swallowed his semen. He tastes like the sea. Marlene told me that all men really want is a woman who makes them feel fully accepted with all their flaws and there is no better way to show acceptance than by opening wide. Otto certainly seems very happy when I do.

I was a little worried that Otto might think me wanton, but he assures me he trusts me absolutely when I tell him that almost everything we've done together is a new experience for me too.

The other night, I persuaded him to let me be the one to go on top. It was a position I'd seen on the back of a playing card pinned to Isadora's dressing-room mirror, which I'd studied from all angles while she was on stage and I was supposed to be doing my make-up.

I had to make a guess as to exactly how we would fit together.

Fortunately, Otto was very patient. He was also extremely hard. It helps, I have found, for the man to be as hard as marble if you're going to try anything other than the traditional way. It also helps for the girl to be very excited too. Luckily, Otto only has to look at me and narrow his eyes with intention and I am as wet as a mermaid in a storm. I quite literally ache for him. It is all I can do not to faint with desire.

Anyway, I have decided that I do like being on top, though it's worse than an hour of hard exercise. My poor thighs were aching for hours. Otto's face made it worth the agony. I love making love with him. I love walking down the street beside him afterwards, acting innocent, knowing what we've been doing all night would even make the prostitutes on the Ku'damm blush.

To keep me from falling pregnant, he pulls out at the very last minute. I must admit I have a secret desire to hold him in place while he comes in me. It is most peculiar. It is as though something deep inside me – something animal – takes over at those moments, and I want to entwine my soul with Otto's in the most ancient and wonderful of ways. To hell with what the neighbours back in Surrey would think. One day I want to see myself fat with Otto's baby. There, I've said it. I love him that much. In my mind he is already my husband.

Sunday 16th October 1932

I am so excited I can barely hold my pen! Today has been the best day of my life. Oh, I never imagined I could be so very, very happy! I am just about ready to burst. Otto and I always spend Sundays together. Usually we have lunch with his mother and sister before we go for a walk in the Volkspark. Today, Otto insisted we take the tram all the way to the Grunewald of all places and have lunch in a little restaurant there. I have to admit, I was a tiny bit annoyed with him. I love his mother's cooking and the Grunewald is such a long way away. But Otto said it was important. He said he wanted to take me to a spot much admired by his maternal grandparents.

Well, when a man says something like that, you really don't want to argue with him.

We arrived at the Grunewald and hiked for what seemed like hours before we came to a lake. It was cold but that made the lake rather beautiful. The grasses around the edge were dusted with frost. A mist rolled over the water. It was like a picture from a book of fairy tales. We walked all the way round it to find the perfect spot. Eventually, Otto took off his coat and spread it over a fallen tree trunk so that I could sit upon it without ruining my skirt.

'Otto,' I said. 'It's really rather chilly to want to sit here for long.'

He put his finger to my lips and bade me be quiet for just a moment.

'I want to give you something,' said Otto.

He was nervous, I could tell. I had seen that nervousness once before when the boy who lived in the rectory proposed to me when I was just fourteen. This time, however, I knew I would not laugh if Otto came out with the four words I was hoping for. I was sitting on my hands to keep them warm. I got my left hand out, just in case, and subtly slipped off my glove. I wanted to be ready.

Otto reached into his pocket.

'I don't have the money to buy you a diamond ring,' said Otto. 'But I spoke to my mother and she said that you should have this. My sister has my grandmother's wedding ring and her necklaces. My brother has our grandfather's watch. This pearl was always going to be for my future wife.'

'Future wife? Are you proposing to me?' I asked him.

Otto licked his lips and nodded.

'I think I am.'

'Then please ask me properly,' I told him.

'Yes. Yes, of course.' Otto immediately dropped to one knee.

'Kitty Hazleton, will you be my wife?'

First off, I squealed but of course I said 'yes'. I said 'yes' again and again. I shouted it to the treetops, so loudly that I scared up some birds from the branches. I jumped up from my seat on the log and threw my arms round Otto's neck. He lifted me off my feet and whirled me round and round. It was the most perfect moment of my life.

We kissed for a long time, but eventually we had to come back to the real world. We had to go back to the Prenzlauer Berg. There were people to tell. Of course, Otto's mother and sister already knew that he was planning to propose because he had taken the pearl, but they would doubtless be waiting on tenterhooks to hear my answer.

We held hands all the way home.

'This pearl belonged to my grandmother,' Otto explained to me as we sat on the train. 'She was considered to be a great beauty and she caught the eye of a

French artist who came to Berlin in the 1880s. Grandma posed for the artist and he gave her this in lieu of payment. I suppose he thought she would sell it. She never did. She gave it to my mother. And now I have given it to you.'

'It's exquisite,' I said.

I didn't mind that it wasn't the diamond ring I had hoped for. I knew that it meant the same thing.

'I know that my grandmother would have been very pleased to know her pearl found such a good home.'

We're going to get it set into a beautiful necklace. I've decided it's so much nicer than a plain solitaire. Bettina will be absolutely green.

Kitty Schmidt. Kitty Schmidt. Kitty Schmidt. Frau Katherine Schmidt.

That is going to be my new name. I can't wait!

Monday 17th October 1932

Dear Mummy and the dogs (and Papa too, if he can bear to read a single word I've written),

I am writing to tell you the most wonderful news. I am engaged to be married! I can hardly believe it. Can you? Of course you can't.

I know it is traditional for a man to ask the girl's father's permission first, but how could my lovely new fiancé have done that when you haven't answered a single one of my letters in the past five months? Anyway, I hope you will be pleased for me. I believe I have found you a most wonderful son-in-law even if you never get to meet him. His name is Otto Schmidt and he is twenty-three years old. He comes from an excellent family here in Berlin. He is studying to be a lawyer, but I met him in our place of work, which is a nightclub. There, the cat is out of the bag. A nightclub. There never was a Hildebrand or an office job. I have been living in a fleapit hotel and working as a hostess in a transvestite bar. I hope you were both sitting down when you read that.

But all that is to change. Otto and I will marry as soon as we have completed the paperwork. On that subject, Mummy, I shall need you to send my birth certificate as soon as you possibly can. I can't get married without it. After that, I will move in with him and his family in the Prenzlauer Berg. Mummy, you would love Otto's mother. She is a very kind lady and she makes the most tremendous strudel. His father, unfortunately, is dead, but I understand he was a great man, beloved by all who knew him. Otto has a sister, called Helga, who wants to be a doctor, and a brother, called Gerd, who is a sort of soldier with the Sturmabteilung. You might have heard of them. They all support Adolf Hitler. Helga is the sister I wish I'd had. A far better influence than Bettina. Gerd is a nice chap, too. He saved another boy from drowning when he was only twelve.

I am so happy to be joining Otto's family. Most of all, I am so happy to become Otto's wife. Mummy, I'm sure you never would have predicted that I would end up with a singing lawyer and a German one at that, but I know he is the right match for me. I am over the moon. I know you will be too.

With lots of love from your only daughter and your soon to be son-in-law,

Kitty and Otto

xxx (for the dogs)

Monday 17th October 1932

Dear Diary,

So, I have sent my letter to the Aged Ps. I hope they will be even half as pleased as Otto's mother, who clutched me to her bosom as soon as she knew I'd said 'yes'. She told me that the news that I had agreed to marry Otto made her almost as happy as the day he was born. She said she could not imagine a better match for her dear son and that I should consider myself to be her daughter from that moment forward.

Helga also smothered me with kisses and told me I was the sister she'd never had. What fun we would have together! How lovely to think that one day, when we were both eighty years old, we would be sitting together on a porch, reminiscing about this day. Our children would grow up together. What fun times lay ahead.

Otto's mother told him to put on the gramophone and open a bottle of sekt and supper was a jolly affair. At least, it was very jolly until Gerd came home. He was in that horrible uniform again. He had spent the evening putting a troop of small boys from the Hitler Jugend through their paces in a local community hall. Apparently, the SA is getting very popular with boys under the age of ten. Anyway, he was as serious as usual. Otto made some joke about playing toy soldiers and Gerd did not even crack a smile. Rather, he told Otto that the future of the Reich was no laughing matter. The young boys who had been practising endless drills that evening might one day be called upon to defend good German lives.

'Kitty is becoming a German,' Helga chipped in then.
'What?'

Gerd's eyes narrowed when he looked at me.

'I asked Kitty to marry me and she has agreed to become my wife,' said Otto.

'Isn't it the happiest news you've ever heard?' Helga clapped her hands together.

'Indeed,' said Gerd, in such a way that we were left under no illusion that he was anywhere near as excited as the rest of us. Still, he had the grace to lift a glass of sekt to his lips in a passable impression of somebody wishing us well. And Helga and Otto's mother didn't let silence reign for long. The gramophone went back on. Though only for a little while because Gerd informed us all that he needed to go to sleep as soon as possible. He had important SA business to undertake in the morning.

Gerd doesn't like me. That much is pretty sure. I think he despises me as much as Otto loves me. How could two men born to the same parents have grown up to be quite so different? Otto is so gentle and open-minded. He is at home in any company. Gerd is stiff in his bearing and just as rigid in his opinions. If he were not going to be my brother-in-law, I don't think I would seek him out as a friend.

Anyway, now that we are engaged, Otto is less worried about being seen accompanying me into the hotel after dark. We told Enno our good news – apart from Otto's family, he was the first to know – and he seemed very pleased for us. He offered us half the wurst he had been eating as an engagement present. I declined.

'Ha!' Enno laughed. 'I suppose you've got your own sausage now.'

Otto gave him a very stern look.

We went upstairs to my little room. How I used to hate it with its peeling green wallpaper and heavy dark wood furniture that put me in mind of my grandmother's house. Now I am fond of it. Otto has changed my whole world.

You know, I do believe that being engaged has made our lovemaking even better. There is not the faintest shadow of doubt in my mind when I climb into bed with Otto. I know that he loves me more than anyone and will never leave me for another girl. And I will never look at another man. We are promised to each other for ever and it is the most wonderful feeling on earth.

I am never happier than when he is inside me. When we are face to face and I feel him move so carefully as he tries to make me come. I love it when we press our lips together as he fucks me. I wrap my arms and legs round him. We could not be closer if he opened his mouth and swallowed me whole. Even when we are both entirely spent, I am loath to let him go.

I am crazy about him and I intend to remain so for the rest of my life.

Tuesday 1st November 1932

Today I saw that old man from the café. The one who wanted to be my slave. He was standing outside the cinema, with his hands in his pockets. I called out 'hello' and wished him a lovely day. 'I hope you've found your perfect goddess,' I told him. After all, he helped me find my Otto.

The old man looked rather confused and shuffled away without returning my cheerful greeting. Perhaps he didn't recognise me. I didn't have my boots on. Perhaps he was simply embarrassed.

Sex, sex, sex. How it moves us. Now that I have Otto, I understand that old man and the people who come to the club so much better.

Sex drives people to such desperate measures. Otto says the reason there are so many English visitors to the club is because we are all horribly repressed back home. I told him he could count me out. But he has a point. Here, in the clubs, no one bats an eyelid if a woman dresses as a man and kisses another woman. Or a man decides he wants to be kissed by a great big brute with a beard.

I hope that one day the whole world will be as free as Berlin.

23

Berlin, last October

Kitty was right. How uncomplicated our lives would be without sex or the promise of it.

In late October, Nick Marsden, my old friend and colleague from Venice, came to Berlin for a conference. We hadn't seen each other since that crazy night back in the summer when we had both got very drunk indeed and he had finally made a move on me, which, for a while, I reciprocated.

I was pleased and relieved when I got Nick's email. Ever since that evening in Venice, silence had yawned between us. I'd heard from Bea, our mutual friend, that Nick was OK with what happened and that I shouldn't be angry with myself about it, but I was very glad when, at last, I heard from him. His email was as jolly and friendly as ever.

'Thomson,' he wrote. 'Or should I say "Dottore"! I'm coming your way. I'll be in Berlin from Friday morning until Sunday night. Giving a talk at eleven o'clock on Saturday morning, but otherwise pretty flexible. Let's meet.'

I already knew he was going to be talking on the Saturday morning, of course. I'd had the conference time-table for weeks and was planning to attend several events. I hadn't been planning to attend Nick's event because I didn't want the first time we saw each other to be with me looking at him from the audience, but now that he'd broken the ice of course I would be there. I found I was looking forward to it.

But there was one other person I knew who might be attending the conference. Steven, my ex-boyfriend, had always taken every chance he could to travel on the history department's budget and this conference was right up his street. I had heard nothing from him, however, and I wasn't about to contact him. In fact, I hadn't heard anything from him since that night in Paris – my birthday – when I freaked out as he started to make love to me as though I were an object. The lack of connection between us that night had disturbed me greatly. It confirmed that something between us had died when we broke up. There was no getting back together.

For that reason, when I walked into the lecture theatre where Nick would be delivering his lecture I was doubly nervous. I still wondered if it would be a little strange to see Nick after what had happened last time we were together; then there was the danger that Steven would be at the lecture too. And what would I say to him?

The last year had been a catalogue of romantic disasters and my split with Steven had precipitated the whole thing. His rejection had made me vulnerable in Venice and later, when I was feeling vulnerable again in Paris, he had reappeared to add to my confusion. Since I had finally burned my bridges with Marco, I was trying to put *all* the shadows behind me. But while it was unlikely that Marco would ever appear to test my resolve, Steven was quite another prospect.

Of course, he was there. I didn't notice him at first as I walked into the theatre and nodded at a couple of my new German colleagues. Nick was already on the stage, talking to the professor who had coordinated the whole event and working out how to use the slide projector. I gave him a shy wave, which he reciprocated by giving me a big smile and mouthing that he would see me as soon as the lecture was over.

I glanced around the room furtively, looking for Steven. When I didn't see him, I relaxed. I chose a seat three rows from the front and draped my coat over the back of it before popping out of the theatre for a moment to visit the ladies' room. When I returned to the place I had earmarked, I found Steven sitting in the seat right next to it.

'Well, fancy seeing you here,' he said.

He said it as though we were just old friends. There was no hint in his demeanour of the anxiety I had been feeling when I thought about the possibility we would meet again.

'I put my coat here earlier,' I said, wanting him to be quite clear that I had not seen him across the room and decided to make a beeline for him. Had I not left my phone and my wallet in my coat pockets, I might have abandoned it altogether in order not to have to interact with him at all.

'I must have subconsciously known it was yours,' said Steven. 'Pheromones.'

On stage, Nick was sitting down beside the lectern, waiting for the room to settle so that Professor Klein could introduce him. He looked in my direction, of course. When he saw Steven, his expression was visibly pained.

'This is your friend, isn't it?' Steven nodded towards the stage. 'The guy from Venice?'

'Yes,' I said.

'I wasn't going to come to this lecture but I thought I'd better pretend to be serious about my subject. I'll have to give some kind of report.'

'I don't think you'll be disappointed.'

'I've heard he's hot stuff. In the lecture theatre, at least.'

I blushed. I don't know why. As far as I knew, there was no

way that Steven could know Nick and I had ever crossed the line from being colleagues. He had to be making a snide reference to someone else. We moved in a small world. Undoubtedly, Nick and Steven had met some of the same students during their tenures at Oxford and London respectively. I could easily imagine Steven seducing a female graduate who had once rebuffed Nick's charms. Steven's comment made me feel oddly protective of Nick.

But perhaps he was making a dig at me. Had he decided that our attempt to rekindle our relationship failed because of someone in Venice and, putting two and two together, decided that someone must be Nick? It was more plausible, I supposed, than the truth.

There were a great many questions I wished to ask Steven. Had Kat used the telephone number I gave her and called him before she left Paris? I thought perhaps she hadn't. I'd been following her progress in the gossip columns. She had, as I'd predicted, soon left Calum, the actor who had insisted she be auditioned for a part in the Augustine du Vert biopic. She was now dating a far bigger star and had been cast as the female lead in a big-budget action movie. No, I suspected Steven didn't ever hear from her at all. But I very much doubted that meant he was alone most nights.

The conference leader was back on stage. He announced that the event was about to start. Steven turned to look at Nick and I couldn't help sneaking a glance at his profile. His perfect nose. His lips. Those lips that had been everywhere, on every part of my body. How was it possible that so much intimacy had left us almost strangers?

We sat through Nick's lecture. I'd seen him talk before. Even on the very driest subjects, Nick could usually find an historical anecdote that would have the whole audience rolling in the aisles. But that day he was surprisingly lacklustre. He couldn't seem to hit his stride. He presented his slides as though he couldn't wait to get through them and get out of there. From time to time he glanced in my direction and I thought his expression was questioning. I wished I could tell him that whatever he was thinking was wrong. I hadn't invited Steven to join me. I would never have chosen to sit with him. Should I have scooped up my things and moved to the other side of the room?

'Got time for a coffee?' Steven asked afterwards.

'Actually, I promised I'd have lunch with Nick.'

'Great,' said Steven. 'I'll join you. Be interesting to have a chance to talk to the man away from his legions of adoring fans.'

'I don't know if that's a good idea.'

'Why don't we ask him?' said Steven. Nick had extricated himself from a small knot of keen students and was drawing near. Steven stuck his hand out.

'Steven Jones,' he introduced himself. 'Great talk. And I understand you're having lunch with my lovely friend here. I hope you won't mind if I join you?'

I longed for Nick to say, 'Actually, I do mind.' But of course he didn't say that. Instead he said, 'Great,' and plastered on a smile to match mine.

We went to Lutter and Wegner on the Gendarmenmarkt. It was a cheesy place – all wood panelling and candles in wine bottles – a skilful recreation of times long past. All the tourists went there, but the food was always great and Nick and Steven both agreed that they wanted to eat something properly 'German'. Something meaty and stodgy and perfect for the cold autumn weather. I ordered the *sauerbraten*. I'd become rather partial to it since Herr Schmidt introduced me to the stuff. Nick and Steven tussled to take charge of the wine list.

I had never before found myself in such a strange position, being fought over by two grown men. Oh, they thought they were being subtle about it, I'm sure, but they were constantly in competition with each other, firing barbs on every subject. And they were both so attentive to me. I need only take a sip from my glass and one of them would rush to refill it. At one point, they both grabbed for the wine bottle at the same time and almost upended it over me.

When Steven and I were together I had never thought of him as possessive, but now, with competition in the form of Nick, he was unlike I had ever seen him. Nick too, was different from the man I knew. It was as though they were two robins, puffing out their chests.

When the bill had been paid, with more tussling that ended with them splitting the tab and treating me, I told them I was going home.

'I'll walk you,' they both said at once.

'No need,' I said to both of them. 'I'm going into the office.'

It was an excuse. I didn't want to have to choose.

'I'll call you later,' Nick and Steven said simultaneously. Then, while they were glaring at each other, I made my exit.

I suppose it was nice to know that I was a desirable woman. Two men wanted me and were prepared to make fools of themselves to be with me. I should have felt uplifted by the thought, but the truth of the matter is that it never feels good to be wanted too badly by someone you don't want in return. Rather than being flattering, it becomes an embarrassment and an opportunity to cause accidental hurt. I wondered how many people ended up with someone they really loved, who loved them in return. How many people settled? Would I do exactly that in the end?

Having told Steven and Nick I was going to the office and set off in that direction, I doubled back on myself and went back to the Hufelandstrasse. Herr Schmidt was playing classical music as usual. This time, he was listening to the desperate yearning song of Marguerite in Berlioz's *The Damnation of Faust*. It gave me pause. I recognised the piece because I had read about it in Augustine du Vert's memoir and listened to it so that I might know what had moved her. *The Damnation of Faust* was the opera that had premiered on the night she realised she had lost her true love to another woman.

I wondered what Herr Schmidt was thinking about when he listened to Marguerite's lament. It was hard to imagine the old man transported by passion or lust. He was so self-contained and polite. But once upon a time he too must have been a young man full of young men's passions, just like Nick and Steven. Who had been the object of his most ardent desire? Had she reciprocated? Had they in fact spent many happy years together under this roof? Did he miss her? Or did the happy memories of their time together still keep him warm?

Of course, while I was in Herr Schmidt's apartment, I had looked for clues to his past. I was incurably nosy and though Clare was right, Schmidt was a common name, I couldn't help thinking of Kitty's diary and wondering if there was a connection. However he had already explained that the young woman in the picture on the mantel was his sister, who had moved to Hamburg and lived there until her death in 1999. The nephew he often spoke of was her son. He hadn't mentioned a brother.

Marguerite's aria reached its finale. I hovered on the bottom step until I heard her last note. Then I heard Herr Schmidt moving around in his room and decided I had better go upstairs before he caught me snooping.

24

Thursday December 22nd 1932

Dear Diary,

Something simply terrible has happened. It was lunchtime. I was at the usual place. Otto wasn't with me because he has lectures on a Thursday, so I was eating sauerbraten with only my book for company. All of a sudden, a shadow fell across the page I was reading and I was aware that someone was standing in front of my table, blocking the light and waiting for me to notice. I looked up. It was Gerd.

'The man in your hotel told me I would find you here,' he said.

I have grown used to Gerd's way of launching straight into conversation without bothering with the niceties of 'hello' or 'how are you?' I asked him how he was just the same.

'I am well,' he said. He didn't look it. He looked positively green.

'Sit down?' I suggested. 'Have you had any lunch?'

'I do not wish to eat,' he said. He pushed his fair hair back from his face with some agitation.

'Gerd, is there something the matter?' I asked him.

His face was so grave that suddenly I began to panic.

'Has something happened to Otto? Or to Helga? Your mother?'

He shook his head.

'Has something happened to you?'

'In a manner of speaking,' he said. He swallowed hard. 'Kitty, I can keep this to myself no longer.'

He reached across the table and took both of my hands. I had an awful feeling I knew what was coming. Alas, I was right.

'Kitty, from the very first moment I saw you, I knew that life would never be the same again. I tried not to let it happen but I have failed to control my mind as I ought. Every day the sensations grow ever stronger. I cannot eat. I cannot sleep. I cannot do anything but think of you.'

'Oh dear,' I said.

'I am in love with you. I cannot help myself. So you must help me instead. You must tell me that you love me too. Without you, I cannot survive.'

I pulled my hands away. 'Gerd,' I said firmly. 'I think you should stop right there. All this will seem very silly tomorrow.'

He looked crestfallen. I hoped I had nipped any real embarrassment in the bud. I tried to go back to eating my sauerbraten. I even offered him a taste of it, but moments later he returned to his theme.

'This is not a silly matter! You must not marry my brother,' he said as he thumped the table. 'I cannot bear to see you with him when you should be mine. He is not the man for you, dear Kitty. You are flighty and wayward and you need a guiding hand. I recognised that the instant we first locked eyes. I saw your soul pleading for the kind of direction only I can give. Otto is not strong enough to tame you.'

This was much more like the Gerd I knew. He couldn't even declare his love to his brother's fiancée without trying to assert his superiority.

'Gerd, please.' I held my hand up to indicate he should stop.

'Otto is a degenerate. He will only drag you down.'

I shook my head. I folded my napkin and put it on the table to indicate that I had finished my lunch and was ready to leave.

'Gerd,' I said. 'I think this conversation is a mistake. I am in love with Otto and I intend to be in love with him for the rest of my life. I have promised to marry him and I will do so at the earliest possible opportunity. After that, you and I will have to see each other every day because I will be living in your family home. You will be my brother-in-law. I don't want there to be any awkwardness, so I am prepared to pretend that today's little debacle didn't happen. If you would please do the same, I would be most grateful.'

When I finally dared look him in the eye, there was no hint in Gerd's face whatsoever that he had just been dealt a mortal blow by the woman he loved. It was the strangest thing. I knew he wouldn't be happy with what I had said, but I was surprised to see that there was no trace of tender disappointment at all. Rather, his eyes blazed with what can only be described as fury. I could tell he could not believe I would turn him down. His pride, not his heart, was bearing the insult.

'I'm sorry, Gerd,' I said. 'Now, if you'll excuse me, I must go. There are some letters I wish to write before I go to the club this evening.'

'The club,' he sneered. 'Yes. That is the best place for a woman like you. I must have been mad to ever think you would be intelligent enough to be my wife. You're a woman of loose morals. No doubt you have loose knickers too. I can't see what else my brother would see in you.'

'Well,' I said. 'If that's how constant your love for me is, then it's probably for the best that I didn't decide to run away with you after all.'

'Don't mock me,' he said. 'Don't ever mock me. You don't know what I can do.'

He recovered himself enough to heil that bloody Hitler man before he walked out.

I don't know what to do. I can't tell Otto. He'll go berserk. It's not as though we can make sure we never see the silly man again. I can only hope that Gerd is just as keen to forget the whole incident as I am. But his transformation from the nervous suitor to the arrogant spurned officer of the Sturmabteilung was so dramatic and so awful that he has left me as badly shaken as if he had pointed a gun at my head.

Otto is going to be here in ten minutes. I must compose myself. I'll feel safe again in his arms.

26th December 1932

What a terrible Christmas. And I had been so looking forward to it. I spent it with Otto's family, of course. Gerd would barely speak to me and he found any excuse to argue with Otto. Their exchanges became so heated that Frau Schmidt actually cried.

Otto enraged Gerd by telling him that the Party was full of weak-minded pansies who should put on a skirt and come to the Boom Boom if what they like is dressing up. I have learned that the worst possible insult you can hurl in a National Socialist's direction is to suggest that he and his cohort are not properly 'manly'. Thus insulted by Otto, Gerd tried to regain his dignity with his fists. That was when Frau Schmidt burst into tears and went to her bedroom. Helga says she does not know why Otto and Gerd have become so antagonistic of late.

I hope that this is not about me. I can't get what Gerd said out of my head at the moment.

'Don't mock me. Don't ever mock me. You don't know what I can do.'

1st January 1933

Dear Diary,

Happy New Year! How quickly a year has flown by and how much has changed in the meantime. It seems almost impossible that this time last year I was sobbing in my bedroom, awaiting news of my terrible fate after being caught kissing Matthew Spencer. If you had told me then that in twelve months' time I would be engaged to be married to the most wonderful man on earth . . .

He is sleeping beside me as I write this. What a raucous night we had. New Year's Eve – Silvester as they call it here – is celebrated even more enthusiastically than it is back in England. The club was open, of course, and we all had to work. Marlene and I created a smashing new routine for the occasion. She played the old year, dressed as a crone in a long black cape, and I played the New Year in my birthday suit and a nappy! Well, I wasn't really naked but Young Hans assured me that from the back of the club, you couldn't tell I was wearing anything much at all, which was exactly the effect we were after. The crowd was absolutely wild for me.

When the club closed, we shared a bottle of champagne with Schluter and toasted a prosperous year.

Back at the Hotel Frankfort, Otto and I welcomed 1933 in our own special way. Schluter let us bring home a half-finished bottle of wine – the good stuff. We had a little picnic in bed. And then we made love. It was perfect. We are so in tune with one another's bodies now that he only has to look at me and I dissolve in a puddle of ecstasy.

We lay head to tail, so that I could pleasure him while he pleasured me. As I took him into my mouth and gently sucked him, he carefully parted my lips to find my clitoris – my pearl as he calls it. It was hard to concentrate on showing Otto my love when every flicker of his tongue drove me just a little wilder. He is such an expert. I came long before him. The taste of him as he came in my mouth was as good as any champagne. And now he is sleeping. It is strange how after we make love, he is exhausted while I am exhilarated. He has filled me with energy and now I can't sleep at all. I will just have to lie here and make plans for 1933. I believe it will be our best year yet.

We are invited to his mother's house for lunch today. I am relieved that Gerd won't be among us. He is at a training camp in Bavaria, learning how to defend the Nazi honour in the snow. I rather hope he stays there.

25

Berlin, last October

I was making notes on Kitty's diary when my mobile beeped. Steven had sent me a text message, asking whether I was really going to work all weekend. Didn't I want to show him Berlin's nightlife?

I hesitated, thinking back to Paris. I remembered the tension that had crackled between us as we sat on red velvet chairs in the Opera Garnier and later across a scrubbed wooden table in that Italian restaurant. Just thinking about it made my skin prickle. Was it ever going to be safe for me to be around Steven? Would I ever be able to be in his presence without feeling that subconscious urge to have him pull my body against his and kiss me passionately?

I could not risk it. I made my excuses and agreed instead to meet Steven for lunch the following day. Sunday lunch and daylight. I would be safe. I told him to meet me at the Ku'damm, outside the branch of H & M that had once been Heaven and Hell.

'Fate keeps pushing us back together,' he said.

'Do you think it's fate? I rather think it's just that we move in very small circles.'

'You used to be such a romantic. The old Sarah believed in fate.'

'The new Sarah has read her Dawkins.'

Steven laughed.

'I couldn't believe it when Kat phoned me in Paris, telling me you guys had just been to a swingers' club.'

I shook my head. 'I didn't know it was that kind of club.'

'We met up and she told me that you'd dumped me for some guy in Venice. Seems pretty clear to me it didn't work out.'

'You're talking about Nick?'

'Yes.'

'It wasn't him.'

'Oh, really. Then who was it?'

'No one you know.'

'But obviously someone very special.'

I nodded. Steven's probing was starting to become frustrating to me and not because he was being unnecessarily nosy. It was because I knew that if I told him about Marco, it would sound ridiculous. Besides, it was over. I had heard nothing from Marco since my last furious email. I changed the subject.

'Do you ever hear from Kat these days?'

'Not often,' Steven admitted. 'She's quite the star. She doesn't spend much time in London any more. She's always in Hollywood. In fact, she's rumoured to be on the shortlist for Tom Cruise's next leading lady – and I don't mean in a film. All she has to do is convert to Scientology.'

We both laughed.

'I'm sure she'd pull it off. Does it ever make you sad?' I asked. 'That's she's moved away?'

'Not half so sad as it makes me not to see you.'

His fingers sneaked across the table in search of mine. When they were close, I thought I could almost see a spark jump across the gap. Our electricity, our chemistry was still strong. Before his fingers could actually touch mine, I lifted my hand to ask for the bill. Safe again for just a moment.

★   ★   ★

After lunch, Steven asked if we could go to the Helmut Newton collection. I couldn't refuse. I'd told him I was free until four. As we walked there, we linked arms. He bought my ticket, despite my protestations.

'I'll expense you,' he said.

'Ever the romantic,' I teased him.

The exhibition was challenging from the start. At the top of the stairs were four of Newton's gigantic nudes.

'He may have created these images that we've come to think of as fetishistic, but I think Newton really liked his women.' I was quoting Anna Fischer. Straight from her thesis.

They were indeed strong images. While Newton's women were naked, they were by no means vulnerable. I couldn't help but compare their athletic beauty with the modern aesthetic, which demands that women are either the kind of thin that can only be achieved with an eating disorder or cartoonishly pneumatic. Neither were they waxed into a pastiche of prepubescence. It was hard to imagine any of them giving an interview to a women's magazine in which they coyly shared with the readers their self-hatred.

'When did it start to change?' I wondered aloud.

I thought of Kat, with her extraordinary body confidence. She would have made a good model for Newton. She was proud of the way she was. She knew the power of her beauty and she used it.

'You would have made a good Newton girl,' said Steven. 'You've got the physical strength. You've also got that indefinable thing inside you. And a timelessness. Look at this. Don't you think this photograph is just like Manet's Olympia? She may be naked but she's got all the power.'

I wasn't reminded of Olympia. I had another scene in mind. The sumptuous surroundings that were typical of a

178

Newton set-up. Velvets and silks. Antiques. Jewels. The trappings of wealth. The defiant stare of the model.

That was how I had felt when I'd looked into the mirror at the palazzo. Not the first time perhaps, but definitely the second, when I knew for sure that I was being watched. My image, reflected back at me, was like a Newton photograph. Had I held all the power in that moment? Though I was looking at Newton's black and white Amazons, Marco was back in my head.

'I have missed you,' said Steven suddenly. 'It doesn't seem to matter how long we're apart. I see you and boom – all the old feelings are back.'

I continued to look at the photograph. I couldn't trust myself to look at him. He seemed to follow my gaze to my fingers and soon our hands were entwined.

'What happened in Paris? I thought that we were getting back together and all of a sudden you're freaking out about how I really see you. I wonder if what actually bothers you is that I am the one person who does genuinely see you. I can see beyond the strait-laced image to what's really going on beneath.'

I shook my head. 'I don't think there's anything going on beneath,' I insisted.

'But there is. I saw it in Paris when we were watching the dancers at the Crazy Horse and I saw it in London when we were at L'Infer. There is a side of you that is wild. So wild that you're afraid of what might happen if you indulged it. I think you like to be watched and I think you like to watch other people.'

Steven was so close to me now that I could feel his warm breath on the side of my face. He talked quietly, forcing me to lean closer still to hear what he wanted to say, until his lips were actually brushing my face with each word.

He took my chin in his hand and turned my face towards his so that our lips were millimetres apart.

It would be so easy to give in. If he was right and I did want to be led astray, then Steven would certainly help me in that regard. He would not judge me for indulging my desires. It would not be safe to let Steven choose my path for me. If I was ever going to explore those parts of myself properly, it would have to be with someone I could truly trust.

'I don't feel safe with you,' I said.

'I understand.'

But he still would not let me go. He held my face in his hands, daring me to keep resisting him. He held me until my phone started ringing. It rang and it rang and it rang. A museum security guard started towards us, as though we hadn't noticed.

'You'd better get it,' said Steven.

It was too late. The caller had been sent to voicemail. But whoever it was had broken the spell. I was grateful to them for that. Saved by the bell.

'I should go outside,' I said. 'To listen to the message.'

'I should get going too,' said Steven, with a shrug of disappointment. 'I'm supposed to see one of my colleagues give a talk at four. I'll see you around.'

'It seems unavoidable.' I smiled.

Steven left me with the most tender kiss he had ever placed on my lips. I closed my eyes so that I didn't have to watch him go. Some things were never meant to last, no matter how much you tried.

Outside, I listened to my voicemail. The caller was Nick. He said he needed to see me before he went back to Venice. It was important. Very important. Bea would skin him alive if I didn't catch up with him. He sounded so flustered, I had to return his call straight away.

26

Venice, last October

The Palazzo Donato was as silent as a grave. It was hard to believe that the house had once been the scene of wild parties that scandalised the whole of Venice. Silvio remembered how he had arrived at the house as a fourteen-year-old. Back then, Marco's grandfather, the man after whom Marco was named, was still alive. The first Marco Donato had made his fortune and bought back the palazzo that had been built by one of his ancestors. Since the eighteenth century, the Donato family had seen many ups and downs but when Silvio arrived, they were on a very sharp upward trajectory. They needed staff. The house buzzed with activity by day and by night.

Marco's grandfather soon ditched Marco's grandmother for a younger model. He had chosen a film star. The entire male staff of the house had hidden in the garden gallery to watch her sunbathing in the nude. While she was the mistress of the house, there were parties every evening. So many famous faces arrived at the watergate: politicians, princes, dazzling silver-screen beauties. So much alcohol was drunk. So much flesh was bared. Almost every gathering ended in an orgy. Rumours spread throughout the city that the Palazzo Donato was the most exclusive bordello in the world. If any paparazzo had found his way into the courtyard garden, he could have lived off the proceeds of his pictures for the rest of his life.

Silvio, still just a teenager, quickly shed his naivety and learned the power of a reputation for discretion. Night after night, he received enormous tips just for keeping his mouth shut.

Now, the partygoers were gone. Ghosts.

Silvio hoped he had done the right thing.

Marco was sitting in his chair by the fire in the library. On his knees was Remi Sauvageon's sketchbook filled with his loving portraits of Augustine du Vert. Marco had read Sarah's research into Augustine's short life. He knew it hadn't ended well. Her death from tuberculosis had sounded so crushingly lonely. Marco could imagine nothing worse than such a solitary death and yet that was what awaited him if nothing should change. Marco tucked his own picture of Sarah on her first day at the library between the pages, imagining as he did so a pressed flower. A moment of life fast fading.

When he walked around the palazzo now, all he saw were ghosts. He remembered the parties, just as Silvio did. He especially remembered the Martedì Grasso party that had ended so badly. He heard Sarah's voice. But there were other voices too, from further back in his past. And the dream of the accident was back. Every night, he was back in the car. Every night, he had a chance to make things different. Every night, he chose not to act and the nightmare ended the same. The flames were all around him again. There was nothing he could do to escape them. He put his hands to his face but it was already too late. He felt as though he would burn for all eternity. For what he had done, that would hardly be too long.

27

Monday 27th February 1933

Dear Diary,

There has been such drama in Berlin tonight. While Otto and I were working at the club, unknown to us the Reichstag was burning down. The Reichstag! That's like the Houses of Parliament going up. We heard about it from Enno, who dropped into the club for a drink after his shift. Of course we had to go and see it for ourselves. It was the biggest conflagration I have ever seen. We could feel the heat from hundreds of yards away. The firemen had no hope of putting it out, though from where we were, we could see them doing their best. We could only stand and pray that no one was inside when the building went up. They would not have stood the slightest chance.

I found the whole thing quite exciting but Otto was very grave as he walked me back to the hotel. He says there is something fishy afoot. He says he does not understand how anyone was able to get into a government building and cause such a blaze without being interrupted. It would have taken more than a box of matches to set such a tremendous fire. I suggested to him that perhaps the Reichstag burned so well because it was full of papers. All those law books! Perfect for a bonfire.

'Exactly,' said Otto, rather darkly.

Tuesday 28th February 1933

Schluter says that the Reichstag fire is being blamed on communists, but he has other ideas. Just as Otto does. Apparently Gerd has been strutting around all day like a prize cockerel, making grave pronouncements about the dangers communism poses to the decent ordinary German.

This morning, an emergency meeting of Parliament was called and civil liberties were suspended. When I asked Otto what that meant, he said it means the end of the world as we know it. He says the change of law is not just about catching the people who set the Reichstag on fire – assuming it wasn't the Sturmabteilung in any case. Otto has no doubt that Hitler and his ilk will use the fire as an excuse to start cracking down on their enemies. He is as vehemently opposed to the funny little man as his brother Gerd is so passionately for him. When I asked Otto who Hitler's enemies are, he told me they are 'people like us'. He said there are things happening behind the scenes – laws being made – that the people of Germany will not fully understand until those laws are used against them.

Otto seems to be unusually upset about the whole thing. I tried to make him feel better as best I could. I asked him to sing for me, since singing usually brings him out of himself. When he said that he didn't feel like it, I sang for him instead. I sang 'The Song is Ended'. Our song. Otto clutched my hand. He asked me if I had heard anything from my parents. We need to get married as quickly as possible, he says, so that he can take care of me properly. I told him I had still heard nothing but it didn't matter.

'Tonight,' I said. 'Let me take care of you.'

I ran a bath for him in the shared bathroom on my hotel floor. I put a notice on the door to make sure that nobody burst in on us, though from the smell of the hotel's other residents, I doubt some of them even know there is a bathroom here.

While Otto sat in the bath, I soaped his back as though he were a small child. The feel of his smooth skin sliding beneath my fingers was as soothing to me as I hoped it felt to him. I traced the muscles of his chest with a sponge. I brought a flannel right up between his legs. It took a moment, but at last he began to stiffen as my ministrations crowded out his worries.

'Isn't that better?' I said.

Otto agreed. 'With you, I can forget the outside world.'

After a while, I took off my slip and climbed into the warm water with him. The bath was small, but it was just big enough for the two of us, if I sat on top of him. Otto rubbed the soap between his hands and applied the suds to my breasts, paying extra attention to my longing nipples.

'You would make a beautiful mermaid,' he said.

'Perhaps I will incorporate that into my next act,' I told him.

'I don't think I want anyone to see you wet except me. You're too enticing.' He reached up to kiss me.

I moved myself into position above him and sank down slowly upon his cock. Otto closed his eyes in utter bliss. Carefully, I slid up and down his manly length. I put my hands on his chest to steady myself and teased him with my undulations. Otto put his hands on my waist to help me move but I would not let him set the pace.

'You're driving me crazy,' he said, as I refused to speed up.

'I want this to last for ever,' I told him. 'Or at least until the water goes cold.'

Eventually, I was starting to be almost as frustrated as he was. I could feel my own ecstasy building within me. At first it was just a tingle in my most intimate place but soon it was an itch that must be scratched. I began to move more quickly, like a rider taking a horse from canter to gallop. I braced myself with my hands on the side of the bath. I moved faster and faster, taking my cue from Otto's face.

'Don't stop,' he said. 'Don't stop! Don't stop!'

1st March 1933

This morning Enno complained that someone caused a flood in the third-floor bathroom.

8th March 1933

Dear Diary,

Another terrible thing has happened. Marlene did not come to the club last night. We joked backstage that she had likely found herself a handsome man who was keeping her busy in the bedroom. The truth was much less pleasant.

After the club closed, Isadora decided he would drop in on Marlene at home. Just to check that she wasn't laid up with the flu, which has been going around. Both Schluter and Old Hans have been laid low. When Isadora knocked on the door at Marlene's place, there was no answer, but as he left the building, he looked up at Marlene's window and saw the curtains move, proving that his instinct was right. She was in.

'Hey!' Isadora called up at the window and threw a small stone against the glass for good measure. Marlene opened the curtains just a crack and gave Isadora notice, by subtle hand signals, that he should come up to the door again. Just as Isadora was about to knock a second time, Marlene opened the door and yanked the boy inside by his collar.

'It was a terrible sight,' Isadora told us this morning.

Marlene had spent the day in bed all right, but not because she'd met a man or been laid low by flu. On her way home from the club two nights ago, she was approached by a handsome young buck who asked her whether he hadn't just seen her on stage at the Boom Boom. Marlene was so taken by the fact that such a good-looking fellow would choose to talk to her that she confirmed she was indeed Marlene of Boom Boom fame. The young man asked if he could walk with her awhile. When he suggested that he and Marlene step into the park for 'some action', Marlene thought that her luck was in. That couldn't have been further from the truth.

As soon as Marlene and her beau were inside the park the mood changed. Her pretty young man was joined by his friends. All of them youthful and handsome. None of them wanting sex with a transvestite. They were out for a fight. They kicked Marlene to within an inch of her life. They broke her nose and one of her cheekbones. They blacked her beautiful eyes.

'And when they had finished,' said Marlene, 'they stood around me in a circle and clicked their heels.'

We all knew what that meant.

15th March 1933

After we heard about the beating, Schluter sent word to Marlene that she should stay away from the club for as long as she wanted to. He would make sure that her rent was still paid. She needed time to recover and she should take it. But Marlene responded that she would not be cowed by bullies. She was back at the club just this afternoon. When she had her make-up on, the black bruises around her eyes were all but invisible.

When Otto heard the story, he grew graver than I had ever seen him. 'This is happening more often. It used to be safe here. People used to be open-minded. Nobody cared what their neighbour wanted to do in his spare time so long as it didn't bother them. It's the Party that's behind this, mark my words. The election results have made them cocky.'

Marlene wouldn't hear it. Didn't want to.

'Otto, darling. Picking up the wrong fellow is a hazard of being one of my kind. You're wrong to imagine that this is a new trend. I should have been more careful. I should never have gone into the park. As if a young bloke like that really wanted to be with an old cow like me.'

'You're not an old cow,' I assured her. 'You're beautiful. Even with that black eye.'

Marlene squeezed my hand. She looked so sad and vulnerable. It's hard to imagine that I ever found her intimidating. She continued to explain that such attacks were part of life for a transvestite. There was nothing political in it. But I felt that she was repeating the story as much to convince herself as the rest of us.

Otto was very serious when he walked me home. He told me he was concerned about me living alone in the hotel.

'You mustn't worry,' I told Otto. 'I can handle myself.'

'I saw how well you can handle yourself the first time I met you, remember?'

'Oh, the boots. Well, I was trying to extricate myself politely. He was old enough to be my grandfather. If he'd carried on licking my feet for much longer, I would have kicked him in the head, have no fear.'

'It's not funny, my darling. We need to be more careful. Perhaps you shouldn't work at the club any more.'

'And do what instead? My German still isn't good enough for me to get an office job and you can't afford to keep me while you're still studying. Besides, I love being at the club. I would go crazy if I had to be a *hausfrau.*'

'My mother and sister would keep you company.'

I tried to seem grateful, of course, and told him I thought that would be lovely, but I wanted to be among my friends at the Boom Boom. Now more than ever, actually.

'Besides,' I said to Otto, 'how dangerous can the Party really be? For the most part, the people who trumpet their involvement with Adolf Hitler and his friends seem to be rather inadequate. They are the sort of people who like jobs with plenty of rules. They are unimaginative and angry in a very passive way. Most ordinary folk see the Nazis as ridiculous,' I said. 'No one wants Berlin to change.'

Otto told me I am too trusting. He says that the years of hardship have left a nasty streak of anger and envy behind and that Hitler is dangerous because he is promising an easy redistribution of wealth.

'He is pitting people against each other. He is making people think that the reason why they don't have what they want is because their neighbours have it instead. Specifically, if their neighbours are Jews.'

'I don't believe that people are really taking all that much notice of him.'

But Otto's right about one thing. You see those horrible armbands much more often now. Apparently the symbol painted on them is called a swastika. Even the way they look is menacing. They remind me of a bandage around a gunshot wound. And they certainly seem to have got their claws into Gerd.

28

Berlin, last October

Later on the Sunday afternoon of the conference weekend, I met Nick for coffee and cake before he headed to the airport and thence to Venice. I asked him if he had enjoyed Berlin.

'Would have been better if I'd spent more time with you,' he said. 'But I definitely couldn't live here. Too many ghosts.'

'But isn't that what you once said about Venice? Now there's a city full of ghosts.'

'Yeah, but they're happy ghosts. They're ghosts that went out on a high. This place is different. It's sad.'

'I like it,' I said.

'Good job,' Nick told me. 'Since you're staying here. Though you know there's a position going in our department back in Venice. You'd be a shoo-in. We'd love to have you back. Bea especially.'

'I've only just started here,' I said. 'I need to give Germany a chance.'

What I didn't say was that I also needed to put a great deal of space between Venice and me. It would be a long time before I could even look at a picture of the city without feeling a knife-twist of melancholy in my heart.

Nick didn't push it. The conversation moved on to the other attendees at the conference: which lectures had been worth seeing and which turned out to be a waste of time. He touched on the subject of Steven. He tried to make his enquiry sound casual but I knew that he was fishing.

'It was nice to see him,' I said. 'Not as hard as I imagined. Perhaps exes can be friends.'

Nick seemed to cheer up at that. All the same, when it was time for him to go, Nick hugged me but didn't try to kiss me. Instead, he presented his cheek for a kiss, like a reluctant nephew. I responded like a dutiful aunt.

He straightened up and I got ready to wave him off. He was walking towards the taxi rank when he suddenly stopped and doubled back.

'Oh,' he said. 'I can't believe I nearly forgot. I told you I had a reason to see you before I left. Apart from enjoying your company.'

He set his case down on the pavement and opened it up. He hunted around in a pocket in the lid.

'Bea sent this for you.'

He handed me a Jiffy bag that felt as though it contained a book.

'She said that I wasn't to look at it. Feels like a book though. Perhaps it's an annotated copy of *Fifty Shades of Grey*.'

'If I'm lucky,' I said.

Nick took the opportunity to kiss me this time.

I waited until he was gone before I opened up the envelope. I took it back into the café with me and ordered another pot of tea. It was grey outside and the drizzly weather made the café seem especially inviting. Plus, I didn't think that Bea's envelope would really contain anything risqué that I should only read in private.

Inside the padded envelope was another envelope. Bea had inserted a handwritten note in between. I pulled it out.

Dear Sarah,

I hope Nick remembers to give this to you! I'm dying to know what's inside it. Of course, you will trust I haven't peeked. Having said that, perhaps I should have done. I may well be sending Nick onto the plane with a letter bomb! But I don't think so. Though this envelope's contents may be explosive for you in some other sense.

It happened like this. I thought I was being stalked! I had the distinct sense that someone was following me when I left the university the other day. I was not wrong. He pounced as I left the Campo Santa Margherita. It was an elderly chap. He asked me if I was your friend. I told him I might be but why was he asking. He thrust this envelope into my hand and told me you left something behind last time you were at the Palazzo Donato. I was to get it to you. Urgently! But he said I shouldn't trust it to the ordinary post.

That's why I've sent it with Nick. I hope he doesn't forget. You know what a dreamer he can be. If he's standing there in front of you as you read this, at least give him a kiss for his troubles. And make sure you let me know what is inside it! Your friend was so serious when he entrusted me with getting this to you that I'm sure it must contain some hugely precious artefact. If I've inadvertently smuggled one of Italy's greatest treasures out of the country, I shall be most upset!

Lots of love and kisses,

Bea

xxx

Inside the inner envelope was a diary and yet another note. I put the diary, which was blue and A5 in size, to one side while I opened the pale cream envelope that had accompanied it. This note was written in Italian. It said:

Dear Signorina Thomson,

I know you like to make a study of diaries. Here is one that you should read at once. For your own sake and for Marco's.

Yours sincerely,
Silvio Fiorangelo

It was a moment before the name made any sense to me. When it did, I was astonished. Silvio had written to me? Silvio the old retainer from the Palazzo Donato? It made no sense at all. Then I opened the diary. I recognised the sweeping handwriting at once but the words were in Italian again. It took me a little while to translate them.

'*I am writing this under duress,*' the first paragraph began. '*My psychiatrist thinks it might aid my recovery to set down the story as I remember it. He is worried that I am being too harsh on myself. He thinks that writing rather than talking might enable me to properly reconnect with the facts of the matter rather than indulge my feelings of guilt. I've told him that my guilt is a fact of the matter. After all, I know exactly what I've done.*'

I stared at the page. Did Marco know I had *his* diary in my possession? He almost certainly didn't, otherwise why would Silvio have written the covering letter? I closed the cover and my eyes as well, as though that might absolve me of having read something I shouldn't. Make it disappear like the diary in my dream with its vanishing writing. I opened my eyes again. The book was still there.

When was this diary written? The cover said 2001. I reread the first paragraph. Marco's unhappiness was so obvious. He was writing under duress. I was reading out of prurience. I shut it again before anyone saw me looking at it, as though they might have known what it was and judged me for it.

I didn't drink my tea. I left enough euros on the table to cover my bill, put Marco's diary in my bag and headed home right away. I told myself I wasn't going to read the diary. Not if Marco hadn't expressly asked me to himself. But I think I already knew that I would, and I wanted to do so in the privacy of my own study. I hurried across the Volkspark as though I was evading arrest. I felt furtive. I was, after all, carrying stolen property.

What had possessed Silvio to take Marco's diary and give it to Bea? He didn't know her. He barely knew me. Why did he think I could be trusted with such a personal possession? If I told Marco that I had the diary, he would be within his rights to give Silvio the boot. And yet . . .

When I got to the Hufelandstrasse, I was grateful that the door to Herr Schmidt's apartment was closed and I didn't have to make up some excuse to avoid conversation. Half an hour after Nick had handed me the parcel, I was alone in my bedroom, with the diary on the bedspread in front of me. I got out my Italian dictionary. Feeling just as much guilt as the diary's author, I opened the first page and dived into Marco's past.

29

Wednesday 22nd March 1933

Dear Diary,

At last, a letter from Mummy. It was waiting for me when I came downstairs for breakfast this morning. Enno handed it over, commenting as he did so that it felt rather thick.

'Maybe some money, eh?' he said.

'I certainly hope so!' I told him.

There was indeed a money order for twenty pounds – such riches! – and three sheets in my mother's extravagant handwriting, bringing me up to date on everything that had happened since I ran away to Berlin. It seemed my father hadn't decreed that I be cut off from the family after all. Quite the opposite.

The Grange, Surrey
Monday 13th March 1933

My Darling Darling Kitty,

Thank goodness you wrote. We have been so very worried! Then to get your letter saying that we've forgotten you exist! Oh, you'll laugh when you hear what really happened. You must think we are terrible parents.

Of course the minute your father heard about that silly little incident at the finishing school, he went straight to Germany to fetch you home. He got to Munich less than forty-eight hours later only to have the horrible headmistress tell him you'd gone to Berlin in pursuit of that terrible Cord Von Cord boy. So your dear father took the overnight train straight to Berlin and presented himself on Cord's doorstep first thing in the morning. When he discovered that Cord had seen you but had sent you off into the city on your own because he was already engaged to be married, your father caused the most awful scene. Cord's fiancée and her family were at the house at the time. I don't believe she was his fiancée for much longer.

But since you weren't with Cord, the trail was cold. Your father spent five more days in Berlin searching high and low. He went to the Adlon, of course, since that is where Cord last saw you, but they said you'd checked out that very day with no forwarding address. So Papa visited all the girls' hostels in the city and showed your photograph to everybody he met but no one had any idea where you might be at all. He thought he saw you on the platform at the Lehrter Bahnhof and chased hundreds of yards to catch up with you, only to discover it wasn't you at all but a boy dressed in girl's clothing. Can you imagine? An actual cross-dresser in the train station! What a funny lot those Berliners are!

He came back to England quite broken-hearted. I told him you would not be lost for long. You always were a resourceful sort of girl. I felt certain you would have found yourself good lodgings and perhaps even a job and that you would write to us soon. But no letter came. Every morning, I would wait for the postman to arrive. Every afternoon I would write another letter to you and put it in the top drawer of my bureau. You will be able to read them all when at last you are home.

The months passed. We were getting more and more desperate. I know your last exchange with your father was an angry one, but I could not believe you would not have sent even a postcard to let us know where you were.

And then in September, we were invited to dinner at a neighbour's house. You don't know the Bradshaws. They moved in after you left for Munich. Well, I didn't want to go but your father insisted. Well, darling, thank goodness he took a strong line with me. Margery Bradshaw is no great conversationalist – in fact she is rather a bore – but that evening we got talking on a very dull subject that unexpectedly brought joy to my heart. She told me she and her husband had been waiting all week for a cheque from the building society and it hadn't turned up. Neither had a birthday card sent to their son from her mother. A birthday card that contained a postal order!

The more Margery complained, the more other people at the party added to her chorus of woe. Mrs

Johnson said she too had been waiting for a birthday card that never arrived. She knew her mother would not have forgotten. The Major said he'd assumed that year's dearth of Christmas cards was due to his having made a fool of himself at his niece's wedding. Well, perhaps in his case that was true, but it was all stacking up. Almost everybody who lived within two miles of us was missing some of their post. Eventually, Papa asked everyone to tell him exactly what they thought they ought to have received. He made a note of it and together with Mr Bradshaw he went to the police the following morning.

Well, it turned out that our postman – that shifty chap with the eyes too close together – had been going through the mail, opening envelopes in the hope of finding money inside and, when he couldn't seal the letters up again without it being obvious they had been tampered with, he would hide them in the attic of his house with the intention of disposing of them later on. Of course, he hadn't been hiding all the post, because then we would have discovered his crime altogether sooner. He was too clever for that.

But your letters were among those found in his attic, my love. He had opened every one. How I hate to think you might have thought we'd forgotten all about you! Not for one second. Of course, Papa was angry about the whole Cord affair, but when he thought we might have lost you altogether, he quickly got over that.

Oh, I am so relieved that you've written again. And with such good news! An engagement!

Your father is not sure what he thinks about your sudden betrothal but I have a feeling he will come round to the idea. Otto sounds like the perfect gentleman. Training to be a lawyer and musical with it! I am so glad he is musical. I could not bear the thought of you ending up with someone without a creative bone in his body. I did exactly that with your father. Oh, of course I love him but from time to time, I wish he would surprise me and I know he never will.

But I digress. Now that we know what has become of you, we need to know when you are coming home to England. We will have a lovely party for your new German boy! Write back at once so that I know you have received this. I am rather paranoid about the post these days. I'm not sure it's safe to send your birth certificate this way.

Papa sends a kiss, as do the dogs.

Your ever loving,

Mummy

xxx

It was so wonderful to hear from Mummy. I read her letter over and over and pressed it to my face so that I could smell her perfume. Patou's Joy. To think that postman might have rendered me estranged from my family for ever. Thank goodness he had been caught out. I showed Otto the letter that evening.

'I knew they wouldn't have cut you off,' he said. 'A woman as wonderful as you must have wonderful parents. They must have been so worried.'

'We must arrange a trip to see them,' I said. 'I know they will love you.'

I hesitated for a moment before I dared suggest, 'You know, perhaps we could have our wedding in England. Now that I know they haven't cut me off after all. My parents' house is rather large. We could have a marquee in the garden. Mummy would love that so much.'

'So long as you would love it too,' said Otto. 'We will marry wherever you like. All that matters to me is that you are happy.'

'Then how about you make me happy now?' I suggested.

I took him by the tie and led him to the bed. 'Take your jacket off and make love to me at once.'

'You are a terrible domina,' he said. 'I should have guessed that the first time we met.'

'I think I'm quite good at being a domina, actually,' I said.

'Perhaps terrible is not what I meant.'

'Your English could do with improvement,' I nodded. 'Perhaps you should conjugate some verbs. And every time you get one wrong, you will have to take off another item of clothing. And then you can take all my clothing off too. I don't suppose it will take very long.'

'It will be even faster if you are the one who has to conjugate her verbs. In German.'

To tease him, I decided I would conjugate 'zu ficken'. To fuck.

'That's it!' he said. 'You got that wrong. You bad girl. Bend over the bed at once.'

He picked me up and plonked me down on the pillows. I quickly wriggled out of my dress.

He is so good at giving me pleasure. I wish with all my heart that I had saved myself for him. If I had known what was coming, I would never have looked twice at Matthew Spencer or Cord Von Cord. At least I know that I will never have to look for anyone else.

'Otto Schmidt,' I told him. 'I love you so much I think my heart may explode.'

'I cannot wait for you to be my wife.'

'I cannot wait to be your wife. I can't wait to take your name. Though "Kitty Schmidt" sounds like some sort of cat ailment,' I teased. It earned me another tap on the bottom.

1st April 1933

What a horrible day. The Nazi Party called for a boycott of Jewish shops. It turned out their boycott included Jewish-owned nightclubs too. When I tried to go to the Boom Boom this afternoon, my way was blocked by a bunch of mean-looking thugs in the same hateful brown uniform that Gerd never seems to take off. They asked me what I thought I was doing, working for a vile Jew. I told them it was none of their business and they should be more polite. I pushed past them to the door, but one of the young men caught my arm and gripped it so hard it made me squeal.

How I wished that Otto were there, but in retrospect, I was very glad he wasn't. He would not have stood by while those thugs tried to threaten me. He would almost certainly have challenged them to a fight and goodness knows what might have happened then.

The club opened as usual. It was a quiet night but by no means empty. Some of the customers told me they had quite deliberately chosen to come to the Boom Boom that night in defiance of the Party's pathetic attempt to tell them who they should or should not consort with.

Schluter made an announcement that everyone who had made the effort to support him should have free champagne. I downed half a bottle as news filtered in of trouble all over town. The Nazis had even beaten Jewish women and old people as they tried to go about their business. How they can live with that kind of brutality on their conscience, I will never know.

30

Berlin, last October

My conscience was overruled and my curiosity got the better of me. I was reading Marco's diary. I should have returned it; that would have been the honourable thing to do. But then I thought how desperate Silvio must have been to try to get the diary into my hands. First he had stolen from his employer and then he had accosted Bea in the street. He might have ended up without a job. And with a black eye, had he got any closer to Bea in that dark alleyway.

Silvio wanted me to know something important.

For that reason – at least, that's the reason I settled on – I continued to read Marco's essay for his shrink. It was slow work. It was written entirely in Italian and I wanted to make sure I got every nuance. If I was going to break so many rules about trust, then I wanted at least to get the translation right.

The date at the beginning of the account was February 2001 but I knew that, since I had been working at the hospital in 1999, the accident must have occurred earlier that year. Was this Marco's account of it? Turned out it was much more than that.

The Girl Behind The Curtain

1st February 2001,
Venice

My name is Marco Donato. I was born in this city twenty-two years ago. I didn't have a silver spoon in my mouth – there's no way you could ever consider my family to be nobility – but I was born to all the privileges that money can bring. My grandfather had built a very successful cruise line. My father was presiding over a big upturn in the family's fortunes. I was blessed in so many ways. I would never want for anything. I had a wealthy father and a beautiful mother. It was as though I was the child in the fairy tale, born to the king and queen. I was their only child.

As I grew older, it was obvious that my advantages weren't just material. I was always good-looking. My nurse told me she could hardly walk down the street when she had me in a pram, for all the old ladies and young wives who wanted to get a good look at me. I liked the attention, she said, and I would always reserve my biggest beams for the pretty girls. I was flirting before I could talk. What's that saying? Smile and the world will smile with you? I had no idea there was any other facial expression. Everyone smiled at me.

Later, at school, I was popular. The girls wanted to be with me. The boys wanted to be me. I found schoolwork easy and my teachers were kind. The only shadow in my life was that, as I went into my teens, my parents' marriage began to falter. They were both busy with their love lives, so they left me to run pretty wild. I went to high school in the States but during the vacations I was back in Venice and I was allowed to throw parties at the palazzo. There's no teenager more popular than one who has a place where his friends can hang out without being nagged about smoking and homework. A teenager with a palazzo at his disposal is really something else.

As it was, my friends came from similar backgrounds. They were as privileged as me. We were arrogant with it. We scorned those who had less than us, never for a moment considering the origins of our own wealth. We acted as though we had earned the right to swagger around Venice, ordering people about like we were worthy of their respect and deference. I am eternally grateful that Silvio seems to have forgiven me for being a teenage prick. I don't know what I would have done without him and yet, before my accident, I treated him with less kindness than I treated the family dog. If Silvio ever thinks I got my comeuppance, he doesn't show it. He's always been a better man than I.

It was in the summer of 1999 that I made the fateful trip. Gianni, my oldest friend, was about to go to the States to study at Stanford for four years. We had to give him a proper send-off so we decided on a boys' weekend.

There was a definite fin de siècle buzz in the air that summer. It was as though everyone was determined to live large just in case the doom-mongers were right and New Year's Eve saw the earth explode in a giant fireball just because the computers couldn't handle a date change. I arranged to meet my friends in Berlin. We had heard that the scene there had to be seen to be believed. The underground clubs were legendary. Not that we were going to be staying anywhere grungy; we booked into the Hotel Adlon, which had recently reopened. We may have liked to think of ourselves as wild and crazy, but we all appreciated clean sheets and American-style sanitaryware.

There were five of us on that German jaunt. Me and my

best buddies. Gianni had scoped out the nightlife. He was a great fixer. He knew everyone worth knowing. With Gianni as part of our gang, we knew we'd have no trouble getting in anywhere we wanted to go. There wasn't a door on earth that was closed to that guy. We had the world at our feet. If only we'd deserved it.

I'm sure you understand what a gang of young men can be like. Individually, we were all perfect young gentlemen, our mothers' darlings, future members of the European establishment. But when we were together and far away from the influence of Venetian high society, we were feral. We were the kind of baying idiots you would cross the street to avoid. With our arrogant swagger and our awful manners, we were a perfect advert in favour of the heavy taxation of inherited wealth.

When we got to Berlin, we didn't waste any time getting into the party spirit. We met in Gianni's suite at the Adlon – of course he had scored a free upgrade by flirting with the girl on the desk – and opened a few bottles of Cristal. It's not that we were connoisseurs, simply that Cristal was the most expensive thing on the wine list. We got through a couple of magnums in an hour.

We were drunk even before we headed to the first club.

We had a packed itinerary of debauchery to follow. Gianni had things organised. He knew where to find the best music, the best girls, the best drugs. We ate at the city's finest restaurant, then travelled by limousine to a rough part of town where we danced ourselves into a frenzy in an old beer cellar. We threw our money around. We made ourselves very unpopular with a lot of poor young German guys. How could they possibly compete?

It was around midnight that we went to a place called

the Boom Boom. Gianni said it was the hottest place to go. It was a relatively new opening but it was based on a club of the same name that had been popular during the Weimar years. It was well-known for its exotic transvestite cabaret and also for its amateur night, which was the real draw for us that evening. We wanted to see people make fools of themselves. Perhaps, when we were drunk enough, we might even make fools of ourselves.

We took a table right next to the stage and ordered the most expensive wine in the place. The waiter brought us a bottle of barely drinkable fizz. We still had to work out that the most expensive was by no means necessarily the best. Still, we were so drunk that anything better would have been wasted.

The show began. We were in high spirits, but even mob-handed, when it came to heckling we were no match for the club's experienced master of ceremonies. Or perhaps I should say 'mistress'. The transvestite, who was at least seven feet tall in her heels, with her blonde hair piled up on her head like Marge Simpson, got so fed up of Gianni's howling that she pulled him up onto the stage and demanded that he dance with her. Gianni joined in the fun. It was comical but good-natured. Gianni had a good sense of humour. We all did. We were young, we were good-looking and we were very very rich. What was there to be unhappy about? Gianni was even persuaded to sing a duet with the enormous trannie. Together they murdered 'Everything I Do' to the delight of everyone present. It was a terrible rendition of a terrible song.

But there were other people at the club who took their music seriously. When the tuneless duet was finished, a girl took the stage. We'd seen some strange-looking creatures that night and, as far as we were concerned, this girl was no exception. She was by no means a traditional beauty. She was wearing the kind of outfit you would have expected to see in a lap-dancing club and her hair, which she wore in spikes, was dyed a lurid green. She was small and almost spherical in shape. The boys at once started to comment on what her figure was lacking. It didn't seem to bother the girl, though she must have heard every word. She walked on to that stage with the confidence of a true professional and even blew kisses in Gianni's direction. But there was one other thing. The girl must have been born with a cleft-lip; she had a lurid scar right in the middle of her face. A slash from nose to lip like a vicious duelling scar. There was a little notch where her Cupid's bow should have been.

It makes me feel ill now to think about what happened next. We started howling and barking. Gianni even threw a couple of French fries at the stage but the girl didn't flinch and, in any case, the mistress of ceremonies soon slapped us down again. The club grew quiet. The rest of the punters were waiting respectfully for the girl to begin her act. Perhaps they'd seen her before and they knew what was coming.

As soon as the girl opened her mouth, it was obvious where her confidence came from. Her curious – some would say, Hell, we did say – ugly appearance belied a beautiful voice. Even Gianni shut up and listened as she sang.

The song she chose was 'Song to the Siren'. She accompanied herself on the piano. I didn't know the Tim Buckley tune at all until that night but I was immediately captivated by its lilting tune and mournful lyrics. The audience was held spellbound by this siren indeed. And as she sang, she seemed suddenly beautiful. I couldn't take my eyes off her.

The song finished. We applauded. And then we barked some more. I would like to say that the girl's enormous talent for singing made me continue to overlook her packaging now that the song was over, but it didn't. Not yet. And when Gianni dared me to chat her up, I can't say I relished the prospect.

We had this game. I'm not proud of it. We called it 'pig hunting'. In Italy, of course, hunting boar is a popular pastime. We took the metaphor into the clubs. Our wild pigs were the girls we didn't consider to be attractive in the least.

Gianni slapped a hundred Deutschmarks on the table. Each of the other guys followed suit, so that my prize, should I undertake the mission they had chosen for me, would be half a grand. It wasn't as though any of us needed the money, but the cash somehow showed the seriousness of the bet. It made the challenge real.

'All right,' I said. 'I'll do it.'

I got up from the table to a round of applause. I was frustrated with my friends for that. They must have known they were making it more difficult for me by giving me such a send-off. I would have thought it was immediately obvious to my 'target' that something was afoot and I didn't expect her to be especially welcoming when I arrived at her table with half a bottle of champagne. But to my surprise she smiled broadly and invited me to sit down with her and her friends, who gave me a curt hello and returned to their conversation. They seemed to know I was a dick, even if she didn't. I poured the champagne.

'That stuff is terrible,' she said, looking at the label as she pushed her glass away. 'Now, what can I do for you, young man?'

With that she immediately put me on the back foot. Young man? It was both charming and quietly patronising. She must have been about the same age as me.

'I just wanted to congratulate you on your performance,' I said. 'You've got a beautiful singing voice.'

'Thank you.' She accepted my praise as though it was sincere, which I suppose, in a way, it was. She did have a beautiful singing voice. I wasn't lying. But now she was looking at me expectantly. 'Carry on,' she said.

'And I like your hair,' I said.

'I do it myself.'

'I thought so,' I blurted out. This made her throw her head back and laugh.

'I'll take that as a compliment, coming as it does from a boy who still lets his mother buy his clothes.'

It was true that, compared to her friends in their creative and exotic threads, I was dressed rather squarely for the Boom Boom. We may have thought of ourselves as rebels, but we couldn't shake the Italian urge for elegance.

'What's your name?' she asked.

I thought about lying but I didn't really have the energy to keep up any kind of pretence. I was too drunk. I told her the truth. 'Marco Donato.'

'Silke,' she said. 'Silke Fischer.'

It sounded like 'Silky' and for some reason, it made me think of a seal, slipping through the water.

She held out my hand and we shook. I noticed at once how smooth her skin was. Her fingernails were painted a deep blood-red. She had the most elegant hands. I found myself wondering if she paid them special attention because her face . . . Her face.

I looked at her. I was trying so hard not to look at her lip that I stared deep into her eyes instead. Perhaps that was when I started to fall for her. Her eyes were dark and compelling. Hypnotic. A smile flickered at the corner of her mouth as though she could tell she was drawing me in.

'Your friends are calling you,' she said. 'They want their terrible champagne back.'

She pretty much shooed me away.

When I got back to the table, I was greeted like a hero with much backslapping and congratulation. I had only poured the girl a drink. You would think I had persuaded her to strip in the middle of the club. As the boys marvelled at my smooth-tongued abilities as a chat-up artist, I was glad to see that Silke already had her back to me. She could not see how I was being lauded at her expense. She was too busy talking to the friends she had arrived with, who suddenly seemed very sophisticated and grown-up compared to my crowd of overgrown schoolkids. I was sure she must have thought me an idiot. Ordinarily, I wouldn't have cared, but there was something about the way she had smiled at me, as though she saw a kindred spirit beneath all the bravura.

And then Gianni upped the stakes. He announced in front of the table. 'A thousand Deutschmarks says you can't persuade her to go to bed with you.'

If I hadn't accepted this dare I would never have heard the last of it. I decided I would take Gianni's money and bring Silke in on the joke. She didn't have to sleep with me, but if she pretended to, she could take half the money. And it was an excuse to talk to her again.

31

Berlin, last October

How did I feel when I read about Marco's dare? I wasn't thrilled, I can tell you. But I wasn't entirely shocked. Back in 1999, Marco was a young guy. I had done some pretty cruel things at the same age; my girl friends and I had flirted outrageously with people we had no intention of ever seeing again. With that in mind, I tried not to judge him. But why was this young girl significant? Where was the story going? Was she the passenger who had died in Marco's car?

There was also the fact that Marco had been in Berlin. The moment I read those words, I felt my perspective on the city shift ever so slightly. Until I read those words, Berlin had been my place. Everything I discovered was new and original. It was mine alone. Now I knew that Marco had been here too, I would have to wonder if he had seen what I'd seen. Of course he must have walked under the Brandenburg Gate. He must have seen the Reichstag. He probably had his photograph taken at Checkpoint Charlie. To think of him in Berlin with those friends I had never met made me sad. And he was at the Boom Boom. I thought of Anna and Silke singing the same song. When Marco described Silke, I could see Anna's face in my head.

I wanted to talk about it, but the only person who knew I had Marco's diary was Silvio. I hadn't even admitted the truth to Bea. I'd told her Silvio was returning an old notebook of mine.

That's the problem with lies. They leave you isolated.

The following evening, I saw my landlord. He climbed the stairs to bring me a parcel that had been delivered earlier in the day, while I was at the university. It was a package of books I had asked my mother to send to me. It was heavy and I felt terrible that Herr Schmidt had tackled the stairs to bring it to me rather than leave it in the hall. I invited him in.

'I don't want to disturb you,' he said.

'I'd appreciate the company,' I told him. That was the truth. Plus, I was intrigued to know more about him. As a young girl, I'd heard plenty about the Second World War from my grandparents, but I had never heard the story from the German perspective. I hoped that I might be able to draw Herr Schmidt on his experiences. I also wanted to thank him for having given me those old diaries; they were exactly what I needed to kick-start my project.

But Herr Schmidt did not seem to want to know about Kitty Hazleton. When I told him that she had fallen in love with a man who shared his surname, Herr Schmidt merely said, as had Clare, 'It is Germany's most common name.'

Herr Schmidt did not stay to talk.

It was strange the way that Herr Schmidt did not want to discuss the contents of the diaries even though he had pressed them into my hands but I decided that perhaps he just felt guilty for having hung on to them for so long. With every year that passed, the chances of getting them and the items he'd found with them back to their owner faded. I'd calculated that if Kitty Hazleton were still alive, she would be ninety-seven.

My search for her had not got far. It was complicated by

the small but important detail that she was a woman and, unlike a man, had almost certainly changed her name after marriage. But I had sent messages to some Surrey-based Hazletons via Facebook, in the hope that one of them was a relative. It would be a wonderful thing to reunite her with her diaries if I could.

Would I reunite Marco with his? How could I do it without drawing his attention to the fact that Silvio had betrayed his trust? The diary seemed to accuse me from its place on my desk. But I think I already knew I would not do it before reading the rest. Marco's diary had become my constant companion; every moment I had, I read a little more. It was slow work, almost as hard as translating Luciana's diaries had been. He used a lot of slang. His handwriting was recognisably his but it was erratic and untidy in places as though even to pick up a pen caused him pain. Sometimes he wrote in a kind of shorthand. The story wasn't always chronological. Parts of it didn't quite make sense. He frequently broke off from telling his story to rant at his supposed reader – the psychiatrist – for wasting his time making him write the story out when it was so clear where the guilt lay. The possible scenarios ran through my mind. I thought I knew what I was going to discover. The punchline would be the car accident, of course and his culpability in it. Driving a powerful car way too fast. Had he also been drunk? I hoped not. I wasn't sure what I would think about that.

I read on, staying up late to finish another page. It caused me especial pain that he was writing about Berlin. About the Boom Boom Club of all places. Because I had been there so recently, I could picture the moment Marco met this Silke all too clearly. She was too real. When I read that he had found her beautiful while she sang, I felt a bubble of jealousy even though I'd sworn to myself that I didn't want him any more.

It shouldn't have mattered what had happened in his past. Who he'd cared for. It was none of my business. Why had Silvio thought I should read it at all?

And yet, when Marco talked, I wanted to listen. Even if the story was for someone else. I remembered an email he had sent me many months earlier, in which he joked that I was his confessor. In that case, however, he had been telling me about stealing something from a shop as a seven-year-old. His nanny had discovered the theft and marched him back to return the sweets and apologise.

This was different. There was no marching back from a death.

Berlin, 1999

So, I took Gianni up on his second dare. I'm sure he thought I would get slapped down. He didn't know I had a plan. This time I went up to Silke and told her I was secretly gay and my friends suspected. Would she be kind enough to leave the club with me to put them off the scent? There was five hundred Deutschmarks in it.

'Five hundred? And I just have to leave the club with you?'

'You'd be doing me an enormous favour.'

'Sounds like easy money.'

We left the club arm in arm. As we walked past my friends, they had the decency not to clap us out. When it looked as though Gianni might say something distasteful, I drew my finger across my throat. It was bad enough that I had taken them up on the bet; I wasn't such an arsehole that I wanted her to know about it.

As soon as we were outside, Silke turned to me and said, 'OK. I'm going back inside. If you'd just like to hand over the money. It's been very nice working with you, Herr Marco Donato.'

'What? Wait,' I said. 'You can't go back inside yet. What will my friends think?'

'You really are bothered what your friends think?' Her eyes flashed mischief. 'Well, if your reputation is so important to you, I suppose I can spare you a little more time for your five hundred marks. It was getting rather hot in there anyway. You can walk me home.'

'Is it far?' I asked.

'Why? Do your shiny shoes hurt?' Silke asked me.

I was expecting only to walk Silke back to her apartment – almost like a gentleman – and leave her there. I would make something up for the benefit of the boys. I didn't expect her to invite me in. Why would she? I was a stranger.

But if we were strangers when we left the Boom Boom together, the sensation didn't seem to last for long. In the noise and hustle of the club, it had been difficult to have a conversation. Outside, on the quiet street, it was much easier.

We spoke in English because I didn't know any German and, while Silke knew some Italian, she knew English better. Her ambition was to study in London but that was expensive and would probably never happen. The idea that money might be an object in any scenario was completely alien to me.

She was cultured and funny. She wasn't just a singer. She told me she played cello as well as piano.

'Cellos aren't that portable,' she said.

In the daytime, while she was waiting for someone to notice her and make her a star, she told me she worked at an old people's home. It wasn't high on her list of dream jobs, but she told me that she quite enjoyed it. 'There are some good people in there. They make me laugh. They have a good perspective on what really matters in life. Which is useful if you intend to be a megastar, as I do. They'll help me keep my feet on the ground. And what about you? What do you do when you're not splashing money on bad champagne?'

I was embarrassed. I could hardly tell her I didn't have to earn a living. In theory, I worked alongside my father, but in practice, I spent most of my time on vacation. I'd dropped out of university because it interfered with my partying. I told Silke that I worked for a shipping company. I didn't tell her the company bore my family name.

'That must be interesting,' she said. 'Gives you a chance to travel the world.'

I had seen so much of the world I was rather blasé about it. Silke had never been outside her country.

We got to her apartment building. It was one of those huge, ugly square buildings that had sprung up during the Soviet era. I had never seen such a hideous building in my life. Growing up in Venice, perhaps, had left me with an aversion to bad architecture. I looked up at it.

'Are you coming in?' she asked.

I hesitated.

'If you come in, I will let you leave,' Silke laughed. 'I promise. It's just that we were having such a nice conversation, I thought we might carry on for a while.'

She was right. We'd been having a great conversation and I was in no hurry to cut it short. I followed her into the building. She told me she shared the flat with a girl friend who was away for the weekend. Though the building was grim, Silke and her friend had made their apartment very cosy. Glamorous, even. Beautiful silk curtains hung at the windows. The lighting was rather romantic.

'What can I get you?' Silke asked. She opened a cabinet to show me an array of drinks. There was even a bottle of tequila with a lizard in it. I remember that because, some hours later, we opened the bottle and she dared me to take a slug.

That's the last thing I can really remember about that night.

I slept on the sofa. I had drunk so much that I could barely move. There was no chance I was going to jump on Silke. She didn't seem to mind. She untied my shoelaces and slipped off my shoes. Then she lifted my legs, so that I was lying flat out on the cushions. She covered me with a quilt that smelled faintly of her perfume. Then she kissed me lightly on the forehead and went into her bedroom.

It was the following morning that it happened. She woke me with a cup of coffee. It was horrible coffee. But then any coffee except Italian coffee is pretty vile to me.

Silke was even prettier without her make-up on. She had beautiful skin, luminous and fine as porcelain. Her eyelashes were long and dark. Though her scar was more prominent when her face was bare, it had a beauty and a bravery to it. I had the sudden urge to kiss it.

She sat down on the arm of the sofa, cradling her own coffee in her hand, and watched me, with her head tipped to one side, as though she wasn't quite sure what had washed up in her living room.

'You're still here,' she said. 'Whatever will your friends think about that?'

I was supposed to leave Berlin on the Monday morning, but I found I didn't want to. Instead, I cancelled my flight and told my friends I would be staying. I wanted to see

Silke again. I stayed for another seven days. During that time, I monopolised every spare moment she had.

Silke's flatmate was back in the apartment during the week, so nights were spent at the hotel. During the day, Silke had to work. I hung around aimlessly, drinking bad coffee in dingy cafés, just waiting for her to finish her shift and appear in my room, still dressed in her old people's home uniform. She would bring tapes of her favourite music with her. She was determined to educate me. It's thanks to her that I heard of Jeff Buckley, son of the man who wrote 'Song to the Siren'. His is the only voice I can stand to listen to now. It suits my mood. Especially since I know he died by drowning. I feel I might follow him into the water.

But you won't let that happen, will you, so I suppose I have to carry on.

Silke was so unlike anyone I had ever met before. She said I was unlike anyone she'd ever met either. She really didn't know anything much about me. I suppose she had guessed that I came from a family with money – I was staying at the Adlon, after all. Silke gave me a different kind of access to Berlin. We went to the kind of places I never would have found on my own or with Gianni and his bunch of monied drifters.

I felt at home in the city when I was with her. Perhaps it's just that I felt at home with Silke. I liked that she came to me with no preconceptions. With my friends gone back to Italy, I could be the Marco I wanted to be. The Marco she made me want to be.

Those words: 'The Marco she made me want to be.' Having translated that telling line, I closed Marco's diary. I wasn't sure that I could bear to read on. I put it back inside the envelope and into the shoebox, where it nestled alongside Kitty's diaries and her teddy bear.

'You seem a bit preoccupied,' said Clare when I met her the following day.

'Thinking about work,' I lied. How could I tell her that I was consumed with jealousy at the idea of a man I had never kissed sleeping with a woman I had never met?

So much of my life was in the past. With Kitty and Marco I spent my time moving between the Berlins of the 30s and the 90s. I asked Clare to tell me about her adventures in Internet dating to take my mind off all the ghosts. But though I tried to concentrate, I was constantly being pulled back into my own thoughts. I made an excuse to leave early.

An hour later, I was back with Marco again.

Venice, 1999

I stayed in Berlin for a whole extra week but eventually I had to go home. I promised Silke that it would not be long before I was back, however, and in the meantime we would write and perhaps even call.

As soon as I got back to Venice, I bumped into Gianni. He was in the café where we always used to go and hang out pretending to be ordinary Venetians. Or 'peasants' as we called them. We were not the kind of guys I'd like to have as friends now.

'What happened to you?' he asked. 'Did you pick up some transvestite?'

'I just wanted to get a better look at Berlin,' I said. 'Nothing wrong with that.'

'Nothing wrong with it, sure. But when did you become such a culture vulture, Marco Donato? There had to be something else keeping you there. Come on. You can tell me. You've spent the past week in a German dungeon being flogged by a big-breasted dominatrix, haven't you?'

'Perhaps I have,' I said. I wasn't going to be drawn. But I have to admit I was relieved he didn't seem to have considered the prospect that I had stayed in Berlin because of Silke. He had obviously believed me when I told him that I'd snuck out of her flat and left without leaving my number after our night at the Boom Boom.

Life in Venice continued as usual. I'd been seeing a girl for a few months and she seemed pleased that I was back from Germany and readily accepted my explanation that I wanted to see more of the city's culture. She also readily accepted the gift I had picked up for her in the airport.

My girlfriend's name was Katrina. She was what anyone who knew me back then would have described as 'my type'. She was a model. She was tall and slim as a breadstick with long dark hair that swished behind her like the tail of some exotic pony. All the guys were envious of her. But the truth was I didn't even want to kiss her. To stay as slim as she did, she starved herself most days and when she didn't have the willpower to starve herself, she stuck her fingers down her throat and threw up. Every time I got anywhere near her, I was almost overcome by the smell, a combination of Dior's Poison and the whiff of stomach acid. But she looked the part. She wore the right clothes and she went to the right places. My friends were impressed and that was good enough for me.

Or was it? I wasn't sure any more.

I had been sincere when I said goodbye to Silke and told her I would be in touch. But I had been back a week and I hadn't picked up the phone to call her. It wasn't that I didn't think of her – I thought about her often. I thought about her whenever I slung my arm round Katrina's bony shoulders and she turned to me in a cloud of scent and sickness.

I don't know why I didn't tell Katrina I wasn't interested. I suppose I was too worried about my image. A man like me just didn't have a girlfriend like Silke. A man like me dated models like Katrina. Nothing less than physical perfection as validated by a full-page spread in Vogue. I didn't have enough courage in my own desires to tell Gianni and the others that I wanted something different. To want something else was to refuse a whole cultural norm. It was to go against my upbringing.

But I couldn't get Silke out of my mind and at last I did pick up the phone and call her. She took my call as though she had spoken to me only yesterday and she wasn't in the least bit surprised to hear from me again. She was effortlessly cool. It made me want her even more.

I was going to London later that month. I asked her to join me there. If she could get a week off work and somehow arrange to get a passport quickly enough, I would pay her airfare. The following day she made a collect call to tell me that the time off was arranged and I should send her a ticket. She was overjoyed at the prospect of a trip to England. As she reminded me, it would be her first trip abroad.

As soon as I got that call, I was torn. I had wanted her to say yes. Of course I had. But then I began to worry again. What if that crazy week in Berlin was just a one-off? What if she got off the plane and I saw her as my friends saw her – a lumpy German girl with ugly clothes and stupid hair? And a face that had been sliced in two by Mother Nature and stitched back together by a butcher?

I toyed with the idea of pretending I hadn't received her letter. There was no chance she'd just turn up; she couldn't afford to fly to London to meet me if I didn't pay for the ticket. But the feeling that I wanted to see her finally outweighed my fears. I sent her the ticket. I even paid for her to fly business class, which was something she would tease me about when we were face to face again. After that, I arranged a hire car. Not just any hire car. I used my father's credit card to hire a red Ferrari.

And after I had taken that step, our next meeting could not come quickly enough. I couldn't wait to see her. My plane arrived two hours before hers did and I waited at the airport, anxiously watching the new arrivals even before her plane had taken off from Germany.

When she finally appeared, she was just as I remembered, except that her hair was no longer green but a bright, cerulean blue. In her long blue dress, she was like a mermaid far from the sea. My siren. When she saw me waiting for her at the gate, her face broke into an enormous smile that told me I had made the right decision. We would have a great time together. I had no doubt. I was still smitten, though part of me had hoped I wouldn't be.

The heart is an unruly beast. The person who invents a potion that allows us to fall in love only with the most 'suitable' other will make a fortune.

We didn't go into London. I had been to the city before, so it was easy for me to tell her that I wanted to go somewhere neither of us had ever been. Wouldn't it be more fun for us to discover something new together, making new memories only for us? That was why we were going to drive straight to the Lake District. In reality, I was still nervous that we might bump into someone I knew.

Though Silke was more beautiful to me than the Venus di Milo, I noticed even as I carried her case through the airport that most of the attention she attracted was less admiring.

I wanted to protect her from the people who stared at her. It started in the airport. By the time we got to that stupid red Ferrari in the car park, I was stiff with the tension of glaring at everyone who gawped at my dear girl. I was angry on her behalf, but I noted that I was also slightly angry with her.

It was three in the morning and I was tired of translating. I put the diary down again. Was I beginning to hate Marco or was I just jealous? A cottage in the Lake District was another of the romantic clichés to which I had once aspired. Marco had taken her. He'd taken Silke. He would almost certainly never take me.

Silvio had made a mistake in sending me this diary. Unless he wanted me to give up all hope.

I should send it back. I didn't have the stomach to read about a romantic weekend. Especially not when I knew it couldn't have a happy ending and yet the repercussions of it still reached into my life. For Silke had to be the girl who had died in the car crash, didn't she?

32

Friday 13th October 1933

Dear Diary,

There was another incident on the street two nights ago. A gang of Brownshirts turned up at the Beluga Bar just after it opened. They watched the whole show and had plenty to drink before they went to the office backstage and beat the theatre manager to a pulp. Their justification? They said he was supplying young girls – very young girls – for sex. It isn't true. There's never been even the slightest whiff of that sort of behaviour about the Beluga. And the Brownshirts were not so bothered about morality that they didn't make off with the club's takings and several bottles of whisky.

Otto spoke to Gerd about it and Gerd assured him that kind of behaviour is not acceptable in the SA and that if the story were to be confirmed to him by an official source, he would make sure the perpetrators were punished. But then Gerd spoke darkly about the likes of the Beluga Bar's manager doing well to keep a low profile in any case and perhaps even think about closing down. The rowdy SA boys were reflecting a growing public opinion, he claimed. People were concerned about the morality of the clubs along the Ku'damm.

'You should tell your boss the same,' Gerd told Otto. 'Things are going to be very different around here soon.'

Otto is convinced that Gerd's pronouncement was in fact a veiled hint that the Boom Boom will be next, so we have made a plan. Last night, after the show ended and we were all in the empty bar, eating supper and complaining about the evening's amateurs, Otto asked if he might address us all just for a moment. He looked so very serious that we all grew quiet without question and let him take the floor.

'Ladies and gentlemen.' He included Marlene and Isadora in the 'ladies'. 'None of us can have failed to notice that the atmosphere in this part of town has been getting rather strained. Marlene has already felt how ugly things are getting and we all know what happened backstage at the Beluga Bar two nights ago. I've worked here for three years now. I've seen rowdy punters and we've all met men so scared of their feelings for beautiful creatures like Marlene and Isadora that they can only express their awe with their fists, but this is different. There's been a shift in political feeling. Maybe even public feeling. There's a sense that we're not so welcome any more.'

Marlene nodded in agreement.

'As some of you know, to my great bewilderment and embarrassment, my younger brother Gerd is a member of the Sturmabteilung. In fact, he's quite the rising star. I spoke to him last night about this spate of beatings and he denied that it is SA policy. But he said we should know that Germany is changing, and some of those things we love most about Berlin may not be tolerated for too much longer.'

'Tolerated by whom?' Isadora asked.

'By the Party,' said Marlene. 'The bloody Party. Just lay it out for us, Otto. We know you're only the messenger.'

'Well, my brother, who is "only the messenger" for the Party, is of course referring to clubs like this. He's referring to men dressed as women, girls who like girls and boys who like boys. He's referring to anyone who might exchange their sexual favours for money. He's referring to foreigners.'

Otto looked at me. I felt my heart skip and not in the usual good way.

'He's referring especially to Jews,' said Schluter.

My mind went back to that awful day in April when the SA boys barred the doors to every Jewish business on the street.

Otto continued, 'According to my brother, there is no official policy regarding the "cleansing" of our streets here in the Ku'damm, but there's no doubt he was letting me know that, unofficially, the club's days are numbered.'

'We can't shut down!' said Isadora. 'We've been here for years and we make people happy. Why should we give in to the small-minded pricks?'

'Because they're small-minded pricks with big fists,' said Marlene.

'I'm not suggesting we shut the club down,' Otto continued. 'But I do think we need to be prepared. No one should keep any valuables here. And we need to start thinking about an escape route should we find ourselves under attack. Schluter, is there any way out of this building except by the front door and the door on to the alley?'

'Of course not,' Isadora interrupted but Schluter silenced him.

'Actually, there is. Through the cellar. Behind the wine racks, there is a passageway. It leads from the cellar beneath this club into the cellar of the Paradise Hotel. From there, you can get into the cellar of the department store and from there into the U-Bahn tunnel. From the U-Bahn, you can get to Timbuktu if you're so inclined.'

'This is good news,' said Otto. 'Schluter, you're going to need to move those wine racks so we can get around them quickly, but they need to be placed in such a way that the passageway is still hidden should someone follow us down.'

'We can sort that out right now,' said Schluter.

'So we have our escape route. What we need to work out now is how we will signal the need to escape. The SA waited until the show was over to beat up the guys at the Beluga. They don't want the general public seeing what they're up to. We need to let each other know that the bastards are in the house without alerting them to the fact that we're on to it. Handily, they usually wear their uniforms.'

'So we could just ban people in uniform,' I suggested.

'I don't think that's going to work.'

'We all need to agree on a song that signals that trouble is brewing. Any one of us can call it. For example, Marlene, maybe you'll be on stage and you'll see something going on at the back of the room. When that happens, you can say, "For my next song" and, while we play the song we've agreed on, everyone backstage can be getting ready to go.'

'Which song?' I asked.

Everyone immediately had a suggestion but Otto refused them all. 'It can't be too popular. It can't be a song that people are going to ask for night after night.'

'How about "The Song is Ended"?' suggested Schluter.

Otto and I shared a look.

'You do know it?' Schluter asked.

'Yes,' said Otto. 'Of course. I think we all do.'

The other people gathered around the table that evening agreed.

'It's the perfect choice,' said Marlene. 'Hardly anyone requests it because the lyrics are in English, but everybody at least knows the tune, so it won't seem odd if you start to play it.'

Otto agreed. 'Then that's the song we choose. Now, we must clear the escape route and have a practice run. Whoever is on stage at the time we give the alarm, someone backstage must be allocated to gather their street clothes for them and be waiting in the wings as soon as the curtain comes down, so they can do a quick change.'

Together with Marlene, I set about writing down the names of everyone in the room and allocating them a second – someone who would collect their things.

An hour later, we all knew how to find the passageway out of the cellar and we had all learned by heart what our duties were should the terrible moment ever arise.

'It's all rather exciting,' said Isadora, but I could tell he didn't really believe that. It wasn't exciting. It was frightening. I wished it weren't necessary but I knew Otto was not one to make us go through such a rigmarole for fun.

We said goodnight to each other especially tenderly that night. The enmities that are present in any workplace had been weakening over the months since Marlene was beaten and now it felt as though we were an unshakeable team.

'See you tomorrow, everyone,' said Schluter. 'The show must go on!'

As we walked back to the Hotel Frankfort, Otto asked me if I thought he had gone over the top. He hoped he hadn't scared anybody.

'What you had to tell us might save our lives,' I said. 'With luck, we'll never need to put the plan into action. The SA idiots who did over the Beluga Bar will be punished and calm will be restored. Think of the number of people that come over here on a Saturday night. I can't believe they're all going to stay away just because Herr Hitler says so.'

I thought I had done a pretty good job of convincing Otto that I was perfectly calm about the whole thing, but, in the end, I couldn't keep my eyes from misting up on me.

'Don't cry, my sweetheart.'

'I'm sorry,' I said. 'It's just that I can't believe that the next time I hear our song, I might have to run for my life. I wish we'd chosen something else.'

'We couldn't choose anything too popular,' said Otto. 'Or we'll all be running for cover three times a night. No one ever asks for "The Song is Ended". It's too much of a stretch for a bad singer.'

'Will you sing it to me now?' I asked Otto. 'Just here. Just for the two of us, while the only thing it means is that you love me and I love you back.'

Otto nodded and started to sing for me. His voice, though he was keeping it quiet out of respect for the neighbours, still filled the room and my heart. By the time he finished singing, I was in floods of tears.

Otto stayed the night with me. He said his mother and sister wouldn't mind and he no longer cared what his brother thought. Party morality was no kind of morality to which he wished to subscribe. As far as Otto was concerned, Gerd might as well be a stranger to him now. He would remain civil to him so long as it was useful for keeping the rest of us safe. That was all.

'With luck,' he added, 'this is just a phase. When the German people get bored of young Adolf as they've got bored of every politician before, I'm sure it will be business as usual.'

When we made love it was with an added intensity. Otto had insisted that the plans we'd made that evening would by no means inevitably be pressed into action, but it was as though at some very deep level we both knew differently.

For that reason, we made love so sweetly. I wanted to take everything more slowly than before. Whereas previously I had joked that Otto should be as quick as he could because I needed my beauty sleep, I didn't feel I could be so flippant again. I wanted our lovemaking to last for hours. I wanted it to be the kind of lovemaking that we could both look back on, if we ever found ourselves apart. I wanted to imprint myself upon him and bear his mark upon me. In me. I wished last night for a baby.

Otto kissed the tears from my face.

'My sentimental darling,' he called me.

In the morning, he pinched my cheeks and told me to cheer up.

'Though, if you're going to insist on making love to me as though every time might be our last, I'm perfectly happy if you worry for a little while longer.'

I am worried. When I first arrived in Berlin, I was surprised and impressed by how liberal the city seemed. London seemed quite stiff and reactionary in comparison. But that does seem to be changing. We all make jokes about Adolf Hitler but there are obviously an awful lot of people in this country who find his rhetoric compelling rather than ridiculous. I take much more notice of politics now than I did before. Gerd might almost be proud of me.

33

Berlin, last October

As intrigued as I was by the deepening seriousness of Kitty Hazleton's situation in 1933, another Berlin story had taken me over.

I continued to read Marco's diary. I didn't want to but I couldn't keep away. I kept reading even though I was burning with jealousy as he described the time he spent with Silke. She had spent days in his company and nights in his arms. She'd had so much more of him than I ever did. I could hardly bear to think about it. There were moments when I wanted to tear the diary into pieces, but I had the feeling that I needed to read to the end, and so I carried on, with my Italian dictionary beside me, deciphering Marco's handwriting and reading his secret story, even though my envy was driving me insane. I began to wonder whether Silvio had sent me this diary to scare me off or make me think I'd had a lucky escape. There were plenty of reasons here why Marco could be considered damaged goods. Yet I had to know more.

Marco spared me no detail.

Venice, 2001

We were together for four nights and they were the most amazing four nights I had experienced in my short, overprivileged life. I could think of nothing more wonderful than spending the rest of my days in a small cottage in the Lake District with this crazy, blue-haired woman. But of course, I wanted my cottage dream to run alongside my Eurotrash existence. And on Friday night, the Eurotrash was calling me. Specifically, Gianni was calling me. He called me all day long. Finally, when Silke was sleeping – as had become the pattern of our afternoons – I walked out into the lane and called him back.

'Hey, bro. I heard you're in England. What are you doing? Come to London tomorrow night. We're having a party. Cameron Diaz is going to be there.'

'Cameron Diaz?'

'Yeah. You know that American guy who came on my boat last year? Well, he's set up his own film production company. Cameron is doing a film with him.'

'Who else will be there?' I asked. I knew Gianni wouldn't be offended by the question. It was automatic. We were all of us quite transparent when it came to how we decided to spend our precious weekends. If the faces didn't fit . . .

Gianni reeled off a list of names, which contained scions of just about every great family in Europe. If by 'great' you mean rich.

'Tell me you're coming, bro. Won't be a party without you.'

'I'll think about it,' I told him.

'Think about it? Where the hell are you anyway? Who are you with? You've got awful mysterious since that trip to Berlin.'

I laughed it off but I wanted to go to the party. I also wanted to spend more time with Silke, though, and we were supposed to be in the country all weekend. It should have been easy, right? I should have taken Silke with me.

She would have loved to go along, I'm sure. She would have been fascinated by my friends and their trashy, spoilt ways. We could have laughed about it afterwards. But for some reason, the opinion of those trashy, spoilt people still mattered to me. When Silke woke up and came to find me, I had a flashback to the very first time I saw her. She was crumpled from sleep. She looked vulnerable. It made me hate her for just a second. I had a weird visceral reaction of horror to the thought that I might have saddled myself with someone who might need my care.

'I understand,' said Silke when I told her that Gianni had called and we needed to cut our romantic holiday short. 'I wouldn't pass up the opportunity to party with a proper movie star either. So when are we going?'

'If we leave after lunch, I thought I could drop you off at the airport at five. There's a flight at six thirty.'

'What? You're dropping me off?'

'Yes.'

'But I don't need to go back for a couple of days. I thought I was going to come to London with you.'

'I know, but . . .'

'But what?'

'Gianni. I mean, he's only expecting me. I haven't told him. I can't explain it,' I began.

Silke's eyes flashed. 'There's no need to. I understand what's going on. You don't want to introduce me to your fancy friends. Is it the same crowd you were with in Berlin? Those braying idiots? You haven't told them about me, have you?'

'Of course I've told them about you,' I lied. 'They saw me leave the club with you that night. They know I spent all that time with you in Berlin. They knew back then that I was interested in you.'

Silke snorted.

'But they don't want me to come along to the party? There's something else, isn't there? There's a girl. You've got a girlfriend. She doesn't know you've been here with me and you've got no intention of letting her find out. Either she'll be at this party I can't go to, or you're frightened that someone who knows her will be there and they'll pass on the gossip.'

'There's no other girl, I swear.' That much at least was true. I'd told Katrina it was over the day before I left for the UK.

'Then why won't you just take me along?'

How could I tell her? Because you look so different. Because I am frightened that people will judge me for being with you. Because I don't have the strength to defend you from their stares.

'Forget it,' she said, shaking her head. 'I don't want to come to a stupid party anyway. I saw what your friends are like the night we met. I'd rather spend the evening with the old people at work.'

For the moment, the conversation was over, but for the rest of the day Silke was distant. She had every right to be. I did my best to make it up to her. I took her out to dinner in the local town. I took her shopping – though there wasn't much to buy. But I stopped short of doing what I should have done, which was tell her I wasn't going anywhere without her by my side. And the following morning, we began the long drive back to London.

We had not been on the road for long when Silke asked if she could drive. I wasn't quite sure she should – she had very little experience of driving anything, let alone such a powerful car. But I was so desperate to mollify her and make up for having hurt her that I pulled over, let her climb into the driver's seat and take the wheel for the first time.

And it was fine, for a while, until I took a call from
Gianni and Silke was reminded where we were heading
and why.

'I can't believe you don't want your friends to meet me,'
she mumbled. And then she put her foot down. She had
been so nervous of driving my car, but suddenly she
seemed very confident indeed. I watched as the figures on
the speedometer crept upwards.

'Silke,' I said. 'Slow down. The limit's fifty on this sort of
road.'

She just put her foot down harder.

'Silke, please.' We were doing seventy, but it felt a good
deal faster, because the road was so narrow and bounded
on both sides by high hedges.

'Silke,' I begged her. 'Please slow down.'

By now the speedometer was showing ninety. On a
straight piece of motorway we would have been fine, but a
bend was coming. To this day, I am not sure whether Silke
tried to negotiate that bend at all.

We ploughed into the hedge that concealed a stone wall.
The car was hurled into the air. I remember glimpsing the
road above our heads and then . . .

You know how time seems to slow down when you're in
danger? In reality, everything is happening in seconds, but
somehow your brain arranges things so that you seem to
have time to think and work out what best to do, even
when you're hurtling at warp speed towards oblivion. The
car rolled and bounced but landed, by God knows whose
hand, the right way up. I was wearing my seat harness.
That kept me from the windscreen. Not so Silke. She
hadn't wanted to wear her harness because she said it hurt.
So there was nothing to keep her in her seat. A blow to her
head had left her unconscious.

I scrambled out of the passenger side of the car and raced to pull her free. For the first time ever, she felt heavy to me. It was hard to move her. I remember shouting and shouting that she needed to help me free her legs, but she was out cold. She didn't seem to hear me at all.

In the end, I did manage to pull her out of the car but I was too exhausted to move far away, so that when the petrol in the engine caught fire, I couldn't move quickly enough to avoid being engulfed by the fireball.

What happened next, I don't remember. I can only tell you what I was told. Apparently a farmer was coming in the other direction. By some strange providence, he was a volunteer fireman and knew at once what he should do. He pulled me clear of the car and put out the flames with his shirt. He thought I was dead, so he left me while he tried to resuscitate Silke. When a further vehicle came along, he sent the driver to find the nearest phone and call for help. He didn't have a mobile phone. My own was burning along with the car.

The fire service and an ambulance arrived quickly, but not quickly enough. They kept me alive while we waited for a helicopter to land in the farmer's field. I was taken in the helicopter to the nearest burns unit. Silke – who hadn't been caught in the flames – was taken by road to a closer emergency room.

I would never see her again.

That's it. That's what you wanted. You wanted me to put the whole story down so that I can be released from my guilt by the truth. But guess what? In this case, the truth isn't going to set anybody free. It hasn't worked. Silke is still dead and it's still my fault. Even this living death is more than I deserve for what I did to her. So please don't try to tell me my guilt is unnecessary. I killed my lover and my best friend.

I don't deserve to live. I want you to consider this my confession and my suicide note. By the time you read this I will have settled the score. Please apologise to Silvio, since he will almost certainly be the one to find me. I hung around for too long. It's time to make amends.

34

As I read Marco's description of the accident and his desperate last paragraph, my heart ached for him. How cruel it seemed. One moment to be driving along a country lane on a blissful summer's day. The next to be having an argument that might have been avoided and an accident that changed two lives for ever. Ended one life altogether.

I don't know why I hadn't guessed that this would be the outcome of his story. Silvio would not have tormented me with so much detail about their short relationship otherwise. He wanted me to know something about the depth of Marco's feelings for Silke because it would help make sense of how he had been since. But the diary stopped at the suicide threat. Had Marco tried to kill himself? Was that how Silvio came to be in possession of his diary?

Suddenly, it felt as though there was no time to waste. Though Marco had written this story out in 2001, his threat was as real to me as if he had made it that day. I had to reach out to him. I had to break the silence.

Dear Marco,

I know I said you would never hear from me again but I find I can't keep my promise. I am writing to you with somewhat strange and embarrassing news. I find myself in possession of one of your diaries. It is from the year 2001. I am ashamed to say I read it. I am sure you know what it contains.

You'll want to know how I came across your diary, of course. I toyed with the idea of telling you that I stole it on the day I discovered your secret office but the truth is stranger still. I was going to say I stole it because, if not me, then it seems the real thief could be only one person. It was given to me by Silvio, via Bea, my former colleague at the university. He tracked her down and was insistent that the diary end up in my hands.

I know I should not have opened it. Or I should have sent it straight back to you as soon as I realised what the parcel contained. But perhaps it is a good thing that I didn't follow my moral compass. I feel I know you much better now.

Why didn't you tell me what really happened in 1999? If you had shared this information with me, then so much misunderstanding might have been avoided. Our relationship seems to have been characterised by secrets and concealment when I might have been able to support you.

I think I was unduly harsh when I wrote to you back in September. I was heedless of your hurt as I reacted from my own. I understand at last why you might feel you need to hide away. If you can bring yourself to forgive me for that, then perhaps we can start again?

Sarah

What next? Would my email open up a dialogue or another wound? I sat in bed with Marco's diary on my knees. I pressed my lips to the cover, as though I hoped I might be able to absorb some of the pain. Like kissing a small child 'better'. Poor Marco. For all this time, I had always assumed that he was behind the wheel when the accident happened. That would have been enough to make anyone feel bad, but in time, had it been that straightforward, his feelings of guilt might have passed. Anyone can make an error of judgement on an unfamiliar road. This was different. Marco believed that Silke had crashed the car through darker reasons than lack of experience. He thought the accident was a direct consequence of his inability to accept the way she looked. His prejudice. And it wasn't difficult to follow his logic.

Was it his fault after all? No. It couldn't be. Silke might have put her foot down because Marco's actions – or lack of action – had hurt her, but that could not make him as responsible as if he'd grabbed the wheel and yanked it, sending them into oblivion. Of course we are responsible for our actions towards other people but we're equally responsible for the way we react to insult, aren't we? Silke could have told Marco to grow a pair when he refused to take her to the party. She could have told him to fuck off there and then and taken the train back home. She could have refused to get into the pretentious car in the first place.

My head ached with questions.

'Oh Marco,' I silently begged him. 'Please write back.'

35

Monday 13th November 1933

Dear Diary,

I got another letter from Mummy this morning. She says the news coming out of Germany is playing on her nerves. Papa had a conversation with the Major who thinks it won't be long before there is war in Europe again. All the signs are pointing towards it. 'Sabres are being rattled,' he said.

'Come home now,' said Mummy. 'And bring your dear boy with you. Bring his mother too. And his sister. His whole family. We'll make space for them. But we would rather that you were here than over there. Herr Hitler is a strange sort of fish and the Major says one just can't know what he's going to do from one minute to the next.'

I wrote back assuring Mummy that all was perfectly fine where we were. The Major retired so long ago, how can he possibly know what's going on?

I certainly didn't tell Mummy about Marlene. Or about the incident at the Beluga. Or about the doorman from the Paradise Club who turned out a couple of SA boys who got a bit rowdy. He was found kicked to death in an alleyway two days later. You don't need to be a detective to work out who did it, though of course the detectives are not working especially hard to solve the crime at all.

The newspaper reports are right. Berlin is changing. Since Hitler gained power, he has been steadily changing the law to take even more. There is a feeling in the air, like when you know that it's getting too hot and there has to be a storm. There has been a drop in visitors to the club, even on amateur night. Schluter says this is how Hitler works. Just the threat of violence is enough to keep people away. Rumour is a powerful weapon of control.

I won't be bowed by it, however. I have been working on a new act. Marlene is making me a special costume based on one worn by the Follies in New York. When I first come out on to the stage, I will be wearing a long dress and looking as chaste as a novice nun. But the skirt will be held on only by poppers, so that I'll be able to whisk it away in a jiffy. I am also working on two new songs and a dance. I'm doing 'Burlington Bertie' as an opener. People need a laugh more than ever.

Tuesday 14th November 1933

Otto and I almost had our first argument this evening. We were talking about the Paradise Club murder. An arrest has been made, but not of any member of the Sturmabteilung. Instead, the police have arrested the old man who runs the tobacco kiosk near the U-Bahn station. It was obviously a set-up. That old man can barely speak for coughing. How could he possibly have kicked another man to death?

'I don't like what's going on. Perhaps you should go back to England like your mother suggests,' said Otto.

'What? And leave you here? No way.'

'I would follow you as soon as I finished my studies.'

'If Berlin is safe enough for your mother and your sister then I'm staying too.'

'I'm not sure it is safe enough for them, but you are different. You have an English passport. No one will stop you from leaving. Please. Go home to Surrey. At least, visit your parents so you can reassure them in person that you're OK.'

'I have been writing to Mother almost every day.'

'It's not the same. She will be much happier if she has seen you. Besides, don't you need to start planning our wedding? I'm sure it will be much easier for you to make arrangements if you are there in England yourself.'

'We should set a date,' I said. 'We don't need to worry about money. Papa will take care of all that. Just tell me when you want to do the deed.'

Otto got a faraway look in his eyes as he considered his diary.

'June 20th,' he said. 'I'd like it to be that day.'

'Is there a particular reason?'

'It's my father's birthday. My mother is always so sad on that day. I would like her to have a reason to remember the date with a smile. I think he would approve.'

'Then that's the day we will marry,' I said. 'How exciting! I'll be a June bride.'

I threw my arms round his neck and kissed him passionately.

'I'll wear white,' I said. 'Though I know I really oughtn't.'

'You are a bad girl,' Otto agreed. I flung myself on to the bed and he followed afterwards, biting me on the bottom.

'When you are Frau Schmidt, I shall have you tied to the bed all day long.'

'Darling,' I told him. 'I can't wait.'

36

Berlin, last October

Marco Donato. It seemed that ever since the first day I heard his name, I had been waiting to hear from that man. Since I had confessed to him that I'd read his diary, my wait was more agonising than usual. I couldn't help but imagine what might be going on in the palazzo. Had my confession cost Silvio his job? Had my prurience cost me any chance of being able to reconcile with Marco and apologise for the misunderstandings that had driven us apart?

I could not concentrate on anything. My English-language students' mistakes went uncorrected. When I tried to finish reading Kitty Hazleton's diaries, the words swam before my eyes. My thoughts were always with him. Sometimes, I saw him as the broken boy in the hospital bed. Sometimes as the broken man who hid himself away in the Palazzo Donato. Sometimes I saw the man of my dreams, damaged but enigmatic. Still sexy as hell.

Then at last, he wrote. It had taken three days. I opened his email with trepidation, expecting a short message of bile. I would deserve it. But that was not what I got.

Dear Sarah,

What can I say? I was surprised to get your email. I was even more surprised by the contents. You have my diary with you in Berlin? That was not what I expected to hear at all.

What do I think about it? I'm still not sure. I was angry, definitely. I have known Silvio my entire life and I would have called him the most honest man in Venice, Italy, the world. I have always been able to trust him. But perhaps there are moments when trust has to be broken for our own good. I have no doubt that Silvio sent you my diary with the very best of intentions. Don't worry about him losing his job, dear Sarah. It is I who needs to worry that Silvio might find reason one day to leave me. I would be lost without him, as I'm sure you appreciate now that you and I have met in the flesh. The broken flesh, in my case.

Still, I wish he had discussed my diary with me. I wish he had discussed with me how I feel about you. Perhaps I could have saved him the effort of subterfuge. Perhaps I would have sent you the diary myself. If I had believed that you would want to read it . . .

The truth is out. You know about the accident and the circumstances leading up to it. That you've written to me gives me hope that you don't think I'm the devil. Or perhaps you're saving your bile for later.

Of course, you know part of what happened next. I woke up in hospital in a room so white and bright that for a moment I wasn't sure I hadn't died and gone somewhere. Not Heaven, exactly, but somewhere else for sure. It would be a couple of days before the hospital was able to track down my parents. My father was in the States with his lover. My mother was in Sicily at the family villa with hers. I was entirely alone.

At first, I couldn't find my voice. And when I did find it, I could remember only a fraction of the English I had learned over the years. The nurses didn't seem to have a lot of time for me. I didn't know at the time that I was in one of your NHS hospitals and they were rushed off their feet. Overworked and underpaid, they didn't have time to try to decipher my Italian as well.

But eventually, someone had to tell me what had happened out there on the road. At last, the doctor came over. He checked my vital signs and told the hospital priest, who was standing waiting for him to finish, that now was the moment. He could reveal all.

The priest, who was Catholic – though he ministered to anyone of any faith – had spent some time in Italy when he was in the seminary. He spoke Italian well. Very formally. He had a kind face. I will never forget it. I will also never forget the hint of pity in his eyes as he looked at me.

The priest laid his hand over mine and I knew everything before he even tried to explain it in his textbook Italian.

'Lei non ce l'ha fatta.'

She didn't make it.

He didn't use quite the correct phrase but his meaning was clear.

He went on to explain to me that Silke had been alive when she was pulled from the wreckage of the car. She died on the way to hospital from a massive cardiac arrest brought on by the trauma of the accident.

The priest needed to ask me lots of questions. They didn't have any identification for Silke. Her passport would later be found by the owner of the cottage where we had stayed. Silke had left it behind in the drawer of the bedside table. I sometimes think she did it deliberately, to scupper my plan to drop her off at Heathrow. Was she thinking that I would give in and take her to the party after all?

'Do you know if she had any brothers or sisters?' the priest asked.

'I don't know.'

I couldn't remember. Later it would come back to me that there was a younger sister. A half-sister, Anna, who adored her. She was Silke's 'mini-me'.

When I was well enough to be moved from the Intensive Care Unit, I was taken by air ambulance to the private hospital where you met me.

By this time I could speak but I chose not to. There were enough conversations going on in my mind. I didn't need to have any in real life. As I lay in that bed, I replayed every moment of my time with Silke over and over in my head. Where did it go wrong? What could I have done differently? And every time I came to the conclusion that the only possible way it could have been different was if I had been brave enough to be proud to be with such a beautiful and unique woman.

She was dead because of me. Because of my arrogance and my cowardice. Because I was shallow.

It didn't help that the nurses at the private hospital seemed to agree with me. It's a funny thing, playing dumb. It's as if you are playing deaf too. The nurses acted as though because I wasn't speaking, I wasn't listening either. But I heard every word those women said and they helped to solidify my guilt.

'Must have been showing off, driving too fast.'

'What a waste of a young life.'

'That's what comes of growing up rich,' said one of them. 'If he'd ever had to work for his money like the rest of us, he wouldn't have been driving a Ferrari in the first place.'

They didn't seem to know that Silke had been driving the car. But that didn't matter. They were right in many ways. If I hadn't grown up rich, the story might have had a happier ending. Perhaps I wouldn't have made it as far as Berlin and Silke and I never even would have met. Or perhaps I would have grown up among people who understood that there are more important things than the 'right car' and the 'right clothes'. Perhaps I would have appreciated that the fact Silke was supporting herself by working at that old people's home so that she could sing in the evenings was way more impressive than the fact that Gianni's heiress girlfriend was getting singing lessons from Kylie Minogue's voice coach. My priorities were well and truly screwed up.

As I lay there in that bed, I thought of a thousand reasons why I should have been the one who died. The nurses amplified my thoughts. Even my parents chimed in with the view that I should not have hired such a fast car. Yours was the only voice that didn't join in the chorus of disapproval. When the other staff told you about the situation, you didn't agree that I had brought my misfortune upon myself. You were kind. You told me funny stories. Sometimes you sang as you were emptying the wastepaper basket or changing the water in the jug beside my bed. You even took care of my flowers and read my get-well cards out loud so that I would have the benefit of the good wishes of the friends who would soon forget me.

Once you touched my hair. You smoothed it back from my face. Do you remember? I craved that physical contact and yet it also frightened me. It forced me to be in the real world for a moment and I wasn't sure that I wanted to be in the real world again. I wanted to drown in my memories. Your voice was like a rope coiling around me, pulling me back to the shore. I didn't think I could make it. I didn't want to.

*   *   *

When I was finally back at the palazzo, I wrote to Silke's parents to tell them how sorry I was. I told them that their daughter had meant a great deal to me. I stopped short of telling them I'd loved her. I didn't hear anything in reply. Why would I? If anything, my letter was probably an affront to them. Me so very much alive and their daughter in the grave.

Meanwhile, my parents put on a rare united front and tried to persuade me to have the best surgeons in the world work on my face. First they made suggestions. I rebuffed them all. Then they told me I was being stupid. Then they begged me to let them help. I refused. My mother was terrified that my face would heal in the wrong way, but I had already decided that it did not matter if my face healed in the wrong way because no one would ever see it again.

The secret room you discovered was always there. When Ernesta the courtesan owned the house, she had the passageway built so that she could hide herself away if an unwanted visitor got past her staff. My grandfather used it when conducting his affairs. Then my father. Now it became my safe place. If I was properly hidden away the rest of the family could carry on as normal without having to worry about me. They soon gave up.

We kept the news of the accident very quiet. My mother told people I had moved to the States. I told her that it would have been better to tell people I'd become a monk. She hired another psychiatrist. I wrote the diary you have in your possession. I tried to kill myself with pills. Silvio found me in time.

My mother died eighteen months later. She had a heart attack. My father blamed it on the stress of seeing me – her only son – in such a state. Though they had been estranged for the best part of a decade at the time of her death, my father took it very badly and chose to stay away from Venice and me from then on. Too many memories. He died ten years later of a heart attack of his own.

With no one but myself to please, I closed the house down. With the exception of Silvio, I let the staff go. At last I could mourn Silke in peace. Until you came back to me.

When you wrote to me about the library, your familiar name attracted my attention, but it wasn't an uncommon name. There must be thousands of Sarah Thomsons in this world. But for some reason, because you had written to me by hand and not by email, I thought I would investigate further. I looked you up on the website. I saw your face. You thought I never looked at you all those times you came into my hospital room? You were wrong.

I never intended to strike up any kind of relationship with you. Not even a friendship. I decided I would let you use the library as my way of thanking you for having tried to comfort me while I was in the hospital. I emailed to tell you that you could come to the palazzo and that was supposed to be that. I don't know what led me to respond to your quick reply with the exhortation that you should 'play harder to get'.

But that was supposed to be that.

Of course, I was in the house when you arrived. I have not left the palazzo since my father's private funeral on San Michele. I had my breakfast as usual and then, just before ten o'clock, I positioned myself in the gallery overlooking the courtyard, ready to watch you walk through.

I heard you before I saw you, chattering to Silvio just as you'd once chattered to me. You were talking about nothing in particular. Admiring the garden, I think. But your voice took me right back to the hospital. It was a strange sensation to say the least. I was both disturbed and comforted. I felt the minute I heard your voice again that you had been sent to me for a reason.

While Silvio showed you into the library, I crept down the stairs and slid into my secret room to watch you as you worked. You took your coat off. You were looking around with something approaching awe. Your mouth was slightly open, in that childlike way you have.

You sat down at last. Luciana's papers were in the box in front of you. You put your hands on top of the box as though you were trying to absorb some feeling through the cardboard.

You were so careful. I was glad to see that. Not that I ever thought you would be any different. And as you opened the box, I remembered your kind hands pushing the hair back from my forehead when I was too weak to do it myself. My heart began to ache.

You returned that evening with a thank you note and when you asked if you might deliver it in person, Silvio sent you away, but he did as you asked and he brought the letter straight to me. I know he was curious as to why I had let you into the library, when I'd sent away all-comers for so long. I didn't tell him that I thought we might have met before. I just told him that you'd written so beautifully and it was clear that you were so keen to know about Luciana, that it wasn't my place to keep you from her diaries.

Silvio knows the truth now, of course. I had to tell him after the day you burst in and found me. He tried to tell me I should go after you, or at least call you at your hotel and insist that you come back, but I was too agitated. I didn't know what to do for the best. I told him you should not be allowed back in and then I wrote you the letter, which he delivered, telling you to give up all hope.

But going back to that night I held your first thank you letter, after your first day in the library, I couldn't sleep. I couldn't wait for you to come back the following day so that I could watch you again. I felt compelled to try to make a connection with you, although as far as my heart was concerned it might be the most dangerous thing I'd ever done. I think I started to fall in love that day.

The simple truth is that I don't deserve anyone's love. Silke died because I wasn't strong enough to tell the world I loved her. She lost everything because of me. I survived as a melted shell of the proud young arsehole I was before. Talk about a parable.

That's why I can't expect you to want to be with me. I am who I am because I am cowardly and proud. You deserve to be with someone you can be proud to walk alongside. I picture you with a man who stands tall and speaks the truth. I am a small man, Sarah, because I was small-minded. My punishment is to have had you come into my life and know that I have to let you go.

Yours,
Marco

I cried that night. I cried for Silke, for Marco and for myself. What should I do? I now knew that I had fallen for a man who would always, in some way, belong to a woman who had come along before me. He had tried to kill himself to be with her. The thought of him swallowing those pills would not leave me. Would he ever get past that? Would I ever be able to occupy the number-one space in his heart?

We were doomed from the start. I had to make this the end.

37

Surrey, 20th January 1934

I have to write this down so that one day I can tell our children exactly what happened at the Boom Boom. God knows I don't feel like writing now but I must. I left my diary in the hotel. Such a stupid thing to do, but I thought I would be able to go back for it.

It was the 8th of December. Otto had no lectures so we spent the afternoon in bed together, eating sandwiches as we sat up against the pillows and making love three times in the space of six hours. We made plans for Sunday. Otto's mother would want us to have lunch with the family, of course, but after that, Otto said we should go to the ice-rink in the Tiergarten to get into the Christmas spirit. I agreed that it sounded like a lovely idea though I haven't worn ice-skates since I was eleven. He promised he would not let me fall down.

Everything felt so wonderful. The thought of Christmas so close made us feel optimistic. It made us so desirous of each other. The little fire in my room warmed the skin on Otto's back as he lay face-down in the pillows, exhausted after our third bout of lovemaking. I put my nose to his warm flesh and breathed in the biscuity scent

257

of him. There was something so comforting about the smell of my Otto. I wanted to breathe him in for ever.

But soon it was six o'clock and we had to get up and get ready for work.

I put on most of my make-up at home, as usual, leaving only the false eyelashes for Marlene to fix when we got to the club. Otto, who had to do nothing more than wash and comb his hair, sat down on the bed to watch me getting ready.

'I am the luckiest man in the world,' he said. 'Because I will be able to watch you get ready to go out every night for the rest of my life.'

'Who says we'll be going out every night?' I asked. 'Won't there be nights when we just want to stay at home with each other?'

I got up and walked across to him. I sat down on his knees and threw my arms round his neck. He kissed me, deeply and passionately. We tipped backwards on to the bed and he rolled so that he was on top of me. He looked down into my eyes and smoothed my hair away from my forehead.

'I don't ever want to be without you,' he said.

'I feel exactly the same way.'

Then, though we really didn't have time, we made love again. We didn't properly undress. He pulled down his trousers and I pushed up my skirt. It was, as Marlene would put it, just a quickie. But how wonderful it was to be filled by him and to feel his urgency as he pushed into me. I never tired of seeing his face as he came. That look of shock, bewilderment and ultimate satisfaction.

'I'll have to go to the Boom Boom smelling of you,' I chided him.

'You have no idea how excited that makes me feel,' he said.

We walked to the club hand in hand. It was a beautiful evening. The sky was clear and the stars were bright. The streets were busy with shoppers, admiring the Christmas window displays. Even the SA goons who hung around on the corner by what used to be the Beluga Bar nodded a greeting.

At the club, Marlene and Isadora were deep in a tête-à-tête about Isadora's complicated love life. Schluter was looking harassed. He said his niece had just announced she wanted to become a doctor and he wasn't sure how on earth the family was going to pay for it. But I could tell he would pay for it. It was obvious that he was very proud of her decision.

The band was already tuning up. Otto kissed me on the end of the nose and went to join them. He was about halfway across the room when he turned and hurried back to me again. This time he folded his arms round me and gave me a proper kiss that made Marlene and Isadora whoop with delight. The band all applauded.

'What was that for?' I asked him.

'It was just to remind you that I love you. I want you to be able to feel my lips on yours for the whole of your act.'

I grinned at the idea. 'I can't wait to feel them in reality later on.'

★　　★　　★

259

At eight o'clock the club officially opened. There were people already on the doorstep when Schluter opened the doors. The fast-approaching end of the year made people want to kick up their heels. One last burst of debauchery before January's clean slate. They were ready to make merry indeed.

As usual, Friday's show would be partly devoted to the amateurs. Marlene would open with her routine, then I would follow with two songs. After that, the amateurs would take the stage. We hoped there would be at least five. Assuming that there were, I would not be back on stage until the very end of the evening.

I spent my time backstage writing another letter to Mother, telling her I had persuaded Otto that we should come to England in the new year and would Papa please wire the money for our passage. Writing the letter made me feel very happy. Otto had taken quite some persuading. He didn't want to have to borrow money off my father to visit him for the first time. But I reminded him that he was keen for me to go back home. If he came with me, I would, and perhaps I would stay for a little longer while he came back to finish off his exams.

I was so excited by the thought of showing Otto around my home town. I felt sure he would love it. I asked Mummy if she would arrange a Sunday lunch at which Otto might meet the extended family. My aunt would adore him, I knew.

I finished my letter and took my place in the wings. The atmosphere in the club was pretty good by now.

The Steinway Sisters, who were in fact two elderly

brothers who liked to dress up as young girls, put in an appearance. They were always extremely popular. Every week, they came up with a completely new act. They would take the most popular song of the moment and come up with a wonderful routine to go with it. That night, they sang 'Was That The Human Thing To Do?' by the Boswell Sisters. They were note-perfect as usual, harmonising beautifully. They had new outfits for the occasion too: matching blue dresses with demure lace collars. They might have been schoolgirls fresh from the convent were it not for their wrinkled faces and stubbled chins.

They were followed by the young man who liked to dress as Jean Harlow. He too was a regular. He was certainly dedicated to his art. Like the sister-brothers, he was constantly honing his routine, making sure that he kept up with the very latest hits. He made a shocking Hollywood goddess, however. I once asked Marlene if she couldn't give him some advice on hair and make-up.

'What? And make him good enough to take my job?' was her response.

Well, Marlene didn't need to worry about competition for the moment. As usual, Jean Harlow gave his best but came nowhere near hitting the notes. And as usual, Otto changed key three times in an attempt to accommodate him, getting so low at one point that 'Love Me Tonight' began to sound like a funeral march. I watched from the side of the stage with Schluter, who shook his head in despair.

'Where are his friends?' Schluter asked. 'Why does

nobody tell him that the crowds only cheer for an encore because they want to laugh?'

I shrugged. 'Perhaps he knows the truth,' I suggested. 'But he loves dressing up so much and this is the only place he can do it.'

'Might not be able to do it here for much longer,' said Schluter. 'Not if Herr Hitler has his way.'

I shivered at the mere mention of that man's name.

'Oh Jerry,' I said. 'Perhaps Adolf will get some Christmas spirit too.'

On stage, Jean Harlow's rendition of 'Love Me Tonight' came to a tortuous, warbling end. Marlene led the applause. There were no more amateur acts that evening. It was my turn to go on.

I was excited to be debuting a new routine and my new costume too. At first glance, it looked like an extremely elegant silver evening dress, but it was held together by a precarious arrangement of buttons and poppers that would enable me to transform it from demure to shocking with just a couple of flicks. I also had a hat. From the front, it looked like the sort of bowler city gents wore to work. From behind, it resembled a cowboy's Stetson.

Otto hit the first note of my first song. Ordinarily, I would already be in the centre of the stage. That night, I was going to try something different. My entrance would be part of the act. I had modelled my new routine on something I had once seen at the Kakadu. First, I gave a high side-kick, so that all the audience saw was my leg. Then I snaked out an arm. Then arm and leg moved up and down together. I hope that from the audience, it looked as though my two limbs were floating effortlessly. Behind the curtain, I was leaning heavily on Schluter so that I didn't fall over. Finally I poked out my head.

The ambience was great. No matter how bad the amateur acts had been, they had certainly warmed things up for me. The crowd clapped along as I sang 'Burlington Bertie' with my personalised lyrics.

Then I galloped through my cowboy song. I'd practised the dance a hundred times but I still felt as though my thigh muscles would snap from the strain of remaining at half-squat – or demi-plié, as Marlene liked to call it – for every chorus.

'Stop complaining. It'll make it easier for you to go on top,' Marlene always said when I moaned during practice.

As I came to the end of the cowboy song I whipped off the last section of my skirt, so that I was standing in my leotard. The crowd whooped their appreciation. The fat guy in the front row looked close to having a coronary. While I was taking a moment before my next song, I called to the barman to send a glass of water to the front.

'Don't want you dying on me,' I told the fat guy, with a wink. 'The night is still young!'

That seemed to delight him. He slapped his thighs and rocked back and forth in his chair. He was having a capital night. Everybody was.

Having caught my breath, I turned to Otto and gave him the nod that told him I was ready to carry on. The lights changed so that I was standing in the centre of a single spot, slightly pink in tone, just as I liked it.

'Ladies and gentlemen,' I said. 'It's been a real

pleasure to sing for you this evening. Thank you for being such a warm and welcoming crowd. To end tonight's entertainment, I'm going to sing one of my favourite songs for you, but not before I've asked you to put your hands together one more time for the fabulous amateurs who gave their all for your delight.'

The crowd duly clapped and cheered.

'And for Marlene, our mistress of ceremonies.'

Marlene pastiched my act by poking her own hefty leg round the curtain. That provoked a gale of laughter. 'And for our wonderful musicians.' I blew a kiss towards my love.

'Thank you everybody and now . . .'

I looked to Otto for my cue.

Then he started to play 'The Song Is Ended'.

Though we had practised our escape half a dozen times before the dreadful day came when we needed to put the plan into action for real, it seemed so much harder than I remembered. I bumped my head on the beam in the tunnel. The beam that we had all been warned of a thousand times. I twisted my ankle, even though I was wearing my flattest shoes.

Perhaps there was a part of me that wanted to be caught. I couldn't bear the fact that up there, in the club, Otto was facing down the Sturmabteilung without me.

'Keep going,' said Marlene. 'Otto will be fine. Idiot though his brother is, I'm sure that when it comes down to it, Gerd will do his best to help him. He'll call the dogs off. Have no fear.'

'Please, God, let that be true!' I exclaimed.

Schluter turned to 'ssshh' me. We were going through the cellar of the Paradise Hotel at that point. The hotel's owner was sympathetic to our plight but he could not be certain that all his staff felt the same way. For that reason, the owner said that he was happy for us to use his cellar as an escape route, so long as we didn't tell him about it. He wanted to remain genuinely ignorant.

Feigning ignorance was the best defence when faced by the Sturmabteilung.

After what seemed like an eternity in the cellars under the Ku'damm, we came out into a service tunnel for the U-Bahn. We walked west, just as Otto had instructed, and emerged into the soft night air somewhere near Charlottenburg. Schluter had friends there, who were going to take us all in until the danger passed. The following day, we would wait for Otto's assurance that it was safe to return to our part of town and gather the rest of our belongings. For now we had to lay low.

I could hear nothing but 'The Song is Ended'. That tune, now hateful to me, would not be chased from my head, no matter what I tried to think about instead.

'Tell me something happy,' I begged Marlene.

She tried to tell me a joke but her usual wit fell flat. I knew that nothing would ever be the same again. I put my hands to my face and breathed in the smell of him that lingered still.

The following morning we heard the terrible news that the club had burned to the ground. The investigators were saying that the fire was caused by someone leaving a lighted cigarette near a feathered costume in one of the dressing rooms. We all knew that wasn't the case. Schluter had always been very aware of the dangers of fire in a theatre. No one dared smoke backstage for fear of a lecture. Besides, to have burned with such ferocity and speed, the fire would have needed some help. It would have needed petrol. Indeed, one of Schluter's spies saw charred petrol cans among the ruins. The cans were never mentioned in the official report.

As for Otto. We heard that he had been taken into custody, together with Arnold, the big bass player, who had stayed behind to back him up. The grounds for their arrest were that Otto had punched a police officer, who was trying to calm down a disagreement between Otto and a customer who was querying a bill. It was the biggest cock and bull story you ever heard. But we were learning that the SA was not overly bothered about the truth if a story would better fit their needs.

'Better in custody than in that fire,' said Marlene, which was true. But I found it hard to believe, as she did, that Otto's brother would make sure he didn't stay in custody long. Not when the club itself had been treated with such brutal disregard. Not when it was clear that the SA had come prepared to destroy the Boom Boom, not just close it down.

Given the way that things had turned out, Schluter decided that it wasn't safe for any of us to go back to within a mile of the Ku'damm even two days later.

'Those thugs will be angry,' he said. 'They must have felt outsmarted when they got backstage and discovered we had already gone.'

'Or perhaps they thought we'd burn to death in the cellar,' said Isadora.

Whatever, it would not be safe to go back for a long time. We stuck together at Schluter's friends' house for a couple of days, then Schluter said to me, 'Kitty, I think it's time for you to go home.'

'But you just said I shouldn't,' I began.

'Not home to the Hotel Frankfort. Home to England. Home to your parents. This country is changing. Right now, it is people like me who are the target of hatred, but it won't be long before the net is cast wider. You're an Englishwoman. There are people in this city who think the English are to blame for the way this country suffered after the Great War.'

'I've never experienced any nastiness because of my nationality,' I protested.

'Not yet but every day, Herr Hitler is focusing the blame on someone else. When he's got rid of us Jews and the gays and the communists and anyone who disagrees with him, you will be next.'

Marlene agreed with him.

'You should go back to your parents,' she said. 'What will you do if you stay here? It will be hard for you to find another job. It's too risky for you to go on the stage in another club. Your German isn't good enough for you to find work in an office. You must go home to England and ask your parents for their help. Get together as much money as you can, then when Otto gets out of custody, he can follow you and you can work out what to do next from there.'

I didn't want to hear it but I knew Marlene was right.

'But I should wait for Otto to get out of custody first and travel with him.'

A week later, however, Otto had still not been released. I wanted to visit his mother and his sister, but Marlene discouraged me. She said it might cause trouble with Gerd. Instead, she had me write a letter to them – she would make sure they got it – and then she insisted that I wire my parents to arrange my passage home.

38

Berlin, last October

The day after I got Marco's email, I was no closer to knowing what I should do. Fortunately it was the weekend, so that when I woke with eyes all red and puffy from crying, there was no need to worry about what someone might think. I stayed in my pyjamas until lunchtime, rereading Marco's words and thinking about his conclusion. We were still no closer to being together. Writing the story out had not, as his one-time psychiatrist hoped it might, changed Marco's mind about the guilt he had carried since 1999. Not even with fifteen years' reflection. At the time it had driven him to a suicide attempt. Now he just seemed numb. I wasn't sure that I had the energy to try to make him see things differently again. Neither was I sure I had the right.

I stayed in for most of the day but I had to venture out in the evening because I'd run out of food. I ate dinner alone in a café, oblivious to the Saturday-night revellers around me. I was lost in Marco's world. Marco's pain.

Eventually, I wandered back to the Hufelandstrasse.

'Sarah!'

I was halfway up the stairs when I heard Herr Schmidt call from the dark hallway. 'Sarah?'

'Yes, Herr Schmidt.'

'I wonder if you have some time to talk.'

269

'Now?' I was surprised. It was almost 10 p.m.

'Yes. If you please.'

His voice sounded wavering. I wondered if he was feeling unwell. I turned and went back down the stairs and followed him into his study, with its warm orange light. He offered to make me some tea. When he turned to go to the kitchen, he seemed unsteady on his legs.

'Are you feeling OK?' I asked him.

'At my age,' he told me, 'one very rarely feels OK.'

I insisted on making the tea myself. We sat down, him in his usual chair and me opposite him on the sofa.

'I need to tell you the truth,' he said.

I cocked my head to one side.

'About what?'

'About my life in Berlin before the war. About the woman to whom those diaries belonged.'

'I didn't think you knew her.'

'Oh, I knew her,' he said. 'I was in love with her.'

'You're Otto!' I said. 'I had my suspicions. I started to think it was you when Kitty described your eyes, the piano-playing, this house . . . Why didn't you tell me the diaries belonged to your fiancée?'

Herr Schmidt shook his head. 'If only. My Christian name is Gerd.'

Gerd the Nazi. Gerd the Stormtrooper. It seemed impossible. How could the gentle man I had come to know, who played the piano so beautifully and with such emotion, have been in thrall to such evil?

'You're shocked,' he said.

'No,' I lied. I sank back into my chair. 'I mean . . . yes. Why did you keep her diary?'

'Because I thought I would see her again one day. I was

sure we would meet again face to face. But I haven't seen her since December 8th 1933.'

Which was the date of the last diary entry, I observed. That morning, Kitty had written about the difficulty of finding the perfect Christmas present for her love.

'The day after the club was burned, I went to the Hotel Frankfort to find her. I promise you I was going to take her somewhere safer. I was going to send her to a cousin in Munich while I sorted things out. She wasn't there so I put her things into a shoebox and brought them here.'

'What happened on the 8th December?' I asked.

Gerd grew visibly distressed. He took a deep breath that seemed to make his whole body rattle.

'When I think now about being a member of the Sturmabteilung, it makes me ill to remember it, but back then, it felt to me as though the SA had given me a purpose in life. I lost my father when I was young. The local mayor took me under his wing because of a favour I'd done him when I was just twelve years old. I pulled his son from a pond. He'd fallen through the ice.

'After that I was the little hero. When Papa died, the Mayor promised that he would be a father to me and he was. But whereas my father was a compassionate liberal, the Mayor had political views of a very different stripe. He was a member of the Party and he encouraged me to join.

'I was young. I was fatherless. I had no rudder to help steer me through the difficult waters of adolescence. I could not resist the siren call of an organisation that was offering to be both father and mother to me. I thought my own mother was rather silly. I wish I had known just how strong she really was. She bore all my lectures with humour. She forgave me when I committed the ultimate crime.

'I was so stupid. My brother, Otto, tried to show me the

error of my ways. But I thought it was he who had been corrupted. He was studying to be a lawyer but to raise money for his studies he worked in a nightclub called the Boom Boom. It was a Jewish-owned nightclub for transvestites and gay people. Berlin was very open-minded back then. The Party was not.

'I was with the group of men who were sent to close the Boom Boom down. I had warned Otto in an oblique way that the moment was coming but I could have done more. I could have told him the very night when we'd be knocking on his door. As it happened, someone else must have tipped them off, because when the show ended, the artists did not even come back on stage for a final bow. They disappeared from the theatre as if by magic. Kitty was with them, of course. It took us a long time to discover the secret passageway that led from the theatre's cellar through the hotel next door to the U-Bahn.

'But my brother, he did not escape. While his colleagues slipped away underground and the customers fled at the sight of our guns, he and the double bass player remained. Otto was in front of the stage in the orchestra pit. He just sat there and waited. They were no match for us. My colleagues pulled him from his piano stool and started roughing him up. I was behind the curtain, looking for the man who owned the theatre, when that happened. Apparently, Otto appealed to me to help him. One of my juniors came to find me to ask what should be done next. I had them bring my brother up into the spotlight. Then I stood in front of him. Over him. I wanted to humiliate him. I was still stinging over Kitty. I'd told her I loved her, you see, but she'd never have left Otto for me. I hated him for that. It seemed like the latest in a long line of insults he'd thrown at me. He was always better than me. He was taller, more clever. He made people laugh. At last, in the Boom Boom, I had the chance to be top dog.

'"Join the Party," I told him. "Join the Party and then we'll know you're serious about being rehabilitated."

'Otto snorted. "I don't need rehabilitation. I'll never join your fucking party," he told me. "Your party is a joke. You prance around interfering with the private lives of perfectly decent people when your leader is the biggest queen this city has ever known." That was when it all went wrong.

'He had insulted the Führer. None of my comrades would stand for that. They laid in to him again, pushing me out of the way to get to him. I didn't join in but I couldn't tell them to stop. Not when he had breached the ultimate taboo. A Stormtrooper's duty was to the Führer even above the country. Family came a distant third. I had to let them do it or take a bullet in the head myself. How I wish I'd taken that honourable path.

'After they had beaten him up, I let them take him away to the police station on some trumped-up assault charge. Later, he was charged again as a pimp under the new law against dangerous habitual criminals. My brother, a pimp. You never heard anything so ridiculous. But it was easy to make it stick because of the nature of the Boom Boom. He was sent to a work camp.'

Herr Schmidt – Gerd Schmidt, as I now knew him – wiped at his tired blue eyes.

'He died three months later of typhoid.'

'When I heard that he was dead,' Herr Schmidt continued the story later on, 'a part of me died too. I knew I was entirely guilty. I could have saved him that night. He might still be alive. I killed him and since that day I have never allowed myself to have what he could not have. I never married. I never had children. I have never allowed myself to dance or sing or laugh. I never even play happy music. I have tried to live as though I too were dead in the ground.'

Shocked as I was by the circumstances of Otto's death, I reached out and took Gerd by the hand. He suddenly looked all his ninety-something years. His guilt and pain were etched deep on his face. I could only feel profoundly sorry for him.

'I was a coward. I was a bully. I was full of envy. I could have saved my brother,' he said.

'You didn't know what would happen to him,' I said, trying to find an excuse.

'I could have guessed. I had seen it happen plenty of times before. I should have put a bullet through my head for what I did to my brother, my mother, my sister and Kitty on that evening at the Boom Boom. It was a long time before I realised how wrong I was. Will you find her? Will you let her know that I'm sorry?'

'I'll do my best,' I said.

'You have to do it quickly,' said Gerd. 'I don't think either of us have much time.'

I squeezed his hand again. His bright blue eyes were liquid with tears. I could tell that he was not a man who had cried often, despite his lifetime of grieving, and I did not want to embarrass him. At the same time, I sensed that what he really needed – needed rather than wanted – was a proper, full-on hug. I got up from my seat and half-knelt in front of him so that I could throw my arms round him. The moment my hands closed behind his back, I felt him shudder with a powerful sob.

We stayed like that for a little while, him crying and me just holding him, hoping he would draw strength from my closeness. Eventually I felt him straighten up a little, a subtle signal that I should let him go.

'I will find her for you,' I promised. 'And she will forgive you, I know.'

I don't know how I knew. I suppose it was the right thing to say. But the funny thing was that, as I said it, I had the strangest feeling it would turn out to be true.

'You are a good girl, Sarah. And you deserve to have all the happiness I have not allowed myself to have. Promise me that one day you will have a husband and a family.'

'That's a promise I can't make,' I said. 'Though I shall certainly wish for it to come true.'

My conversation with Gerd was the impetus I needed. Gerd had spent most of his adult life atoning for what had happened to Otto, but now he was ready to ask forgiveness and move on. Perhaps Marco could get to that place too. I had to help him find it before it was too late.

Though it was late at night and I was tired, I opened up my laptop and began to put down my thoughts. I would not let Marco be so self-indulgent, for, ultimately, that was what it was.

I finished writing to Marco at four o'clock in the morning. I wrote:

Dear Marco,

I still want to see you. Whatever you think, your diary has not changed the way I feel about you except to make me more sure you are a man worthy of love. You have spent the past fifteen years doing penance. Now it's time to stop. I believe that Silke sent me to you. She sent me to be at your bedside in the hospital and she sent me to you in Venice, to tell you that the time for mourning is over.

Silke did not die because of you, Marco. Your terrible accident was just that: an accident. A split second's difference in timing and you would have both lived. You would have sat together by the side of the road, shaking

275

with shock at your near miss. You would have clung on to each other and promised never to have such a stupid argument again. Then you would have realised how silly it was to think your friends wouldn't want to meet her and you would have insisted that she come to London after all and you'd have walked into that party with your head held high and your friends would have loved her. You would have wondered why you ever thought they wouldn't.

I don't believe Silke intended to crash the car at all. She didn't want to die and she didn't want to kill you. She was in love with you. She wanted to shake you out of your cowardice. That's all. She just shook too hard. If Silke was anything like the woman I've come to know through your diary over the past few nights, then she would have been appalled to think that her momentary expression of frustration and pain could end up hurting you so badly.

Imagine a different outcome. Imagine you had taken her to the party. Imagine you had a wonderful night. The following day you would have driven her to the airport and waved her off, promising to meet again as soon as you could. Perhaps it would have been the start of a wonderful relationship but perhaps you wouldn't have stayed together for ever. Perhaps she would have left you for someone else. She could have grown up to be a very ordinary woman who would look back on the time you spent together with fondness but nothing more. Perhaps, while her husband snored on the sofa, she would have put down the book she was reading for a moment and remembered you and smiled to herself as she thought about how young and hot-headed you both were.

And without your grief to seal you in aspic, you wouldn't have stayed the same either. You wouldn't have carried on being so shallow and thoughtless. That's the privilege of the very young. Other, smaller tragedies would have chipped away at your edges. You might have fallen in love and found yourself rejected a dozen times or more. You might have married. You might have divorced. Had you had children, your heart would have been pricked all over with the pain of loving them.

You too, would think of Silke from time to time and you would smile to remember that first night you spent together in Berlin.

What I am trying to say is simply this: I believe that Silke would want you to be happy again. She would want you to live life to the full on her behalf. She might even want you to be with someone like me.

Come to Berlin, Marco. Finish the story.

Your ever loving,

Sarah

I sent my email and sat back, looking at the glowing screen. I hoped I had said the right thing. I hoped Marco would appreciate that I had written to him from a place of love. I hoped he wouldn't think it was sentimental claptrap.

I undressed and got into bed, feeling more tired than I had ever done. However, I wasn't able to sleep. Every time I thought I was feeling dozy, my brain would kick in again, wanting to go over everything I'd said and written and done for pretty much my entire life. It was one of those nights when the past will not stay in the background and the future looks precarious and uncertain.

All the following day, I heard nothing in response to my email. I tried not to think about it, but of course it was the only thing on my mind. I went into the office and I met Clare for lunch. I think I did a pretty good impression of someone without a care in the world, but my hand was constantly on my BlackBerry, waiting for the vibration that told me an email had come through. Fortunately, Clare was too eager to tell me about her latest date to notice that I was distracted and back at the office, no one even looked up from their screens when I came in.

Evening came. I walked back to my flat, narrowly escaping death as I checked my BlackBerry one more time in the middle of the road.

I had an email but it was not from Marco. It was from a woman called Katherine Naylor. It read:

> My grandmother has asked me to write to you on her behalf. She dictated the following as arthritis makes it difficult for her to type these days. She is almost a hundred years old! She says she is very glad you tried to track her down. The diaries are almost certainly hers. I have transcribed some pages she wrote on her return to England. The rest is as she told me earlier today.

I opened the attached file. Another story was coming to an end.

39

It was right before Christmas 1933 that I left Berlin in the middle of the night. My parents had wired the money for my passage as soon as they received my telegram. My mother's response was brief but it reeked of worry. I have to admit that during my time hiding out with Marlene and the gang, I had grown more worried myself. Otto's sister had sent me a letter saying she was certain that Gerd would do what he could to have Otto sprung but two weeks had passed since the night the Boom Boom burned. If Otto had really punched a policeman in the heat of a fight, he would have been home by now. He was being detained under the laws that he had warned me about. The Nazi Party didn't need a good reason to throw someone in jail even then.

Before I left, I gave my engagement pearl to Schluter.

'Take this,' I told him. 'I've got the money I need to get back to England now but I don't know how Otto will raise the cash to follow me. Please, sell the pearl and make sure he gets what you raise for it. He can use it to pay a lawyer and with what's left over he can get out of Berlin.'

Schluter promised that he would get the best price and he did, though alas Otto would never get to use the money.

That night in 1933, Marlene accompanied me to the main train station. It was still strange to see her in her man's clothes. It was strange too, how she changed when she was not in costume. Suddenly, she reminded me of my father with his Victorian manners. She insisted on carrying what few belongings I had. She was a proper gent.

'I'll see you soon,' I said, as we embraced on the platform at the Lehrter Bahnhof.

'Yes,' said Marlene. 'I'll see you very soon indeed.'

I would never see her in the flesh again.

I did not sleep for the entire journey. Even when I was out of Germany and well away from the Nazi bullies, I regarded everyone with suspicion.

My parents were ecstatic to see me. They were waiting on the dock at Dover when my boat arrived. My mother was dressed to the nines. My father had a new car. When Mummy reached out her arms to me, I finally crumpled in shock. Not only had I not slept in four nights, I had not eaten anything either. I was so light and weak that Papa was able to lift me like a child. He laid me down on the back seat of the car and Mummy covered me with her new fur coat.

It was a long drive back to High Trees, my childhood home, which I had left in disgrace a couple of years before, off to finishing school in Munich. My parents spoke in whispers, but I could hear every word.

'What on earth has happened to her? He must have called the engagement off.'

'I knew it,' said my father. 'I knew it. He was never a lawyer. She met him in a nightclub, for goodness' sake. Now she's found out that he's a liar and she's been left heartbroken. Still, at least it happened before the wedding so we won't have any nastiness with a divorce. He must have been a gold-digger.'

I didn't have the strength to tell them the truth. Not then.

Later that day, once my mother had forced some chicken soup down me while I sat propped against the pillows in bed, I did tell her the truth of the matter. She listened with growing concern.

'But why would they put him in custody, dear? It must be more complicated than you imagine. It can't only be because he was working in a nightclub that was owned by a Jew?'

It would be a long while before my mother fully understood the whole story. Years, in fact. At first, the trickle of Jewish immigrants arriving in London would not seem to be such a significant story. After 1939, we'd all know differently. And then my parents would understand that my grief for Otto was not the simple grief of a girl who'd lost a boyfriend. They understood that I had lost the love of my life.

Back in 1933, my parents were still horribly confused, but at least after that first night, my mother did not mention again the Christmas party she had planned. I would not have to be paraded in front of the neighbours. I was in no state to meet anybody. Not without news of Otto. The last thing I wanted to do was celebrate.

Marlene wrote to me in the new year. She told me everything she knew about Otto, which was not much. The last she had heard was that he had been charged with pimping, of all things, and sent to a prison camp. No one had been able to visit him.

Marlene herself was living a very different life from the one she had enjoyed before. She had given up dressing as a woman, she said. Isadora, too, was a changed man. They had not seen Schluter for a while. He had gone to visit relatives. Someone thought he might have got out of Germany altogether and gone to New York, where he had a cousin who ran a club that was almost a twin of the Boom Boom.

I received a last letter from Marlene in 1938. By that time, Hitler had turned his attentions to the gay community. Though Marlene had toned his life down, I doubt he'd really had the willpower to stay away from rent-boys altogether. I can only imagine that he followed Otto to a camp.

In 1941, Schluter wrote to me from New York to tell me he thought it was time to put the money from Otto's pearl to good use. I agreed he should release the funds to an underground group helping Jewish refugees escape Germany. I know Otto would have approved.

During the Second World War, I did my bit for the war effort by becoming a land girl and working on the farm attached to the Spencer family house. I didn't tell anyone about my time in Berlin. It would have been too hard. While they were living in fear of the Blitzkrieg, no one would have wanted to hear how much I had loved my time in Germany. How a German had become my true love.

I tried to find out what had happened to Otto but got nowhere. And then it was twelve years after I'd left Berlin in the middle of the night. The war was over and the Nazis had been vanquished. Otto would be free to contact me at last. But he didn't. And eventually I had to accept that either he was dead or he had made himself a life that had no room for me in it. I had to do the same.

I finally married at the age of thirty, which was very late in those days. My husband was a good man. I don't think he was ever in love with me, as I was never properly in love with him, but we had great affection for one another and once we had our two boys, we were very happy indeed. I made an effort to think about Otto less often. I allowed myself to be truly sad only once a year: on his birthday.

Decades passed. I have grandchildren now. Great-grandchildren. But still from time to time I'll see a familiar-looking young man walking down the street and I'll have to catch my breath before I remember that my long-lost love would be more than a hundred years old now. Otto is eternally young to me. They all are: Otto, his sister Helga and Gerd.

I wrote back to Kitty at once, telling her that Gerd was still alive and was eager to talk to her. The following day I received another email, dictated via her granddaughter.

I assumed that Gerd must have been lost in the war too. I sent a letter to the address in Hufelestrasse in the 1950s. I heard nothing in response. You must tell him that I meant everything I said back then. I forgive him. Otto would have forgiven him. My only feelings for Gerd are those of a loving sister.

A week later, an actual letter arrived from England.

40

Gerd asked me to read the letter to him. We sat opposite each other in his tidy sitting room. I knew now that the table where we had dined together was the table where Kitty and Otto had announced their engagement. I knew that the clock on the wall was the clock that ticked in the awkward silence after Gerd heard the news.

'Are you sure you want me to read to you?' I asked.

'Yes,' he said. 'Because of your voice. When I hear your voice, with your accent, I can almost hear Kitty. It will make it as though she is speaking to me.'

I read aloud.

Otto would not have wanted you to punish yourself for the rest of your life. He loved you and would constantly remind me that beneath the SA uniform, you were still the little brother who had shown such generosity and bravery as a small child. He was certain that had your father lived, you would not have been taken in by the Party. Instead, you would have drawn strength from your papa and become a great force for good.

Losing Otto changed all our lives, but when I look back over the vast plain of years, spreading out behind me, I see there are glittering moments of happiness that I might not have experienced if Otto and I had not been parted that day. I have my children and my grandchildren and I have told them all Otto's story. I hope I have passed on to them even a tenth of your brother's sense of justice, his generosity and his kindness, his ability to see the good in everyone. Even you. Especially you, Gerd.

Know that Otto loved you, and so do I.

Kitty xxx

The following morning, I knocked on Gerd's door as I headed out. He did not answer. I pushed the door to his apartment open. I think I knew the moment I stepped into the study that Gerd was no longer alive. He was sitting at his desk. Kitty's letter was there in front of him, as was a letter in his own hand.

I called for an ambulance and waited while they came and took Gerd's body to the morgue. I helped the policewoman who came on a routine call to gather together the numbers she would need to contact his family. The following day, I met his great-nephew, who came from Hamburg. His name was Otto too, after the great-uncle he had never known. He told me that I should stay in the house for as long as I needed to. He was also concerned that I would not suffer any lasting stress from having been the one to discover his great-uncle's body. Otto was so kind and caring that I did eventually allow myself to cry in front of him. He put his arm round me and gave me a squeeze.

'He was a strange old thing but we loved him,' he said of his great-uncle. 'He always held himself apart from us, as though he thought he was a burden. I wish I'd had the chance to know him better. Makes you think about the perils of wasting time, does it not?'

I agreed.

Otto Schmidt picked up a photograph of his great-uncle and mother as children.

'Life is beautiful but brief. We should make the most of it. What is it they say? Live, laugh, love.'

While the young Otto Schmidt continued to make arrangements for his great-uncle's funeral, I went back upstairs.

As I climbed to the top floor, I checked my BlackBerry and saw that a new message had come in. Thanks to some peculiar feeling of portentousness I waited until I was safely inside my room before I opened it. And of course it was from Marco.

I had a dream last night. I dreamed that I was in bed awake and someone came into the room. It was a woman. She was wearing a long white gown. Her hair was covered with some sort of veil. I couldn't see anything of her face but from the way that she walked, I was sure it was Silke. She went to the window and climbed up on to the sill. She looked out on to the Grand Canal. She didn't seem to know I was in the room behind her.

I sat up and I called to her. I called quietly. I didn't want to startle her. She didn't seem to hear. So I called a little louder.

'Yes, yes,' she said in her accented English. 'Don't worry. You won't be alone for long.'

Then she uncurled from her resting place on the wide stone windowsill. She put a bare foot on to the floor and lowered herself down. She turned to walk towards me and as she walked she took off her veil. But beneath the delicate lace wasn't my dear friend Silke at all. The girl behind the veil . . . she looked like you.

And when I woke up this morning, I reread your perfect email and I could hear it in your voice and in Silke's voice too. I knew by the time I had finished reading that you

were right. It is time to finish the story. So I'm coming to
Berlin to see Silke's grave and I want you to be there with
me too.

I wrote back at once, telling Marco that the moment he
touched down in the city I would be beside him and I would
stay with him for as long as he needed me.

'I think I might need you for a very long time,' he wrote.

'That's perfectly all right by me.'

Marco was coming to Berlin. Everything was going to
be OK.

41

After that, Marco and I emailed every day. Our correspond-
ence fell back into the easy pattern of those early days in the
library, when he was the first person with whom I shared the
news of my day-to-day. I told Marco everything about Gerd's
story, of course. Marco sent me some roses to cheer me up
on the day of Gerd's funeral, though it wasn't the gloomy
affair I had imagined. Gerd's sister Helga had gone on to
have four children. Her grandchildren and great-grandchildren were innumerable. Far from being sent off with a shout
of 'good riddance', Gerd was very well-mourned.

Though Marco's own tale was very different, there were
some parallels between the two. Just like Gerd with Otto,
Marco had taken the decision to punish himself for Silke's
death by swearing he would not allow himself to be happy,
even though it was clear to me from having met Gerd's
family that they had long since stopped blaming him for
his brother's untimely end. But unlike Gerd, Marco still
had a chance to recover that happiness. He still had time
to be in love again. Perhaps to marry and have a family.
Perhaps to be with me.

Still, I felt as though I was holding my breath until he
finally booked the plane for his trip to Germany. It took a
while for him to sort out the logistics. One email ran:

My passport has run out. I didn't even think about that complication. I guess it's to be expected since I haven't left the house in five years let alone the country.

He was making light of it, but I wondered how he would feel when the time came for him to get a passport photo. He answered the question.

'I had to leave the house for that. Fortunately, it was a cold day and I was able to wrap a scarf round the bottom of my face. Add that to a hat pulled down low. I was pretty well disguised for my trip to the photo booth.'

I told him I had been worried for him. It was, after all, his first time away from the Palazzo Donato since his father's death.

'It was strange,' he admitted. 'I walked past the café where Gianni and I always used to meet for coffee. I half expected to see him there, in his usual seat at one of the tables outside. But of course, he wasn't there. I looked him up on the Internet today. These days he is living in New York. His corporate photograph shows he has aged pretty well. He has a wife and two daughters.'

My heart ached a little to read that and I wondered if it had hurt Marco at all to find out. Gianni had a family. It was proof that life had gone on as though Marco had never existed. His friends were leading extraordinarily ordinary lives. And the city? How had he found his beloved home town?

'People always say that Venice never changes, but believe me, I was astonished by how much was different. Shops and cafés had changed hands, of course, and gained sparkling new façades. There were new hotels. Even a new museum. The faces had changed too. Once upon a time, I knew most of the *gondolieri* and they knew me and my friends. They made it their business to know us – we were all of us big tippers. But I recognised hardly any of the men hanging out by the Bacino Orseolo. Then again, I don't suppose they would have recognised me.'

'How long did you stay out of the house?' I asked.

'I walked quite a way,' Marco told me. 'I went as far as the Cannaregio. I walked past our friend Luciana's house. Once I was away from the palazzo's four walls, I was surprised at how good it felt. That long walk made the blood sing around my body. I suppose I would describe the feeling as suddenly being very much alive.'

'I'm glad,' I wrote. 'That lifts my heart.'

Every day after that, Marco would venture out of the palazzo for a while. He said it was easier than he'd thought to be anonymous in the small city. He told me one day that he went to the Peggy Guggenheim museum. It had been expanded during his years of self-imposed exile. He found the carved marble bench that I had admired when I visited back in the summer.

'Savor kindness for cruelty is always possible later,' was the message carved upon it.

'I felt close to you when I saw it,' he told me. 'Thinking of you reading those words back in July.'

I told him that I wished I had been with him when he saw them for the first time. As he slowly came back to the world, walking a little further every day, I wished I could be there to hold his hand. But I knew in some way that it was important for him to make these early forays without me. That way he could make them entirely at his own pace.

But, oh, the pace seemed all too slow to me! I couldn't wait to see him.

At last he announced that he would be arriving in the middle of December. He had hired a private jet. It was the one concession to his condition he'd allowed his wealth to buy him. That week saw the first snow of the year. Just a few flurries. It didn't settle; but the city was beginning to prepare itself for Christmas. All the Christmas markets had been running since the end of November. The smell of *Glühwein* was in the air. My colleagues at the university were in high spirits. There were parties every night.

It was a wonderful time to be a tourist in the city. But Marco was not coming to Berlin as a tourist. I was reminded of that when he told me that Silke's sister had sent instructions on how to find Silke's grave.

Of course, Silke's sister was Anna, my favourite student. It all fitted together. The song. The voice. Her fascination with the power of appearances. I had gently coaxed the story out of her. Her face, when I told her about Marco, was a picture of distress, but she had agreed to let me put him in touch with her and he had asked me to let her read the diary. I had to help her. From Italian, to English, to German.

'To understanding,' said Anna.

I hoped so.

The night before Marco's scheduled arrival in the city, I couldn't sleep. I had worked hard to convince myself that he would come but now my optimism was waning. On the one hand, the journey from Venice to Berlin was not so onerous; just a couple of hours on the plane, and both airports were close to the cities they served. But, as he had pointed out when he told me about his passport, Marco had not left the Palazzo Donato in five years. He had not left Venice since he arrived back in the city direct from the hospital where I had tried to chivvy him back to health. On top of all this, to make a flight to a city that held such strong and difficult memories for him could not be easy. And I wondered how the wider world would seem to him. Of course, he had not been entirely out of touch and it wasn't as though he would be travelling easyJet. But what would he find to be different about Germany? Would anything scare him?

When he arranged the trip I had suggested, tentatively, that it might be a good idea to have Silvio accompany him. Marco had insisted that he would be coming alone and that Silvio deserved a holiday after all these years.

'And I am not afraid of the outside world,' Marco assured me. 'I have merely been sparing it the embarrassment of having to look upon me.'

I worried how he would feel when the world did look upon him. Would he be ready for the stares? Would he pretend not to notice them, as Silke had once done?

Would I pretend not to notice them too?

On the day itself, I woke early. I drank three cups of tea in quick succession, hoping it might calm my nerves. Marco sent me a text message to say that his plane was on time. He reiterated that I didn't have to meet him – a limousine to his hotel was all part of the service the private-jet company provided – but I told him there was no way I wanted to miss a second in his company. I would be at the airport the moment he arrived.

'In that case,' Marco texted me, 'please let me send a car for you.'

An hour later, a limousine appeared on the Hufelandstrasse and I settled into the deep leather seats for the drive out to Schönefeld. I spent half the journey trying not to cry through nerves.

Marco had also arranged for me to be admitted to the private terminal to wait for him there. My heart was in my mouth as I watched the aeroplane touch down. After all, it contained such precious cargo. It seemed like an age until the plane taxied to its allotted berth. Then another age while the doors were opened before finally, finally, Marco emerged into the blustery Berlin day.

I felt a surge of love as Marco carefully descended the stairs. He was wearing a scarf wrapped round the bottom half of his face and a knitted cap over his head. He was carrying his own bag.

I suppose I might have hoped for a more intimate setting for our second proper meeting, but the terminal staff were very discreet. Having opened the doors to let Marco into the building, the hostess disappeared, leaving us alone in the smart airport lounge.

I smiled. Marco pulled down his scarf and smiled back at me. He set down his bag and opened up his arms. I'm afraid I burst into tears as we finally embraced.

'Sarah, my angel,' he called me.

I just carried on crying into the side of his neck until Marco started laughing.

'My love,' he said. 'This is supposed to be a happy moment.'

Finally, I pulled away from him and wiped my eyes. Then Marco wiped a tear away with his thumb and kissed me, for the first time ever, on the mouth.

I wasn't ready for it. He took me by surprise. But oh, it was wonderful! I felt like Kitty Hazleton, kissed by Otto outside the Hotel Frankfort. It was a kiss you could write home about. I saw stars and I heard the fireworks. Feeling me begin to wilt in his embrace, Marco put his arm round my back and pulled me closer to him. I immediately felt safe in his arms.

It felt as though the world had melted away around us but, alas, that wasn't the case.

The limousine driver was waiting to take us back into the city. Marco let the driver take his bag and held on to my hand. We sat side by side in the back of the car, saying nothing though there was so much to say. For now, we just looked into one another's eyes.

42

On his first day in Berlin, I did not see much of my love. The limousine took us straight to the Hotel Adlon. Marco had taken the hotel's most expensive suite, the Royal Suite, with its orange-painted living room like something out of a stately home. It also had a book-lined office that reminded me of the library back in Venice. It was hard to believe the hotel had only existed in its current incarnation since 1997.

I had not presumed that Marco would want me to stay with him and so I left while the butler was still hanging his clothes in the wardrobe. We would see each other later on. I claimed that I had work to do. He had already he told me that he had to make a visit to Silke's family before he could think about doing anything else. Anna had put Marco in touch with her mother and he had written a long letter explaining everything that had happened since the accident in which their daughter died. Silke's mother had responded kindly. The years had mellowed her attitude towards the young man who had been there at her daughter's death. She said she had spent many years thinking about the accident and the events leading up to it and had finally come to the conclusion that Marco could have done nothing differently. Silke had been at the wheel. And young love makes fools of everyone. Which of us hasn't done something foolish in a rush of passion?

She agreed to see Marco as soon as he arrived.

While Marco was with Silke's family, I went into my office

but I found it hard to concentrate on anything. I imagined the conversation he might be having. Who would be there? Silke's parents were already divorced when she died. Would they come back together for this moment of reconciliation and forgiveness? I knew Anna would be there. I imagined how interested she would be to hear a firsthand account of the girl she had idolised. What would her parents have to tell Marco? Would they show him photographs of Silke as a younger girl? Would they tell him stories that he hadn't heard before? Would he love her even more as a result?

As much as I wanted Marco to be reconciled with Silke's memory, I still feared her hold over him and worried that, now he was back in her city, she would reclaim him as hers. I found myself offering her a little prayer. She'd had him for so long. He'd grieved for her for so many years. It was my turn to claim him for love.

Marco texted me as he left Silke's mother's house. He asked me to meet him at his hotel and told me to come straight to his suite. When I arrived, he was sitting on his bed with his head in his hands. I immediately thought that his downcast demeanour must be due to the difficult conversations he'd had that afternoon, but he assured me that he was merely tired from all the travelling and the anticipation of what had actually turned out to be a perfectly pleasant meeting.

'Was Anna there?' I asked. 'Does she look like her sister?'

'In some ways,' said Marco. 'They showed me some photographs.'

'I thought they might.'

'And even as a child, Silke was different from the rest of them. Her mother told me that it had come as no surprise when Silke decided to dye her hair blue.'

'Are you glad you went?'

Marco nodded.

'I think it helped, you know, for them to see that I didn't just walk away and carry on living my vacuous playboy life.'

I squeezed Marco's hand. I didn't like to agree with him but I had a feeling he might be right. If anyone really believed there was blame, here was evidence of punishment.

'Do you want to eat anything?' I asked.

'Silke's mother insisted I ate some of her cake,' he said, with a sad smile. 'All I want to do is lie down and rest.'

We spent our first night together in the Hotel Adlon, in the suite that Marco had booked for his stay. We didn't make love that night. We simply held each other on the big wide bed. It wasn't the right time for anything more. We lay down on top of the sheets fully clothed and wrapped our arms around each other's bodies. We said very little, just listened to the sound of each other breathing. There was something healing in our proximity to each other. Indeed, Marco said as much when he asked me if I was sure I really needed to hear every-thing about his relationship with Silke and the way the memory of her had dominated his life since.

'Sarah, know that I am telling you all this because I want to be with you. I am undergoing some kind of transforma-tion, which started the day you arrived at the Palazzo Donato. This is my scar tissue. I need you to see it properly, before you can say with certainty that there is hope it might be successfully cut away. I'm asking you to perform open-heart surgery.'

As I had predicted, it was not long before I stopped seeing Marco's injuries. When we looked at each other, we were eye to eye.

I felt at home in his arms. I dreamed that we were happy.

*   *   *

The following morning, we had breakfast in bed. I met the room-service waiter at the suite's main door, so that Marco would not have to deal with any questioning stares. But over breakfast, Marco seemed different. He sat a little straighter against the pillows than he had the night before. He smiled at me over the sumptuous breakfast that could have fed four. That said, neither of us was very hungry. I touched only the orange juice and half a croissant. Marco did not do much better.

'How are you feeling this morning?' I asked him, as he toyed with a pain au chocolat as though he'd never seen one before.

'I think I'm ready,' he said. 'We can go there right after breakfast.'

Of course, I knew where he meant by 'there'. Silke's grave.

'Do you need to get her some flowers?' I asked.

'She wasn't that kind of girl,' he said. 'I've brought her something she would like much better.'

He nodded in the direction of his suitcase.

'In the outside pocket.'

I went to look. Inside the pocket was a small square package wrapped in tissue paper.

'Open it.'

Inside was one of the Buddhas from the secret office.

'She gave this to me the week I met her,' he said. 'And now I want to give it back. I have prayed to this little Buddha on so many occasions. I was praying to him the night before you came back into my life.'

I wrapped the little Buddha up again. Marco was standing in front of his wardrobe, choosing a suit for the day. I had already noticed that he had come to Berlin with a suitcase full of brand new clothes. It was hard not to think that he had chosen them for Silke, though I suppose he had not shopped in a decade. He didn't need any other excuse.

'What do you think?' he asked me, pulling out a suit in a dark, sombre blue.

I nodded. The tears were prickling the back of my throat. It was the strangest thing. Here at last was the man I loved and I was helping him dress for another woman. A dead woman, but another woman nonetheless. The effort of sitting on my jealousy made my eyes hot and my head ache. I felt a sense of rising panic, as though if I made Marco look good enough, Silke would reach out from beyond and take him back with her.

Perhaps that was what he wanted. Had Marco really come to Berlin to find closure with the intention of beginning a new life or, like Gerd, was he really just preparing for his own death?

'You look worried,' he told me.

'I'm not,' I lied. 'Except, perhaps for you. It's cold outside. Are you going to be warm enough in that suit?'

Finally, I asked the question that had been on my lips ever since he announced that today was the day he would visit Silke's grave.

'Are you sure that you want me to come with you?'

Marco nodded. 'I don't think I can do it without you.'

I put my arm through Marco's and gripped him tightly as we walked from the car to the cemetery. We walked slowly.

In the days before Marco came to Berlin, I had already been to the cemetery and discovered exactly where Silke was buried. I led Marco to within twelve feet of the grave, then let him carry on alone. I sensed that he would need a moment on his own with the woman who had changed his life so dramatically in such a short time.

Her headstone was simple. It put me in mind of Augustine du Vert's grave in Père Lachaise. There was nothing about it that spoke of the vibrancy of the woman named thereon. Nothing to remind people that here was a girl who dyed her hair all the colours of the rainbow and sang with the voice of a siren.

I watched from a distance as Marco placed the little Buddha on Silke's headstone. He bowed his head, as though in prayer, but I sensed that he wasn't talking to God. He was talking to Silke. I also sensed that she was talking back to him. His shoulders, which had been so tight, seemed to loosen. He stood straighter.

Then, at last, he lifted his head and turned to look at me. He held out his hand in my direction. I stepped towards him, as nervous as I might have been at any ordinary party, meeting the legendary ex-girlfriend.

'Thank you,' said Marco. 'For bringing me here. You'll think I'm mad if I say this, but I feel as though Silke has been talking to me. She's been telling me that everything's going to turn out fine in the end. I think she forgives me.'

'How could she not?' I asked him. I turned to Silke's grave and stood listening for a moment. 'She says you're a silly fool for ever thinking she could hold a grudge.'

'See,' Marco said. 'That's girls all over. You're ganging up on me already.'

Marco put his arm round my shoulder and I put my arm round his waist. I leaned my head on his shoulder. It may not have been the right moment for a kiss, but it was definitely the right moment to remind each other that we were still alive, we were together and there could be decades of happiness ahead of us.

The atmosphere as we got back into the car was much lighter than it had been when we arrived at the graveyard. Marco held my hand in his lap. We drove back to the hotel but we were not there for long. Marco's plane would be waiting to take him back to Venice at seven o'clock. He had warned me that this trip would be a short one; he had to see his doctor in Venice the following day. I wasn't going to ask him to miss that appointment. They were going to be talking about the first operation to give Marco more mobility in his damaged hand.

After I had helped Marco to repack his bag, I went with him to Schönefeld airport. We didn't talk much on the way. I think we were both still trying to absorb the momentousness of what had just happened. Marco had travelled to Berlin and made his peace with Silke. We were free to be together at last. He was going back to Venice to talk about operations. There was forward motion, but I think we were both nervous that saying too much could jinx any future plans.

We got to the terminal and I sat with Marco while his plane was prepared. He had his arm round me. It felt natural already, like we'd always been this close.

'I can't stand to leave you here at the airport,' he said. 'Come back with me to Venice. Come now. We'll send the driver to fetch your passport from the Hufelandstrasse.'

'I can't,' I told him. 'Not yet. You know I have things to do here.'

'Will I see you again?' Marco was suddenly anxious.

I nodded. 'Of course. And once we are together again, I promise I will never leave you alone.'

I wiped a tear from my eye as Marco's private plane climbed into the clouds. I was silent and subdued as the limo driver took me back to my apartment. The building seemed especially melancholy now that Gerd Schmidt had gone and I knew there would be no music to accompany me as I climbed the stairs. I made a cup of tea and took up my favourite spot on the bedroom windowsill. I wrapped the curtain round me to protect me from the cold. Outside the snow was beginning to fall and settling too, making everything look fresh and new. A clean slate. That was what Marco and I had now. We just had to take things slowly.

Then I received his text message. 'I love you,' was all it said. With those three words to hold close to my heart, I knew I'd never feel cold again.

43

Christmas, England, last year

A couple of weeks after Marco came to Berlin, I was back in the UK to receive my doctorate and celebrate Christmas with my family. I had other business there too. Just as I had promised Gerd, I had tracked down his brother's darling Kitty and arranged to visit her to give her those small effects belonging to Otto that Gerd had kept for her over the decades.

I arrived at a beautiful house in the Cotswolds. It was a cold day but it was bright and the countryside was stunning in a glittering cold of frost. A Christmas tree glowed invitingly in a bay window.

A young housekeeper opened the door to the house and showed me in. I found Kitty in a cosy little sitting room. She was sitting in a chair by a bright wood fire, squinting over a crossword. She put it down and smiled at me.

'Got to keep your mind busy,' she said. 'Use it or lose it.'

I agreed with her.

'I still keep up my diary too. Though these days there's nothing much to report except the doctor's visits. I shall have something exciting to write up this evening though. Sarah, I am very glad you're here.'

She offered me some tea and a slice of home-made cake.

'I didn't make it myself,' she explained, holding up her stiff

303

old hands. 'Hands are too shaky these days. Oh, what am I talking about! I never made cake in my life. Baking really wasn't my thing.'

'I feel exactly the same,' I said. 'Life's too short.'

'Besides, once you've eaten cake in Germany, nothing else seems to match up.'

'Gerd made great cake,' I told her.

'Well, that must have been something he learned after I knew him,' said Kitty.

'I've got something for you. Shall I hand it over now?'

Kitty nodded.

I brought the shoebox out of my bag and placed it on the table next to her.

'Oh!' she said. 'Turner and Timpson. I wonder what happened to the shoes that were in there? My mother and I bought them on a shopping trip for my sixteenth birthday. I thought they were terribly grown-up. So what have we here?'

She took off the lid and reached inside. A faraway look came into her eyes as she held the little teddy bear in her hand. And then there were tears.

'Oh, my darling Otto,' she sighed.

She pressed the bear to her face and inhaled, as though her beloved's scent might still linger there.

'You must excuse me. It's funny how the most ordinary things can come to mean so much to us,' she said.

'I understand,' I assured her, thinking of the little white rose. I wished I hadn't thrown that away.

'Otto gave me this bear for my birthday,' said Kitty. 'I called it Little Adolf. It seemed like a good joke at the time. I shall have to call him something else now. Do you think he looks like a Nigel?'

She posed the bear so that he leaned against the cake-stand. She brought out the handkerchief next.

304

'I embroidered this at that finishing school. I was never much good at sewing.'

She picked up the diaries. She opened the red one and promptly shut it again.

'You read all this?' she asked. I admitted I had. 'You must think me a terribly naughty girl.'

'I specialise in naughty girls,' I told her. In the emails I had exchanged with her granddaughter, I'd described the research projects that had led me to be interested in Kitty. I explained once again that Kitty was in good company with Luciana Giordano and Augustine du Vert.

Then I told her everything Gerd had told me about his brother's fate. I had given Kitty's daughter the bare bones of the story to make sure Kitty was somewhat forewarned that there was no happy ending, but she sobbed openly as she heard again about Otto's death from typhoid.

'I'm so sorry,' she said. 'Crazy as it sounds, I can't believe he's actually dead. Just this morning I turned on the radio and heard a Berlin accent. It can still break my heart. I keep expecting him to turn up one afternoon, with his hands in his pockets and whistling our song.'

' "The Song is Ended"?' I said.

'Yes,' said Kitty, deliberately misunderstanding my quoting of the song's title. 'I suppose it finally is.'

By the time I left, Kitty had once again regained her composure. As I got ready to go, she asked me a little about my own life. Was I married? Did I have any children? I told her about Marco and his own Berlin tale. I told her I would be in Venice before too long.

'Thank you for coming,' she said. 'I only wish I'd had a chance to see Gerd before he died.'

'He was a good man,' I said. 'He was very kind to me.'

'I always knew he had that in him. Thank you, dear, for reuniting me with these little pieces of my past. I hope that you and your friend can work things out, my darling. I think you may be just what he needs.'

'I think so too,' I confided.

Kitty squeezed my hand. I said goodbye. As I left, I thought I heard her singing 'The Song is Ended'.

44

After my brief visit to the Cotswolds, I went back to Berlin to put my affairs there in order. I cut short my tenure at the university but remained in Berlin for as long as it took them to find a replacement to take the classes I was contracted to teach. It was just a couple of weeks but it all felt too long until I could be back with Marco.

My friends were anxious for me when I told them that I was giving up my cushy number in Germany to take up a job as a librarian. Librarians were an endangered species, in the UK in particular. But what I didn't tell them – at least, not at first – was that I wouldn't be throwing myself on the mercy of a politically motivated local council, who might cut my job at any moment. I was going to be working as librarian in a very particular private library. Marco's library at the Palazzo Donato.

When I arrived in Venice for the fourth time in a year, I knew that Silvio would be waiting for me at the airport dock. I spotted him at once, standing proudly at the wheel of the beautiful little boat that had been the very first vessel in the Donato shipping empire: the boat that Marco's grandfather had bought with tips from his waiting job.

What I did not expect was to see that Silvio was not alone. As he jumped up to help me load my bags on to the boat and receive my grateful hug, I saw that Marco was with him.

Marco took off his sunglasses and I was immediately lost in those wonderful eyes.

For the first time, we walked through the garden together. The fountain had been switched on and, though it was the middle of winter, the air in the garden was soft and welcoming. The light was as pink and yellow as it had been on my very first day in the city twelve months earlier.

As we passed the rose bush, Marco pointed out a single rose, braving the elements to bloom against the odds. He plucked it and gave it to me.

'What will you give me in return?' he asked.

'You can have every part of me now, as well you know,' was my reply.

'For ever?' he asked.

'For ever,' I said.

As we passed the statues of Orpheus and Eurydice, I could have sworn I saw both of them smile.

We went into the library, the scene of so much flirtation and angst. Marco showed me some new additions to his collection. Luciana's diary and Louis Sauvageon's sketchbook both had pride of place in a new glass display cabinet. Ernestina still smiled down from her place above the fireplace. I could tell that she was pleased with the way things had worked out.

Then finally I was in the bedroom I had so often dreamed about. It was exactly as I had imagined. The enormous bed was made with pure white sheets and it was as soft and fluffy as a cloud. I fell on to the mattress just as I had done in my dreams, with my arms above my head in an attitude of perfect abandon.

Marco hesitated by the door for a moment, just watching me.

'What are you thinking?' I asked him.

'I'm thinking,' he said, 'that we've been here before, you and I.'

'I was thinking exactly the same thing.'

He stepped towards me. He sat down on the mattress and leaned over to kiss my lips.

'Tell me this isn't a dream,' he said.

'I promise you,' I said to him, 'that this is absolutely real.'

Being with him at last was more perfect than I had ever imagined. My most wild and exotic dreams could not compare with the reality of finally being in the arms of the man I loved.

Marco joined me on the bed. He kissed me more passionately than I had ever imagined. When he slipped his tongue into my mouth, I could taste the champagne we had been drinking on the boat trip from the airport. I ran my fingers through his thick dark hair, then down his neck to his shoulders, feeling his muscles beneath his blue cotton shirt.

We pulled apart for a moment and I helped him to undress. He had an erection already. I could feel it through his trousers. Meanwhile, he pushed my dress up to my hips and unclipped the suspenders that were holding my stockings in place. He rolled them down towards my feet and kissed each foot as he bared it.

I got up to help Marco get out of his trousers. He was wearing pure white boxer shorts. I pulled them down over his hips. His cock sprang out to greet me. The skin of his penis was silky and warm. I wrapped my hand round it. Marco slid his own hands over my curves. He registered his pleasure with a delighted groan.

I gasped as Marco's fingers moved to the place between my legs. He smiled with pleasure upon realising how wet I already was. Just at the thought of him. Before he even got there. I murmured my appreciation as he moved to touch my clitoris. Every confident stroke took me a little closer to the edge. At the same time, he continued to kiss me, to caress my breasts with his free hand. When he stopped kissing me for a moment, I felt my stomach muscles contract in delirious anticipation as I watched him lick a finger before slipping it inside.

Everything was just right. The sound of his voice as he whispered 'I love you' in my ear. The smell of his hair as I nuzzled my face in his neck. The feeling of utter completeness that came with having him enter me, filling me so utterly. And nothing could be better than the sensation of having him come inside me. To hear him cry out my name flooded my heart with happiness.

Never had I been so completely satisfied. Marco made me feel as though every part of my body was precious and rare. He touched me so carefully. He worshipped me with his lips and his tongue. I worshipped him too. Touching him transported me to somewhere close to heaven. There was nothing I wanted more than to be with him. We were free of the past and the future that awaited us was perfect.

For the next few weeks, we were like honeymooners. Every moment we could we spent in bed together. I loved to wake up beside him and fall asleep with our limbs entwined. During daylight hours, we could hardly bear to be apart. The Palazzo Donato was the perfect love nest. The silent courtyard was now filled with music and laughter once more.

When Marco asked me to marry him, I could hardly find the words to tell him how happy it would make me. It's a good job I only had to say 'yes'.

Epilogue

That was last year. I've been in Venice ever since. We married within two months of Marco's proposal. There was no need for us to wait. Silvio and Bea were witnesses as we signed our names in the register at the Palazzo Cavalli, overlooking the Rialto bridge. I wore a pure white copy of the dove-grey Dior dress that Marco had picked out for what should have been our first meeting.

We celebrated with a small party at the Palazzo Donato. The courtyard was full of roses for the occasion. Silvio even had the statues of Orpheus and Eurydice moved so they were together again at last. Bea caught the bouquet that I threw as Marco and I sped away in his grandfather's boat on the first leg of our journey to our Paris honeymoon. Later, she admitted that she had dropped the security guy in favour of Nick and they were making one another very happy.

My love for Marco only grows stronger over time. It's not all been plain sailing. He continues to have small procedures that, if they will not give him back the face he once had, will at least make him more comfortable. He has increasing mobility in his hand.

He continues to draw me while I work, but now he does not have to observe me through a peephole in a false wall. Instead he sits in the armchair by the library fire. Sometimes we spend whole evenings there together, reading out loud to one another. One of our favourite things is to read Luciana's diaries again. I read them in Italian and Marco pretends to swoon at my appalling accent.

At night, when we are alone together in the bedroom, I tell Marco about the dreams I had before we were together. He tells me about his own dreams. It is strange how closely they echo mine. Sometimes, when he tells me something from his past, I feel as though I was there. We have no secrets from one another and our plans for the future are all shared.

From time to time, I think about all the women who have shown me through their stories what I might make of my own life. Luciana with her daring. Augustine with her devotion. Kitty with her bravery. They've taught me about taking risks, remaining loyal to love and about finding and offering forgiveness. They've taught me that it is possible for two people to make a bond that lasts for all time. I only hope that one day in the future, someone will read my diary and be inspired to find a love of her own.

Acknowledgements

With thanks to editor Francesca Best and copy-editor Jacqui Lewis for their sterling, speedy work in bringing my trilogy to print. To Emilie Ferguson for spreading the news. To Antony Harwood and Joanna Kaliszewska for brokering the deals. To Victoria Routledge, Jojo Moyes and Serena Mackesy for their support while I thought about retraining as an accountant. To Matt Dunn, Kate Harrison, Stella Duffy, Rebecca Chance and Lauren Henderson for all the tweets, quotes and Facebook fabulousness. To Helena (with an 'a'!) Cutler for reading everything I write and always finding something kind to say. To Mum, Dad and Kate for listening to my complaints when I was cross-eyed with tiredness and felt like I'd never get to 'The End'. Most of all, thanks to Mark, who didn't complain when I interrupted our Italian holiday to plot the whole trilogy out and was equally game to dress in rubber and hit the clubs of Berlin. Any tea-making scenes are entirely inspired by him.

Have you read the first two books in the
Hidden Women series by Stella Knightley?

The Girl Behind The Mask

and

The Girl Behind The Fan

are available now in paperback and ebook.